SOMETHING CHANGED

SOMETHING CHANGED

JULIE TOVEY

Copyright © 2025 Julie Tovey

The moral right of the author has been asserted.

Apart from any fair dealing for the purposes of research or private study, or criticism or review, as permitted under the Copyright, Designs and Patents Act 1988, this publication may only be reproduced, stored or transmitted, in any form or by any means, with the prior permission in writing of the publishers, or in the case of reprographic reproduction in accordance with the terms of licences issued by the Copyright Licensing Agency. Enquiries concerning reproduction outside those terms should be sent to the publishers.

The manufacturer's authorised representative in the EU
for product safety is Authorised Rep Compliance Ltd,
71 Lower Baggot Street, Dublin D02 P593 Ireland (www.arccompliance.com)

This is a work of fiction. Names, characters, businesses, places, events and incidents are either the products of the author's imagination or used in a fictitious manner. Any resemblance to actual persons, living or dead, or actual events is purely coincidental.

Troubador Publishing Ltd
Unit E2 Airfield Business Park,
Harrison Road, Market Harborough,
Leicestershire. LE16 7UL
Tel: 0116 2792299
Email: books@troubador.co.uk
Web: www.troubador.co.uk

ISBN 978-1-83628-477-2

British Library Cataloguing in Publication Data.
A catalogue record for this book is available from the British Library.

Printed and bound in Great Britain by CMP UK
Typeset in 11pt Minion Pro by Troubador Publishing Ltd, Leicester, UK

For James
(with thanks to Pulp for the title…)

NOW

The sign on the door said 'Do not enter'. But a sign wasn't going to stop her. One eyebrow raised, Anna turned to meet Dan's gaze, noting the barely perceptible upturn in the corner of his mouth that gave her tacit approval to proceed. She pushed hard against the swing doors and walked inside.

From the bottom of the stairwell, their son, a sensible teenager who believed that rules were there to be upheld, protested. 'It says you can't go in there. It's not on the tour!' He sighed loudly. 'It's my Open Day for God's sake, not a nostalgia trip.'

His mother ignored him. 'It's not doing any harm,' she called. 'You've got to see this. Come on!'

Clearly, the whole space had been emptied for refurbishment. Anna quickly took it all in, orientating herself, looking for the familiar: the thick pillars, the long line of the bar and, finally, the magnificent floor-to-ceiling windows overlooking the Thames. As it had done so many times before, the view exerted the pull of a magnetic force, drawing her in. Anna inhaled deeply, filled with a long-forgotten feeling of pure, euphoric joy that came from a time when the future held infinite possibility. Placing her forehead on the glass, she was once again awe-struck by the panorama: the grandeur of Tower Bridge to her left, the concrete brutalism of the South Bank in front of her and the elegance of Big Ben to her right. There were newcomers to the skyline – the Shard, the London Eye – but it was reassuringly familiar.

'I'd forgotten about this view,' Dan said as he came up behind her, followed reluctantly by Jack, whose facial expression conceded that, in fact, his mother was right: it had been worth the unauthorised detour.

She turned, her face animated in a way that Jack had not seen before. 'It's even better at night, when all the buildings are illuminated.'

Anna held her smartphone at arm's length. 'Selfie? For posterity?' It was a cliché, but she wondered where the time had gone. Jack and his father rolled their eyes in impressive synchronicity, shaking their heads in resignation, and leant in towards her, fixing their identical, wide smiles as a single touch of the screen froze the moment in time.

On the way down the stairwell to rejoin the authorised tour route, Anna took one last look back. In her mind's eye, simultaneously visible yet elusive, a slender girl sprinted eagerly up the flight of stairs, her dark hair falling over her shoulders, long legs extending from tiny hot pants. A burst of music broke free.

I Wanna Be Adored.

And she was. In those days when adoration and lust were indistinguishable.

THEN

It had been out-and-out war for weeks, in a passive-aggressive kind of way. Mae had stomped around the house, loudly banging items in the kitchen whilst audibly announcing, 'It's worse than the Third World. It's like living with animals.' This was accompanied by Post-it notes deposited next to the weekly chores rota she had drawn up, pointedly identifying jobs that had been neglected. Karl, who, months earlier, had drawn the short-straw box room, spent as little time in the house as possible, returning late to sleep and leaving early before the others awoke. Meanwhile, Simon was going through some kind of breakdown.

'I don't know what I'm doing here – not just here, you know, geographically, but "here",' his fingers jabbed inverted commas in the air, narrowly missing the mug of tea Anna was attempting to proffer, 'generally.'

'But everything's going OK with your teaching practice…' Anna's voice trailed off, half-query, half-reassuring statement.

'Yeah. No. I suppose so. I don't know. I don't even know what I want to do. What am I even doing here?'

SOMETHING CHANGED

And so the conversation moved in ever-decreasing circles, Anna playing the role of amateur psychoanalyst – not, it must be said, because of any innate altruism, but because she was nosey, and also because she felt sorry for him. As he wept, hunched like Rodin's *The Thinker* with his eyes shielded by one hand, she placed her arm around his shoulder in a gesture of comfort.

'Thank you,' he sobbed.

'What for?'

'For listening. For trying to help. Unlike...' he groped for the right words, 'unlike fucking Mae. Fucking mental Mae.'

No, it was fair to say that it had not been the easiest house-share experience. She wondered idly where Karl spent his evenings after his teaching practice had ended for the day and felt an increasing desperation to join him, wherever that might be, if only to gain some fleeting moments of peace.

Until, one day, the decision was made for her. Anna had been vaguely aware of a late-night flurry of activity but, with an early commute ahead of her, she had simply turned over and fallen back to sleep. The knock on her door preceded the alarm clock the next morning. Raising her head from the pillow, dragging herself from the warm cocoon of her bed, Anna opened her door a crack.

'Simon? What is it?'

Karl was standing next to him, looking awkward and apologetic.

'I'm sorry, Anna. We've had enough. We're moving out.'

And just like that, they were gone.

THEN

Quickly realising that they were fifty per cent down on the rent, Anna and Mae debated their options. When the landlord moved back into the house with his wife, occupying one of the vacated rooms, they took the hint and moved out within the week.

It was a time when all of Anna's worldly possessions could fit onto the back seat of an old Volkswagen Polo. Mae turned the key in the ignition and depressed the accelerator firmly.

'Right!' she announced with cheery resolution. 'Let's get going. Faraday Hall, here we come!'

It wasn't a long journey – just a few miles around the South Circular – but in every other respect, it was a world away. It felt strange to be back in university halls again, with its rules and regulations and wardens. She and Mae smiled weakly at each other, unloaded the bags and boxes that contained the sum total of their lives thus far, and headed off to different floors, in different directions, and – ultimately – to different lives.

Anna turned the key she had been given in the lock, shouldered open the heavy door and kicked a box into place to wedge it open. Her heart sank a little as she surveyed her new home: the chaste single bed; the thin mattress; the chipped desk; the white walls pock-marked with Blu-Tack marks made by previous occupants. She rallied herself, resolving to claim the space as her own, tacking up posters of work by Picasso and Klee, a CND poster and a picture of the Red Hot Chili Peppers gazing into the eye of the camera naked save for the socks covering their genitals. On the shelves she placed books by Albee,

Williams, Plath and Lowell; on the desk, her red portable typewriter; by the basin near the door, her toothbrush and a bottle of Body Shop White Musk perfume. As she stood to survey her handiwork, there came a hesitant rap on the open door.

'Hiya!' The friendly Geordie voice belonged to a tall girl who stood, beaming, in the doorway, exposing a Wife-of-Bath gap between her front teeth. 'I'm Sally. And this,' she gestured to the next door up, where Anna's neighbour leant out, his pale, aristocratic face looking at her quizzically, 'is Julian.'

'Hi, neighbour. Julian. Psychology. You?'

'Anna. Postgrad teacher training.'

'Little ones?' Julian called.

Why did people always assume that, if you were female, you must want to spend your days looking after small, incontinent children?

'God, no. Secondary. Secondary English.'

'Blimey!' Sally raised her eyebrows. 'Rather you than me!'

'No. The kids are great. Really.'

From the very beginning, Anna had understood instinctively that pupils were pack animals. They were predatory and on the lookout for fresh meat, whether peer or adult, sniffing out weakness. All it took was an early baring of the teeth, a warning nip at the scruff of the neck, and they would back off. Whilst Anna had seen other student teachers – and, indeed, more experienced teachers at her own school – succumb to the pack, she had quickly established herself as pack leader.

THEN

'Well, if you need any help…' For a moment, Anna thought Sally meant help with her teaching.

'You're Education too?'

A shadow of bewilderment passed over Sally's face. 'No, no. I meant with the unpacking.'

They looked at each other and laughed. In that moment, Anna sensed that Sally was everything she was not: uncomplicated, open, and straightforward – and for that reason, she liked her immediately.

'I'm OK, but thanks. I'm nearly done. I don't have that much stuff, as you can see.' She swept her arm across the narrow confines of the room.

'Well, we usually get together in the kitchen at about six most nights, so, you know, you're welcome to join us.'

And, after two hours of lying on her single bed staring at Paul Klee's *Red Balloon*, that is exactly what she did, shielded by a box of pans, crockery and cutlery – an armour of busyness and purpose that could detract from any potential social awkwardness.

Sally – as she would always be – was at the centre of the group. Her face broke into a broad smile of welcome as Anna entered.

'So – everyone – this is Anna. Anna, you've met Julian and – this is Karen,' a petite blonde smiled and raised her hand in greeting, 'and Phil,' puppyish and sweet, wearing a faded New Order T-Shirt, 'and Jenny,' homely and rounded, sporting enormous earrings that appeared to be made of curtain rings.

Anna smiled, depositing her box and perching on the edge of the kitchen table.

'So, I think that's pretty much everyone. Who have I missed? Ah...'

At that moment, the door swung open and in walked a tall, dark, handsome guy with a battered leather biker jacket slung nonchalantly over one shoulder.

'And this is Dan.'

Dan glanced briefly in her direction, then turned to talk to Phil.

A bit offhand, she thought. *A bit rude.*

However, as Jenny chattered away beside her and Sally brought muddy-looking cups of instant coffee, Anna became aware of his surreptitious glances in her direction. She was familiar with those glances: the ones that moved from breasts to buttocks before sliding down her thighs. So, the guy who was too rude to say hello was checking her out. The trace of a smile played on her lips.

That night, they headed to the ground-floor bar. Sally and Phil played pool. Anna was hopeless at ball games, so she brought a book and half-read, half-watched them as she sipped her drink. Jenny was transformed into her nocturnal alter ego, the Bar Manager, assisted with varying degrees of competence by Dan and the Hulk, a boulder of a rugby player who stood at six foot six and whose shoulders were so wide they blocked out the light.

Anna rolled the sweetness of the drink around her tongue, feeling the warmth of the alcohol as it slid down her throat, her book open but unread, mesmerised by the dull clunk of cue on pool ball. The Hulk watched her as he pulled pints, smiling good-naturedly every time he caught her eye.

THEN

'Hi, is this seat taken?'

Anna looked up, taking in the slender frame of a young, dark-haired man. Given that the seats around her were entirely unoccupied, it seemed an unnecessary question.

'Feel free.' Anna tried to place his accent. 'So, you're... American? Canadian? Sorry, I can never quite tell the difference.'

'American.' He smiled.

'And what brings an American all the way to England?'

'Apart from all the beautiful English roses?'

Anna cringed.

He laughed. 'No, seriously. I'm studying for a masters in War Studies.'

'War Studies?' Anna's eyes widened. 'Is that even a thing?'

'Sure it's a thing!'

'So what's your next step? Are you formulating a cunning military strategy for world domination?'

'Now that's an interesting idea.' He pretended to consider it for a few seconds. 'But no, just a career in the American Navy.'

'Ah!'

The conversation juddered to a halt. He looked down at the book in her hand, flipping it to read the cover.

'Tennessee Williams. Now that's a great American playwright.'

And so the wheels of conversation were oiled, and they talked of literature, art and history until, eventually, they looked up and the whole bar had emptied, and they'd missed last orders. She became aware that her book had been replaced by his hand.

'Are you finished with these?' The Hulk stood over them, gesturing at their glasses. Anna rapidly detached her companion's hand and drained the last dregs from her glass, handing it over.

'Thanks.' She smiled. She picked up her book. 'So, that's me done for the night. It's been lovely to meet you…'

'Ed.'

'Ed. So, I'm off to get some sleep.'

'Can I escort you to your door?'

She'd heard that one before. 'No, I'm fine, thanks. I think I can just about make it there alone and unscathed. Anyway, nice to have met you.'

'Likewise.'

'Closing up!' Dan called, pulling down the shutters on the bar.

Three pairs of eyes followed her as she moved across the room to the stairs, watching her pert bottom in the blue 501s.

The next night, Anna had just got into bed when she heard the soft hiss of paper being pushed between her door and the carpet. A flyer probably but, unable to sleep, she rose and went to investigate. The bright moonlight streaming through the window revealed it to be an envelope on which was written, in a neat mixture of upper and lower-case letters, one word: 'Symphony'. Inside was a poem, which she quickly scanned.

THEN

Fortissimo kisses…
Studied notes played on well-toned fleshes…
Ragged breath rests, then a minor-key chord…
Metronomes sliding…

A cold weight settled in the pit of her stomach as she realised that the poem was, in fact, an extended metaphor for love-making – and, in particular, the poet imagining in some detail making love to her. She placed the sheet of paper face down on her desk and retreated to her bed, banging her shin painfully on the edge of the bed frame and cursing quietly, turning over in her mind who its author might be.

Over the next few days, she commuted to school; taught lessons; carted back exercise books in a tote bag slung over her shoulder; wrote comments like: 'Is it too simplistic to label Lady Macbeth the fourth witch?' She kept herself busy, kept her mind busy. Late at night, as she lay awake in her bed, she could sense rather than hear the presence of someone else on the other side of the door: there were suggestions of a soft exhalation of breath, the whisper of fabric as a body changed position before moving away. Her mind urged her to unlock the door and confront whoever stood there, but in reality, she was paralysed by inaction, too afraid to confront the creep or embarrassed that she might find no one there. Besides, there had been no further poems. One of the guys had clearly written it as a joke.

But then another appeared, so late this time that she did not discover it until morning. The poem announced its maker's jealousy that it had slipped beneath her doorframe where all night it had *heard her breathe sweetly, and by sunrise watched her face bloom.* The very thought – fictitious or not – of being watched as she slept made her feel nauseous.

Quickly dressing, Anna picked up a pen and yanked a sheet of paper from her typewriter.

To whoever has been posting poems underneath my door, she wrote in her tall, upright hand, *I would be grateful if you could stop.*

The message was simple and unambiguous.

She rolled a couple of balls of Blu-Tack between thumb and forefinger and stuck the message to the outside of her door as she left, slamming it shut behind her.

That evening, she lay tensed and alert to any sounds outside her door. None came. Message received and understood.

A couple of nights later, she was undressing for bed, wriggling her skirt down over her hips, when she heard a gentle knock at the door.

She froze, then called out a tentative, 'Hello?'

'It's Ed. Can I come in?'

It was nearly midnight.

'Uh – I'm – I'm not really decent at the moment.'

Silence.

'Maybe another time?' she suggested, desperately.

'OK.'

She remained very still, her skirt pooled around her ankles, waiting, listening.

After some time, she heard his footsteps recede down the corridor. As if released from a spell, she became

THEN

reanimated, one arm covering her bare breasts, the other reaching for her dressing gown. Slowly, she opened her door, checking that the corridor was empty, and re-read the note she had placed there. A feeling of impotent rage swelled within her. She was now sure it was Ed who had written those poems and felt somehow violated and frustratingly powerless. Tearing down the note, she kicked the door and rained down blow after fruitless blow until her fists hurt.

One by one, the doors down the corridor began to open.

Julian peered out of his room, his expression morphing rapidly from befuddled sleepiness to alarm.

'What's happened?'

And so that night they all gathered in the kitchen, quietly passing around the poems and considering what they should do.

Dan looked up, confused. 'It's about music. How is that weird?'

Sally huffed. 'Christ's sake, Dan. It's a metaphor. It's not about music. It's about sex. It's weird and the other one is just pervy.'

Phil chuckled. 'Well, at least we all know what he'd like to do to you with his metronome!'

Sally threw him a look. 'Very amusing, Phil. Obviously, Anna finds all this hilarious!'

Silence descended.

Julian ran his fingers through his hair. 'Actually, come to think of it, I've seen Ed a few times hanging around outside your door.'

'Yeah, me too,' added Jenny, 'really late at night sometimes.'

Sally took control. 'So, guys, what are we going to do? He clearly hasn't got the message.'

Dan stood up decisively. 'Give those to me,' he said, snatching the poems. 'I'll sort him out.' And, turning on his heel, he left.

'Well, as we're all up,' Sally said breezily, 'anyone fancy a cup of tea?'

A few minutes later, Dan returned, minus the poetry.

'Guess who I saw walking back towards your room with an envelope in his hand?' he announced.

Anna looked at him. 'So what did you do?'

'Well, I gave him the poems back.'

'And?'

For the first time, he looked directly into her eyes. 'I told him to forget the girl.'

Her knight in shining armour. Her not-so-charming-prince.

***

'So, have you been subjected to the Hulk's chat-up lines yet?' Phil flicked washing-up bubbles at Anna's face; it was the weekend, and there had been no further sightings of Ed.

Anna laughed, wiping the inside of a saucepan with a damp tea towel. 'Why, are they good?'

'Ah, I didn't say they were good. They're some of the worst chat-up lines known to man. But it doesn't stop him using them. It's like a rite of passage at Faraday. He's tried them on just about every female of the species here – and probably some who aren't.'

Anna dodged another cloud of bubbles.

'Like what? Forewarned is forearmed, after all.'

True to form, as she sat that night watching Sally and Phil play pool, the Hulk took a seat next to her. Phil nudged Sally and, gradually, amused and knowing glances were being exchanged across the room.

'So, Anna, I need to ask you something,' he began, fixing his face in an earnest expression.

'Ask away.'

'Did it hurt when you fell from heaven?'

She smiled and shook her head. 'Not really, I landed on my halo.'

'And, aside from being sexy, what do you do with your time?'

She raised an eyebrow. 'I psychoanalyse sexually insecure men who don't know how to communicate with women.'

He paused to consider this unexpected response.

'And your accent. Do you come from Brighton?'

She knew what was next and launched a pre-emptive strike. 'No, but I have come *in* Brighton.'

He burst out laughing, conceding defeat. 'Fancy a drink?'

Initiation over, she discovered that he hailed from the Highlands of Scotland, that Scotsmen really do go commando under their kilts and that the Scottish whisky they served behind the bar was shite and an affront to Scotsmen everywhere. He was warm-hearted, and he made her laugh; used to towering over most men whenever she wore high heels, secretly she delighted in how small and feminine he made her feel.

At the other side of the room, Dan watched the two of them as they sat thigh to thigh, heads close together to better hear each other over the hubbub. He observed the way she hitched up the spaghetti strap of her top with one finger when it slipped down over her shoulder, the way that she threw her head back when she laughed. Draining his sixth pint of the night, he walked purposefully towards them and fell down on one knee at Anna's feet, grasping her free hand. For a crazy moment, she thought he was going to propose. Slowly, he kissed the tips of each of her fingers, then the inside of her wrist. She watched him in stunned disbelief.

The Hulk shook his head in disgusted disapproval, raised his voice and continued their conversation. 'So, as I was saying…'

The kisses, light and fleeting, moved up her arm.

By now, she had become aware that everyone in the bar was watching. She was unsure if she was the unwitting object of some game between them and felt the heat of a deep blush flush across her cheeks. Gently, deliberately, Dan kissed her collarbone, then her neck, and the sensation shivered deliciously within her.

She needed to stop this now.

Abruptly, she rose, standing over him. 'Dan's obviously had too much to drink.' She extended her hand; he was still kneeling at her feet. 'Come on, Dan. Let's get you some coffee and sober you up.'

THEN

She'd adopted her brisk, no-nonsense Miss Brodie voice and, to her relief, he complied, staggering to his feet. He swayed against her as they crossed the room, as she helped him up the stairs. In the kitchen, with some difficulty, she manoeuvred him into place at the table.

'Right. I'll make you a coffee. A strong one.'

But as she turned from him, he grabbed at her, pulling her back towards his lap, gripping her arms and wrists, trying to kiss her with surprising force.

'You're gorgeous,' he slurred.

'Hey! Let go!' Anna struggled to free her arm. 'Look, I'm not going anywhere,' she placated him, 'I'm just trying to make you a coffee.'

Somehow, she managed to free herself, focusing on the mundane tasks of filling the kettle and heaping spoonfuls of instant coffee into a mug. But then he was there again, a big black spider behind her, pinning her wriggling arms, pressing her hard against his body, cupping her face in his hand and saying, 'I *really* want you. I want you *so much*.' His mouth closed over hers until she struggled for breath. Leaning back, swaying in an arc, she attempted to extricate herself, but his hands anchored her at the waist. As he swung her back up to meet his lips, she lunged to one side and bit his neck.

He cried out, recoiling in shock.

'That's what you get for not knowing when to stop,' she gasped. 'Just be grateful it's your neck.'

His hand nursed the place where she had bitten him. She had not drawn blood, but it would leave a bruise.

'Here.' Anna shoved the coffee at him. 'Sober up. I'm

going to bed.' And then, for the avoidance of doubt, she added: 'Alone.'

***

Anna's love life thus far had followed a predictable route. She was articulate, wrote poetry and thought about most things far too deeply, so it was no surprise that she had attracted a succession of boyfriends who were articulate, who wrote her poetry and with whom she had deep discussions about literature, philosophy and politics whilst lying prone on her bed listening to The Smiths and decrying Thatcherism. It had all been very earnest and intense, though somewhat lacking in the hedonistic fun of youth. She had spent most of her formative years immersed in a literary universe populated by taciturn Rochesters, brooding and misogynistic Heathcliffs and haughty, repressed Darcys, and what all these female writers had taught her was one thing: that romantic love was unfailingly complicated and painful. No girl wanted a Mr Collins. So, whilst the encounter with Dan had thrilled her – all that passion, all that sexual desire – and his feelings were reciprocated more than she cared to admit, she was more fascinated by his subsequent behaviour.

For days, if she was in the kitchen, he'd turn on his heel and silently leave; if they passed in the corridor, he avoided eye contact. When they gathered as a group in the evenings, Dan would steal glances when he thought she wouldn't notice but never speak directly to her. The

THEN

atmosphere between them was like a tension wire. She quickly ascertained that Dan was not like the other men she had known. Despite having taken a two-year gap year that made him older than the others, he had an air of awkwardness rather than maturity. Dan was not an articulate man, and he didn't do words – so she decided to say nothing and see what happened.

It had turned into a blisteringly hot summer with cloudless blue skies and a shimmering heat haze that rose from the melting tarmac. Sally had come up with the idea of a picnic. 'A posh picnic!' Each person would bring a contribution, and it would be held on Wandsworth Common, by the lake.

'The girls will all wear frocks, and we'll play rounders!' Sally announced, like a Geordie version of the Head Girl at Mallory Towers.

In the afternoon, laden with bags and blankets, Anna and Sally made their way towards the common, Sally in a bright poppy print, Anna in a dress strewn with blue cornflowers. The grass had been leeched by the sun to brown paper underfoot as they spread the cloths. In a meandering procession, others made their way towards the edge of the lake, depositing quiches, sausage rolls, strawberries, cakes.

As the afternoon heat faded into early evening, Anna lay back, arms pillowed behind her head, and closed her eyes, half listening to the babble of conversation surrounding her. She felt replete and began to doze.

'You coming for a game of rounders?'

Anna opened her eyes, squinting into the light at Phil's silhouette, and wordlessly shook her head.

'Sweet dreams then!'

She lay alone, listening to the distant thunk of ball on rounders bat; the cheers as someone made a home run; the groans as the ball was hit, splashing, into the lake.

A while later, somebody lay themselves down heavily next to her. She could smell the musk of their sweat. Anna turned her face sleepily, propping it on a cupped hand, and opened her eyes. Dan bent towards her and kissed her like a starving man.

'Come on, let's go.' Having failed to meet any resistance, Dan stood and extended his hand towards her, pulling her upright. Hand in hand, wordlessly, they walked through the gathering dusk.

For some time now, he had imagined her body, naked. His eyes had traced the shape of her breasts beneath her clothes, the curve from her waist to her hips, the small rose-bud lips; had imagined those long, lean legs wrapped around him as his hand pistoned furiously beneath his bed sheets. Now, she stood before the bed, a reality in her cornflower-blue dress, looking into his eyes. Waiting.

He kissed her again, feeling at the nape of her neck for the zip, pulling it down. She gave a little wiggle, and the dress fell over her hips to the floor. He fumbled with the hooks of her bra, tugging and inwardly cursing until she reached behind her and released the milky white flesh of small, firm breasts. He buried his face there, inhaling the smell of her skin. She reached down to his jeans, sliding down the zip, releasing him. His hand moved between

THEN

her legs, easing down the white lace knickers, and he heard her give a small gasp as he slid his fingers into the hot wetness.

He felt her warm breath against his ear. 'I'm not on the pill.'

He reached into his jeans pocket, pulled out the condom he had placed there hopefully earlier that evening, tore open the packet and quickly rolled it on. As he lowered her onto the bed, she guided him inside her; he thrust hard, holding still deep inside her for a moment, then, raising himself on his hands, he watched as he moved inside her body, withdrawing then disappearing like some act of magic. After a while, she raised her knees high, her feet and hands gripping his hips, pulling him towards her, meeting his thrusts rhythmically at first, then faster and more frenzied. He watched as her eyes closed, taking her to some inner space or place he would never know. He tried to focus on the wall behind her in a desperate attempt not to come. At that moment, he felt her body tense and shudder beneath him, her hands clenching into fists. The air filled with her loud, ragged cries. It sounded like she was in pain, and he was briefly afraid that he had hurt her, but he could not hold back any longer. Every nerve in his body was tensed. Just as he felt like he might break, there was the sweet sensation of release as he came, collapsing onto her body in a slick of sweat. Utterly spent, he lay, still gripped inside her, until finally Anna moved beneath him, and he rolled off her body, wiping the perspiration from his forehead with the back of his arm.

He turned to look at her. 'Jesus Christ, Anna,' he said and then, turning to the ceiling, to no one in particular, 'Jesus fucking Christ.'

For hours, they lay in each other's arms, kissing each other's skin, inhaling the scent of each other's bodies. They barely spoke. Later that night, when the corridor outside finally fell silent and she was drifting towards sleep, Dan gently slipped from her bed, dressed, and wordlessly left the room.

As the summer heat intensified, Dan skirted awkwardly around Anna during the day, avoiding eye contact. But each night, when everyone was asleep, she would hear a small tap at the door and the click of the door handle as he slipped into her room in the darkness. It felt exciting, illicit, thrilling, skulking around in secret, away from prying eyes. She found his desire for her intoxicating; for him, it was a physical addiction that was all-consuming and, therefore, terrifying, and against which he knew instinctively that he must protect himself.

The penultimate night of term, the heat had become so oppressive, the weather had to break. Anna was kneeling on the floor packing her possessions into cardboard boxes when there was a knock at the door. It was Dan, standing awkwardly, looking at his feet.

'Can I come in?'

Anna shoved a box aside, and he closed the door behind him. 'Knocking on my door in broad daylight!' Anna exclaimed in tones of theatrical surprise. 'To what do I owe the pleasure?'

THEN

Dan clearly wasn't in the mood for sarcastic jokes. He shifted his weight uncomfortably. 'I just wanted to say… I mean, me and you…'

Anna looked at him. 'Me and you?'

'Yeah.' He paused, looking increasingly uncomfortable. 'About our relationship…'

Anna detected his tone immediately. 'Relationship?' She smiled. 'What relationship?'

Dan looked up. He hadn't expected that. He had been expecting tears, recriminations. 'Right. Yeah.' He averted his eyes, looking over her shoulder. 'I mean, it's been great…' He paused. 'Just, you know, I don't think either of us is into anything heavy.' He thrust his hand into his jeans pocket then instantly removed it, not knowing what to do with himself. Anna watched him, silently. 'Right, OK then.' He gathered himself and turned to the door. 'I'll see you around, then.' The door clicked shut behind him.

Anna sat for a moment, surrounded by the detritus of her life. She inhaled slowly, holding her breath for a few seconds, then exhaled loudly, pulled an empty box towards her, and continued packing.

That evening, fork lightning ripped across the sky; thunder rumbled like tumbling boulders and the whole building trembled. Everyone gathered in the bar for farewell drinks. Someone had turned the main lights off and the lightning strobe-lit the room as they shared holiday plans – some returning home, some working in the city, others excitedly anticipating travels across Europe. Pieces of paper passed from one to another – an address, a phone number. There were promises to send postcards; to stay in touch. Anna wrote her address and number on the torn-off corners of beer mats, the backs of envelopes. She pocketed Sally's number, and Phil's, and the Hulk's.

But she didn't pocket Dan's. He didn't offer, and she certainly didn't ask.

***

15 Rossiter Road,
Balham.
Dear Anna,

Thank you for your postcard. The Cam looks delightful, although I did wonder which part of you got stuck on the punting pole? Had me worried for a moment. Anyway, whilst admiring the eloquence and wit of your prose, I noted with a modicum of interest that you will be visiting the Big Turnip, as I like to call it, next week…

Anna smiled and wriggled herself further up against the white vinyl headboard, which creaked alarmingly. It was certainly not a bed in which to have vigorous sex, although she had tried to avoid thinking about that for the last few weeks. Aside from the creaking, the captive audience was enough to dampen anyone's ardour, observed as she was by an assortment of aggressive-looking Ninja Turtles and a startled-looking Teddy Ruxpin with a cassette tape permanently shoved up his rear end. No, she was spending the second Summer of Love in Cambridge teaching English to a revolving door of Italian and German students, which

THEN

was how she'd ended up here, in the bedroom of her host's seven-year-old son, whilst he shared with his brother next door.

She returned to the Hulk's letter – the rounded, almost feminine handwriting tightly packed onto four pages of memo paper headed 'Ventris Construction'.

Clearly, they were keeping him busy.

So, what news from the Big Turnip? Well, in the latest instalment of 'Rossiter Road: A Story of Four Totally Incompatible Housemates', Julian is bored. It's not surprising really, all he does is lie on his bed and say: 'I'm bored, I'm bored, I'm bored.' Stavros is living at home but comes up at weekends, gets pissed then goes home again. Dan has failed to get a job despite, as he keeps reminding us, his excellent interview technique. He spends all day watching Jimbo and Playbus, drinking cheap wine and muttering, 'I need a fuck' a lot.

Anna paused and re-read the last sentence. On the one hand, she noted with satisfaction that Dan had failed to find another lover. On the other hand, was the Hulk implying that Dan was an utterly superficial bastard who was only interested in getting laid? She read on.

And me, well, I'm having a marvellous time, living the life of a playboy of the western world...

She was impressed with the Synge reference.

...so if you fancy meeting up, give me a ring (telephone number above). Your call will be answered in a polite, professional manner – that is, unless I pick up the receiver, when it will be answered by a bored, pissed-off Scotsman.

Anna laughed out loud.

Hope to see you next week, can't really think of a good reason why and all that stuff. Lots of love...

She rested the last page on her lap and looked up.

'So, what shall I do, Teddy Ruxpin? Shall I phone him?'

Teddy Ruxpin appeared to have no strong opinion on the matter, but the Ninja Turtles gave the impression that they thought it was a good idea. She was persuaded. Anyway, she was bored, and she deserved some laughs.

They arranged to meet at a pub near the Tower of London after she'd dropped her students off for a guided tour. He was already there, standing at the bar, his body half-turned towards the door. Despite his resolution to look cool, his face lit up as she entered. He watched as her eyes scanned the room. He lifted his hand and, when she saw him, her expression betrayed a nanosecond of relief that she hadn't been stood up. Her face broke into a smile.

She was wearing the blue cornflower dress. He noticed slight sunburn on her shoulders that would eventually turn golden, the dark tendrils of fringe that clung to the

THEN

faint sheen of perspiration on her brow. The tip of her tongue moistened the cupid's bow of her lips, and his heart tightened.

'Well, you look lovely!' He gestured at her dress.

She smiled and looked at the white plimsolls on her feet. 'Not exactly a fashion statement,' she laughed, 'but needs must when you're schlepping around London.'

They hovered briefly, suddenly unsure of how to proceed. As he bent to kiss her mouth, she aimed for his cheek, and they met awkwardly somewhere in between.

'So!' Her face flushed pink beneath the summer freckles sprinkled across her nose.

'So!' He lifted his pint. 'Can I get you a drink?'

'Thanks. A chilled dry white, I think.'

They found themselves a corner table and leant over their drinks, smiling at each other. Anna sensed that the atmosphere was different, somehow, from their usual larky banter.

'How's it going as a playboy of the western world, then?' she ventured.

The Hulk spread his arms wide. 'Fighting them off with a big stick, as you can see.'

She grinned. 'It must be exhausting for you!'

He watched her as she picked idly at the corner of a beer mat, the fingers slender and delicate, a small silver ring on her right index finger inlaid with some kind of iridescent blue shell.

'And how's it going with the students?'

'Oh, good. Occasionally, hilarious. There was the student who told me he'd written his answer "on ze backside". Well, I didn't fancy going there to grade his efforts. Of course, he meant the other side of the page.'

He laughed. 'Any more good ones?'

'Well, one day we were talking about food and what we liked to eat, and this girl said, "I like to eat the cock."' She raised an eyebrow in warning. 'Before you get too excited and ask for her number, let me tell you I had to explain to her that a cock and a chicken are not the same thing, in more ways than one.'

The Hulk tried not to splatter his mouthful of beer as he shook with laughter.

And then the strange atmosphere was broken, and the banter was back, and it was fun again.

'How's the house-share?'

'S'alright.'

'Julian still bored?'

'Yep.'

'Stavros still pissed?'

'Yep.'

'Dan still unemployed?' She'd mentioned him last. She didn't want to sound like she was fishing.

'Actually, no,' the Hulk replied in a tone of surprise. 'He's just got a job as a milkman.'

Now it was Anna's turn to try to avoid splattering her drinking companion with a mouthful of wine.

'Seriously?'

He nodded.

'Dear God, it sounds like one of those soft porn films from the '70s.' She adopted the deep voice of a movie trailer announcer: '*Confessions of a Milkman*, starring Dan

THEN

Randall. Delivering the White Stuff to housewives all over London.'

The Hulk laughed. 'Balham may be awash with Dan lookalikes in nine months' time.'

'What a horrific thought!'

Anna got another round in, and they talked and laughed until, suddenly, she looked at her watch and said she had to go – the tour was about to finish. He attempted to prolong the afternoon by walking her to the entrance of the Tower.

'Haven't you got work to get back to?'

'Nah. They won't have missed me for a couple of hours.'

But they had, and he'd got a stern talking-to from his supervisor afterwards.

Recognising the tour guide's yellow umbrella, Anna waved at her students and began to break into a jog. 'Gotta go,' she called. 'It's been good to see you!'

'You too,' he called back. 'Stay in touch, yeah?'

'Yeah!' she yelled, as she was absorbed into the crowd.

He stood there for a minute as the tide of tourists surged past him, looking for the blue cornflowers in the distance until, turning, he walked away, feeling suddenly bereft.

***

Before they knew it, the heat of summer had faded, there was a chill in the early morning air, and it was late September. Julian lounged languidly across the expanse of brown velour, his leg extended, his arm draped along the back of the sofa. A thin roll-up drooped from the corner of his mouth. With his floppy blond hair and high cheekbones, he looked like he'd wandered off the set of *Brideshead Revisited*.

'F*AAA*F week coming up,' he drawled, without explanation.

At a time before everyone had mobile phones, Sally and Anna had eschewed the phone box and had decided instead to call round to Rossiter Road to make arrangements for Freshers' Week. There was an air of unspoken excitement at the new year that lay before them, with its myriad possibilities – even for Anna, who now had a proper, grown-up job at, of all places, a convent school.

'What's F*AAA*F week?' she asked, mimicking the drawn-out vowel sound. 'Not an acronym with which I am familiar.'

'Fuck A Fresher week,' said Dan, coming through the door. 'Fresh meat,' he added, for emphasis.

Anna turned and felt her stomach lurch.

The milk round had clearly agreed with him. He looked tanned and gorgeous, and she fancied him like mad, but she wasn't going to let him see that, not when he was clearly contemplating new conquests. Instead, she adopted a defensive, adversarial position.

'That's sexist,' she retorted.

'Not at all.' They stared hard at each other. 'I'm sure there are just as many *male* freshers out there available to fuck.'

She flinched.

'Or women, if that's your thing…'

THEN

She gave him a withering look.

'So…' Sally said, changing the subject. 'Next Thursday, student union bar, say eight o'clock?'

'Peeerfect,' drawled Julian, taking a drag on his cigarette and inhaling deeply.

The student union bar was heaving, full of newly independent, fresh-faced teenagers high on the endless possibilities of reinvention and intent upon leaving their former, less interesting, selves behind.

'Oh,' groaned Sally, 'we're never going to get served.'

Anna surveyed the tightly packed bodies waving notes at the bar staff and plotted her route. She moved off.

'Diabetic coming through!' she yelled as she shouldered her way through the crowd. 'Sorry…sorry… diabetic!' She felt fleetingly guilty as a guy stood aside to let her get to the front of the bar.

'Thanks,' said Anna. 'I can just feel a hypo coming on.' He nodded sympathetically. In an attempt to assuage her conscience, she turned to face him, smiling sweetly. 'Can I get you anything while I'm here?'

'Pint of Stella, please.'

Anna smiled at the barman. 'Two Cokes please, not the Diet kind, oh, and can you stick a rum in them? And a pint of Stella.'

She passed the pint to the guy behind her, then, clutching the drinks, Anna made eye contact with Sally, who gestured to her right. Someone had had the common sense to open the doors onto the balcony overlooking the river. They moved into the cool air with relief.

'How did you get served so quickly?' asked Sally, raising her glass.

'I said I was diabetic.'

'Oh my god,' Sally exclaimed, furrowing her brow with concern. 'You never told me you're a diabetic!'

Anna shrugged. 'I'm not. But it got me served faster.'

Sally looked at her, open-mouthed.

'Fancy seeing you here!' boomed a Scottish voice behind them. Anna felt a tap on her shoulder and turned to see the Hulk smiling down at her.

'Hello, you!' She grinned, looking beyond him for Dan and tugging at her black Lycra dress. It had been a quick change after a staff meeting that night and she hadn't had time to shower.

'Dan and Julian are at the bar,' the Hulk explained, as if he knew what she was thinking. 'How's school?'

'Oh, you know. Sensible shoes and tweeds.'

She had a fleeting flashback to an excruciatingly embarrassing conversation she'd had with her Head of Department, who'd drawn her aside one day in the staffroom, pointed at her very short miniskirt and explained that we expect pupils to adhere to a uniform code, and, as teachers, we should never underestimate our influence as role models, and please could she just pop into Next on her way home and buy some office-appropriate skirts that were longer than her earrings?

'So it's Dead Poets' Society and all that,' the Hulk joked.

'Yeah, though I try to get some live ones in there, too. At least, Ted Hughes was the last time I checked.'

'Carpe diem,' the Hulk continued.

THEN

'Yeah, carpe bloody diem,' Anna laughed, 'but unlike with John Keating, none of my students has been driven to suicide. At least, not yet.'

Sally chuckled and nodded her head in the direction of the bar. 'Just look at those two.'

Behind them, Julian and Dan were intent on their sole objective of the week: to Fuck A Fresher. The unwitting freshers they had selected were a petite brunette in black stirrup pants and high heels and a bouffant-haired blonde with aristocratic features and the air of the boarding school about her. Julian was projecting a carefully constructed persona of intellectual cool, somewhat thwarted in his attempt to run his fingers nonchalantly through his hair by the sheer volume of mousse he had applied earlier that evening.

'I bet he's talking psycho-bollocks,' Sally laughed, 'encouraging her to release her repressed id.'

'Yeah, well he's certainly got the ego,' quipped Anna.

'Dan's chances look a little better, though.'

Anna observed him, fascinated despite herself. His tall frame hunched over the petite brunette, listening intently as she chattered and gesticulated, looking into her eyes – he was actually looking into her eyes – with an expression of gentle attentiveness, smiling and nodding. A swell of jealousy surged through her veins – there was no smash-and-grab kiss, no sarky point-scoring.

The Hulk placed his hand on Anna's shoulder and put his mouth to her ear. 'They've got a bet on. Tenner for whoever pulls first.'

She suddenly felt sick and moved away, turning to face

the river. Tower Bridge was rising as a boat approached; the National Theatre's digital display advertised *Cymbeline* – a play she'd never read – and an upcoming production of *The Good Person of Sichuan*. She inhaled deeply.

'Best view in London,' she announced, then, 'come on – let's go upstairs. I fancy a dance.'

***

The hand on the wall clock ticked loudly, dragging itself reluctantly from one minute to the next. Unbelievably, it was only 9.25am. Anna could feel herself break into a cold sweat as Emma Dobbs plodded through Shakespeare's fine words with dogged determination.

'The murtherers... *murtherers*?' Emma looked up quizzically, but her teacher was staring hard at the back wall, so she continued, '...steeped in the colours of their trade...'

Anna sucked harder on a Polo mint, desperately attempting to quell the rising nausea. She'd not had time to brush her teeth that morning. The previous night, she'd thought it was a good idea for her and Sally to go on to a party at the art school, after which she'd fallen asleep fully dressed on the sofa at Sally's place. After three hours of fitful sleep, she had managed to keep down a slice of dry toast before dragging herself halfway across London by tube and train, clutching a hastily emptied make-up bag in case of emergency.

In the corner, Karina Martin snorted and rummaged around a nostril with her finger.

THEN

'...their daggers unmannerly breached with gore...'

The combined image of Karina's mucus-covered finger and Duncan's gore prompted a sudden, dangerous lurch in Anna's stomach. She staggered to the sash window, one hand covering her mouth, the other frantically shoving at the window frame.

Bloody. Sash. Window. Bloody. Well. Open.

Anna eyed Plan B: the waste-paper bin.

'...who could refrain, that had a heart to love...' Emma Dobbs continued, nose inches above the page as if this might help her pronunciation.

Finally, the window gave way. The rest of the class watched in horrified fascination as their teacher leant out of the third-floor window and dry retched twice.

'...and in that heart courage, to make's love known...'

'Shut up, Emma!' yelled Karina, throwing a pencil case at her head. 'Miss isn't very well. Miss, Miss, are you alright?'

Anna was very evidently not alright. Her face had taken on a deathly pallor.

'Maybe she's got morning sickness,' suggested Shereen Davies. 'Miss, Miss, are you expecting a baby?'

Excited speculation circulated around the room.

Anna closed her eyes. She daren't open her mouth to quash the rumours for fear of the consequences. As her stomach lurched again, more violently this time, she leant further out, willing the window not to crash down on her like a guillotine, and heaved not only the toast but the entirety of last night's stomach contents a merciful few centimetres to the left of Sister Etheldreda, who was walking below.

SOMETHING CHANGED

Sister Etheldreda looked up, startled, as if receiving a message from God.

'I'm going to get someone,' announced Karina Martin decisively as she strode off to fetch Matron, puffed with self-importance.

'Sip it slowly,' instructed Matron, lifting a plastic cup of water to Anna's lips. 'Don't gulp or you'll bring it all up again.'

Sister Etheldreda popped her head around the sickroom door, and Anna had the decency to inwardly cringe in shame.

'Ah, and how's the patient?'

'On the mend,' stated Matron brusquely.

Anna smiled weakly. 'I'm so sorry, Sister.'

'You don't want to be apologising, my girl. Those tummy bugs can be awful fierce. You want to be getting yourself home. I'll call you a taxi…'

Anna made as if to protest, but Sister Etheldreda raised her hand. 'No arguments. You're going home. Get yourself well.'

As she made her way to the taxi, Anna heard someone call her name. Her colleague, Claire, crossed the playground towards her.

'Anna Thompson,' she said in mock chastisement, looking her up and down, 'are those the same clothes you were wearing yesterday?'

Anna raised an eyebrow.

'You dirty stop-out!' Claire winked. 'I hope he was worth it!'

THEN

But Freshers' Week had not been the thrilling den of sexual debauchery the lads had hoped for. Mostly, it had been a week of throbbing hangovers, cheesy chat-up lines, dodgy kebabs and girls lovesick for their boyfriends back home.

'I think she was secretly a *lesbian*,' drawled Julian, pulling a face before knocking back another gin and tonic. 'A lot of them look perfectly hetero but it's all a *façade*.'

'Who was a lesbian?' asked the Hulk.

'Selina.'

'The blonde with the big hair?'

'Mmm.'

'The one who blew you out because she had a rich boyfriend at Sandhurst?'

'He has my sympathies.'

'What about her friend?'

Julian narrowed his eyes. 'They were probably at it together like rabbits,' he said, exhaling a halo of smoke. 'Dan didn't have any luck there, either.'

'You poor things!' Sally laughed. 'All that testosterone and no takers.'

Anna patted the top of Julian's head. 'Aww, bless. And a missed opportunity for a threesome.'

Julian's face fell. 'I hadn't thought of that,' he said, like a kid who'd just dropped his ice cream.

'I'd have loved to see their faces if you'd suggested that!' The Hulk laughed.

Anna looked up and turned to Sally. 'Your date has arrived!'

A guy was walking towards them looking like Terence Trent D'Arby's lost twin, an image of urban cool with the kind of face that you'd find, appropriately enough, on the cover of *The Face*.

'Hi, Kris!' they chorused as he bent to kiss Sally on the cheek.

'Man,' he grinned, 'the tube, right? It took me – what? Forty-five minutes to get here.'

Sally pulled an apologetic face. 'I should have met you there.'

'Nah, nah, you'd never have found it.' He held up her coat. 'Come on, let's get going.'

And with a wave, they were gone.

'The sole success story of the last few weeks,' said Julian, a tad bitterly, as he watched them leave.

The bar was surprisingly quiet for a Saturday night. One of the bar staff had resorted to reading J.S Mill; the others were leaning against the wall in the far corner, chatting.

'God, it's dead in here tonight.' The Hulk sighed despondently. 'Come on, Julian, pick your ego up off the floor and we'll all go back to ours.' He turned to Anna. 'You can sleep in my bed if you like.' Then, seeing her expression, he quickly added, 'Obviously, I'll sleep on the sofa.'

So, in the absence of anything better to do, she joined them.

The season was turning. Amber leaves scuttled down the streets; the days were shortening and there was a chill in the air. They'd sat patiently as the Northern line made its usual unexplained and interminable stops in dark tunnels, finally arriving at Rossiter Road with the air of weary travellers at the end of an epic journey.

THEN

The TV blasted out from the back room. Stavros sat in his boxers and a large, baggy T-shirt, legs spread wide. He looked at them, scratching the dark stubble on his cheeks.

'Alright?'

'Alright?' they responded.

'Don't mind me,' said Anna, pointing to his boxers, which had begun to gape alarmingly around the fly.

Stavros, a man of few words, merely nodded and turned once again to watch two men kicking the living daylights out of each other on the screen.

'You know what?' announced Julian, clearly unimpressed by the entertainment on offer. 'I think I'm done for the night. See you in the morning.'

Anna and the Hulk stood awkwardly in front of the television.

'Can I get you a drink?'

'Don't mind if I do. What've you got?'

The Hulk looked at the bottle next to Stavros's armchair. 'What you drinking, Stav?'

'Australian rum,' he replied. With eyes still fixed on the screen, he picked up the bottle and swivelled his arm sideways. 'Want some?'

'I'll just find some glasses,' said the Hulk solicitously, as if not swigging rum from a bottle was the height of sophistication.

She heard the tap running in the kitchen.

'Good summer, Stav?' enquired Anna politely.

He continued looking at the screen. 'Yup.'

The Hulk returned with two hastily rinsed glasses and extended one towards her.

'I didn't know they made rum in Australia,' Anna said, looking closely at the label on the bottle.

'Well, let's give it a try.'

The Hulk poured two generous measures, and they knocked them back. Within seconds, Anna felt like her throat and her entire stomach lining were on fire.

The Hulk spluttered. 'Jesus, Stav, is this stuff legal?'

Stavros shrugged.

'Water?' pleaded Anna hoarsely.

The Hulk beat a hasty retreat to the kitchen to fill her glass and she downed it in one gulp.

'Well, that was an experience!'

They flopped on the sofa. Anna removed her black suede courts and rubbed her feet, grimacing. 'They're killing me!'

'Stick them up here and I'll give you a foot rub.'

Anna looked at him doubtfully.

'I'm good at foot rubs!' he protested.

'It's not that. I'm just questioning why anyone would want to go near my feet. Have you done a risk assessment?'

'Potential biohazard.' He laughed. 'Seal off the room! Alert Porton Down!'

Anna laughed and lay along the length of the sofa, her feet in his lap. He began massaging the pads of her toes, moving downwards to the arch of her foot.

She began giggling. 'Not there!'

'Anna Thompson, are you ticklish?'

Stavros stood abruptly and removed his kick-boxing video. 'Off to bed,' he said.

'Goodnight, Stav,' called Anna.

THEN

'Thank fuck for that,' muttered the Hulk. 'Now we can watch something decent.' He lifted her feet and made his way to the TV, rummaging through the video pile.

'The Jam?' he enquired.

She nodded, and he shoved the video into the slot.

'Stick your feet up.'

She obeyed and he sat back down.

Eton Rifles, A Town Called Malice...

'You wanna risk another rum?'

Just as Anna was considering this question, the door slowly creaked open and Dan's head appeared. He looked from Anna to the Hulk and froze. Recovering himself, he attempted a smile.

'Just thought I'd say goodnight. I'm off to bed.' His head disappeared and the door closed.

'Goodnight, Dan,' Anna called after him.

The Hulk laughed loudly.

'What are you laughing at?'

'Him.' He gestured towards the door.

'He probably wants us to turn the volume down. His room's right next door.'

The Hulk shook his head. 'You know, Anna, for an intelligent girl, you can be really stupid sometimes.'

She looked at him, frowning. 'What?'

'It's pretty obvious he was hoping to find you on your own. So he can try to have his wicked way with you and all that.'

'You think so?' Anna secretly hoped that he was right.

'I know so.'

Neither of them spoke for a while.

The Hulk squeezed her feet and looked at her. 'We have a good laugh, yeah?'

Anna – her arms folded behind her head, her face turned towards Paul Weller – replied: 'Yeah.'

'We're pretty good together.'

Anna turned to look directly at him. 'Yeah, we have a good laugh. Why?'

'Well, you know. I just wondered…' He cleared his throat. 'I just wondered how things were between me and you.'

'Me and you? We're good.'

He shifted awkwardly. 'Good – you know – how?'

Anna swung her feet to the floor and sat up. 'What are you getting at?'

He looked at her in sheer frustration. 'Because… because I'm in *love* with you, Anna. I've been in love with you for months. I think about you all the time.'

She didn't know what to say.

'The postcards, that day in the summer when we met, and since then… I thought you felt the same.'

Anna thought back to that day; the way he'd looked at her; the way the atmosphere had been somehow different. Had she really known it then? Had she chosen to ignore it? Worse, had she been *playing* him?

He sat, face flushed, looking at her with terrible hope. She wished she could give him the answer that he wanted to hear. But she couldn't. Uncharacteristically, she stumbled for words.

Eventually, she said: 'I didn't know you felt that way.' But even as she said it, she suspected it was a lie.

'Well, you know now.' He was breathing hard.

'I love you to bits,' she began, adding quickly, 'but not in the way you want me to. I really want to, but I can't.'

He shook his head in confusion. 'What do you mean, you want to, but you can't?'

She didn't answer.

There was a slow realisation.

'You fancy someone else?'

She avoided his eyes.

'Who? Who is it?'

Involuntarily, she looked towards the door. He followed her gaze, open-mouthed, then his head slumped into his hands.

'You have got to be fucking kidding me.'

He tried to compose himself, on the verge of tears, and his anguish turned to a slow, quiet anger.

'Dan? *Dan?*' He spat the words. 'Can't you see what he's like? The only person he thinks about is himself; the only person he cares about is himself; the only person he puts first is himself.' He looked at her. 'Is that what you want?'

For a long time, she didn't answer, then she said, lamely: 'You can't choose who you fall for.'

'Yes, you can, Anna. Yes, you fucking well can.'

He hid his face in his hands, breathing hard, and she placed one hand tentatively on his shoulder.

Finally, he looked up, his expression and his voice composed.

'Do you think it could ever happen? Me and you?'

Anna lowered her eyes. 'I don't know.' She pressed a fingernail into her thumb. 'But I don't want to lose you as a friend.'

For a while he sat, staring at the floor, then he left the room, returning a few minutes later with a blanket.

'You have my bed.'

'No, I'm fine here.' She took the blanket from him and spread it across her. He bent to straighten it and kissed her forehead.

'Goodnight.' He stood, looking down at her for a moment, then turned and disappeared through the door.

Anna huddled beneath the blanket, trembling with the cold, or adrenalin, she could not tell. She looked at her watch. She'd missed the last tube. She lay awake in the dark until 5am when she slipped out of the door and waited on the platform for the first tube train home.

***

Sally sat in Anna's kitchen clutching a fried egg sandwich in one hand and scooping up the yellow trail of yolk that had dripped down her chin with the tip of an index finger.

'So you had a good half term week?' she enquired, watching Anna thump the end of an HP bottle.

'Yeah.' Anna had taken herself home to visit an old school friend who'd just had a baby, thereby missing the school trip to Berlin, which had proven to be unexpectedly momentous. 'He's a tiny little thing. I didn't realise babies could be that small.' Anna bit into the bread and chewed. 'I mean, fair play to her and all that. I couldn't cope with motherhood at the ripe old age of twenty-three.'

'God, no!' Sally exclaimed. 'Got a few years of partying left in me yet.'

THEN

'So, aside from the Berlin Wall coming down, what's the other big news? Anything exciting happened in my absence?'

Sally didn't answer. She finished eating her sandwich.

Anna frowned. 'Everything OK with you and Kris?'

'Oh, yeah.'

'So?'

Silence.

'Come on, spill!' Anna nudged her friend's elbow, laughing. 'What's the gossip?'

Sally didn't laugh. 'I saw Dan a couple of days ago, after a lecture.'

'How nice for you.'

Sally flashed her a look. 'It's not funny, Anna.'

'What's not funny?'

'He had a black eye.'

'Then he needs to be careful who he chats up!'

Sally gave her a measured look, then continued. 'Apparently, the Hulk and two of his mates waylaid him on the way home from the pub one night and gave him a beating. He didn't say why. Phil says he's black and blue.'

Anna sat in silence.

'Anyway, he's moved out of Rossiter Road and back into halls.' Sally screwed the top back on the sauce bottle and took her plate to the sink. 'I don't know what's going on there, Anna,' she said pointedly, running the tap, 'but whatever it is, it needs to be sorted.'

Anna didn't answer.

Sally washed the plate, placed it on the drainer and turned to face her friend. 'Anyway, enough about the lads. Let's sort out the party.'

SOMETHING CHANGED

The End of the Wall party was arranged for early December. The victory of Western capitalism over the communist East was celebrated with copious amounts of alcohol, economy pizzas and a variety of cheap potato snacks.

As a precautionary measure against being in the same house as Dan and the Hulk, Anna had invited her colleague, Rich, an affable guy whose girlfriend had just dumped him and who needed cheering up. He stood, huddled in his grey peacoat, outside the tube station, clutching a plastic bag containing two bottles of wine and stomping his feet to keep warm, the vapour from his breath curling into the air.

'Rich!'

He lifted his hand and saw Anna skipping down the road towards him, cocooned in a grandad coat and the world's longest scarf.

'Come on, lovelorn from Lewisham!' She leant in and gave him a peck on the cheek, and he smiled gratefully. 'Auntie Anna is going to help you to heal your broken heart!'

They felt the thump of the bass before they even rounded the corner. As they neared the house, Anna could hear Soul II Soul's Club Classics blasting out; light glowed from the windows, silhouetting the dancing figures within. People – many of whom Anna didn't recognise – spilled out into the front garden despite the cold, clutching cans and plastic cups. Julian leant against the wall in the hallway like an unofficial doorman.

Anna shouldered her way through the crowd towards

the kitchen, Rich trailing behind her, and flung off her coat. She spied Jenny standing alone at the end of the hallway.

'Jenny!'

Jenny looked around and smiled.

'Jenny, this is Rich; Rich, this is Jenny.' They smiled politely at each other. 'Why don't you two get to know each other whilst I get some drinks?' She pushed her way into the kitchen.

'Well, look who it is.' The Hulk stood, beer bottle in hand, next to Sally in the corner.

After that night in Rossiter Road, he had lain awake in bed, replaying his conversation with Anna in his head, and had made a decision. She wanted to love him, that's what she'd said, and the reason she couldn't was Dan. It was Dan, then, who became the focus of his anger and animosity, and when Anna eventually came to her senses, as she surely must, he would be there, ready and waiting.

He bent to kiss her cheek.

'Ah, a bottle of Grolsch!' Anna exclaimed, nodding towards his hand. 'Save the bottle tops for me.'

'Bottle tops? What do you want those for?'

'The girls at school are tying them to their shoelaces,' Anna laughed, 'I thought I might join them and pledge my allegiance to Bros.'

'Jesus!' groaned Sally. 'Not bloody Bros!'

'I'm nothing if not conversant with youth culture!' boasted Anna.

'There's a line to be drawn,' said Sally emphatically, 'and Bros is that line.'

They laughed.

Anna waved towards the fridge. 'Just need to get some drinks. I brought a friend.' She grabbed a couple of cans and headed towards the hallway, waving one above her head to attract Rich's attention. As she arrived, Jenny moved off, pulling a face at her and shaking her head slowly.

Anna sighed heavily. 'Please tell me you haven't spent the last five minutes talking about your ex?'

He smiled apologetically.

'Oh, Rich!'

He cracked open the can. 'Apologise to your friend for me.'

'Oh, Jenny won't mind. She's a great girl.'

She looked over his shoulder. Coming towards her was Dan. Instinctively, she turned, moved her mouth close to Rich's ear, placed a hand on his other shoulder and stage whispered a joke about one of their colleagues. They laughed, faces close together, eyes locked on each other in mirth.

The hallway was packed, and Anna was right between it and the kitchen. It was hot inside, and Dan was desperately thirsty. To her left, a couple were enthusiastically consuming each other's faces. He'd have to push between them and her to get himself a drink. Weaving through the bodies, he watched Anna and the guy she'd brought with her, who looked like some well-meaning social worker. He watched as she whispered in his ear, noticing the familiarity of her hand on his shoulder; the way that she looked into his eyes before throwing her head back in laughter.

Why was she never, *ever* alone?

He turned himself sideways and pushed awkwardly between the kissing couple and Anna's back. He looked

THEN

down at the low scoop of her dress, the three small moles between her shoulder blades like Orion's belt, felt his groin brush uncomfortably against her buttocks. The social worker type was laughing idiotically.

Anna felt Dan behind her but didn't turn. If he couldn't be bothered to say hello, why should she? And so that night she danced and drank and laughed until Rich said he really thought he should be getting home, and she walked with him to the end of the front path and hugged him goodnight.

Dan stood in the doorway as she made her way back towards the house. The crowd had thinned now; the dancing had stopped, and people were strewn over the furniture and floor.

'Are you with that guy?'

'Sorry?'

'That guy.' Dan nodded behind her towards the front gate. 'Are you with him?'

'Given that I am here, and he is not, clearly I am not *with* him.'

'You know what I mean.'

As she made to push past him, he turned his face towards hers and kissed her. She didn't protest; she didn't resist; she kissed him right back. Finally, he pulled away and, holding her hand tightly as if she might slip away, he found their coats and they left.

***

Light was seeping around the corners of the blind. Anna looked across at her alarm clock. It was 8.30am. She felt a sudden jolt of panic that she was late for school, then remembered that it was Sunday morning. Next to her, a body stirred. Dan opened one eye and looked at her.

'Morning.'

She turned on her side to face him. 'Morning.'

He smiled and kissed her, his hand tracing the dip and the rise from her waist to her hips and down along her thigh. She pulled back, looking into his eyes, and ran her finger down his cheekbone before resting it on his lips. She kissed him again before snuggling into his chest. His heart beat a steady rhythm against her cheek.

They had been meeting like this for months now, slipping away from pubs, bars and parties, always leaving apart, always reuniting at the nearest station before taking the train back to Anna's flat, rocking and clattering over the tracks, engrossed in each other.

Dan buried his face in her hair and inhaled deeply. 'I love the way you smell.'

Anna wriggled. 'I haven't washed my hair for two days.'

'No, I don't mean shampoo or soap. I mean the way *you* smell.'

Anna adopted an aristocratic voice. 'Darling, all those years I wore Chanel when I could have been bottling Eau de Anna!'

Dan smiled, a wide, straight-toothed, toothpaste-ad smile. Self-consciously, the tip of her tongue moved to the small chip on the edge of her front tooth.

'You know what?' he began.

'What?'

THEN

'If we had a kid, with my looks and your brains, it couldn't go wrong.'

'What if it's the other way around?'

He laughed. 'Then we're fucked!'

She hit him with the pillow.

He swung his feet out of the bed. 'Come on, let's get up. I need a coffee.'

At that moment, she loved him so much, it made her chest ache.

NOW

Jack consulted the Open Day schedule neatly laid out across a glossy page, a different coloured box denoting each department.

'Right, so – Politics is green.' His finger slid downwards. 'There's an Introduction to Politics followed by a lecture in the Wilson lecture theatre in fifteen minutes. Hold this a minute, Dad...' He shoved the schedule towards Dan's chest, frowning with concentration, and turned to rummage in the canvas Welcome Bag that had been handed to him by students who had been unusually bright and cheery for 10am on a Saturday morning. 'Mum, can you find the map? It's in here somewhere.'

Dan straightened the crumpled schedule. 'No need, son. I know where the Wilson lecture theatre is.' He nodded to their left. 'Just down there. *Trump and the Appeal of Populism*,' he read aloud. 'That sounds interesting...'

'Well, it'll be interesting to hear what Mueller has to say.' Jack smirked, as if he was an FBI insider. 'I'll bet Trump is wishing he'd never fired Comey!'

They shuffled along the queue moving into the lecture theatre.

NOW

'I like this bag,' Anna said. 'They didn't have all this promotional stuff when your dad and I were students.' She held aloft a branded water bottle, an inflatable beach ball, a wristband and multiple pens. 'We'll try to get some more of those pens,' she added. 'They'll be useful.'

'Right,' said Jack, sarcastically, 'because there's a worldwide pen shortage. This is how capitalism corrupts, Mum. It starts with a shiny pen and before you know it, you've sold your soul to The Man.'

'Well, I like shiny pens,' she replied. 'And anyway, your father and I sold our souls to The Man a long time ago.'

'Right, let's get a seat, then,' Dan interrupted, surveying the room. The Wilson lecture theatre lay before them like a relic from a Victorian time capsule, with its tiered, steeply backed oak seating and the aroma of furniture polish lingering in the air. He sat down, arching his back and rolling his shoulders. 'I don't remember it being this uncomfortable.'

'Ah, in the good old days when you were permanently hungover and before you got a dodgy back.'

Dan brushed a hand over the top of his head. Over the years, the dark, wavy hair had retreated like an outnumbered battalion; after a brief period in his late twenties when the last strands standing had lingered, as if in hope of regrouping and launching a retaliatory strike, Dan (with some persuasion from Anna) had finally admitted defeat and shaved the lot off. He tugged at his shirt, worn loose over his expanding belly, and the buttonholes strained.

'You're not *staying*?' Jack said, more statement than question. 'This is for applicants, not parents.'

Anna looked around the lecture theatre, which was rapidly filling up around them. Smug middle-class parents took their seats next to their offspring, all of whom appeared to be hunching in Jack Wills hoodies in acute embarrassment. She stood up.

'Come on, Dan,' she said. 'Let's go and get a coffee or something.'

'Oh.' He looked disappointed but, after seeing Jack's expression, said, 'Alright, then.'

Anna squeezed past her son. 'Enjoy Trump! See you in about an hour.'

THEN

It was the summer of the heatwave. There had been regular fainters in Anna's classroom and, in the end, in the days before interactive whiteboards and interminable PowerPoints, she had simply taken her pupils outside with books and pens under the shade of the trees. Such was the extremity of the temperature, the deputy head had made the unprecedented announcement that pupils were no longer required to wear ties, or even to fasten the top button of their shirts. Liberated by such a relaxation of the rules, levels of rebellion were signified by how many buttons were left undone, from the virginal one button to the three-button abandon of the aspiring Page Three model.

But outdoor lessons at school were about the only time Anna got to see the sun, as World Cup fever had descended. With the exception of the Hulk, who defiantly wore Scottish blue, everyone else, including Sally, wore Three Lions on their shirts. They spent their time in darkened rooms with the curtains closed against bright sunlight, knocking back cans of Skol and shouting at the TV like they'd suddenly become seasoned football pundits.

SOMETHING CHANGED

It was no way to spend a summer.

'Come on, guys, let's go out! We're British! We spend over half the year indoors in darkness anyway! It's *summer!*'

No one moved. England were playing the Netherlands, and it was 0-0. Phil and Sally were having a bet on whether Lineker or Gascoigne would score the first goal for England. Dan crumpled an empty Skol can in one hand, let it drop to the floor, then reached for another. Julian peered into his cigarette packet and realised he was down to his last two fags, and it wasn't even half-time yet.

Anna perched on the arm of Sally's chair and waved a hand in front of her face. 'Remember the good old days? When we used to drink outside in pub gardens?'

'Sorry, pet, I'm going nowhere. My money's on Gascoigne to score.'

Anna sighed, grabbed a can of Skol and feigned interest in the sweeper system, quietly hoping that England would get knocked out and she could reclaim the alfresco summer with friends that, to date, remained solely a figment of her overactive imagination.

But England didn't get knocked out and by the time they had, unbelievably, made it to the semi-final, football had taken on the status of a national religion. Unable to face sitting through an entire match, Anna had timed her arrival at Sally's to coincide with the end of the game. It was a school night, but there was a party at the art school they were heading to after the match.

Anna raised her fist to bang on the door only to find that it was ajar. She made her way inside, enveloped by the gloom and an eerie silence.

THEN

'Anyone home?'

No answer. She felt a flicker of annoyance. Had they gone to the party without her? She pushed open the living room door. Four faces were ghoulishly illuminated by the bluish-white light of the TV screen.

'Who won?'

'Sssh!' they chorused.

Her eyes turned to the screen just in time to see Chris Waddle kick the ball to the crossbar and four bodies slump with their heads in their hands, groaning loudly.

'Never mind!' said Anna brightly. 'There's always the play-offs!'

Four faces turned towards her, aghast. She wondered if she might have misjudged the mood. Unlike Anna – who had been doing important things all day, like making teenagers literate and writing end-of-year reports using double-speak phrases like 'Christine is a lively presence in classroom discussions' – the rest of them had been drinking since late afternoon.

The art-school party was held in a series of arched, subterranean rooms with little means of natural ventilation, so everyone was sweating like the 'before' image from a Sure advert, even the art-school girls in black with Louise Brooks bobs and the Boho-types with pre-Raphaelite hair.

Men's eyes followed Sally and Anna as they passed. Anna made an effort for art school parties: black Lycra minidress, stilettos, red lippy.

As the others went off to dance, Dan cornered her near the bar. An afternoon of drinking had loosened his inhibitions, but he wasn't yet completely drunk.

'You look gorgeous.'

She looked at him, bemused.

'Like one of those girls in that Robert Palmer video… for… uh…'

'Yeah, I know the one. None of them could play the guitar, either.'

'No, seriously, you look gorgeous.'

'You've got your beer goggles on.'

'Take a compliment.'

She shrugged.

Dan half fell on the sole remaining seat behind him.

'I see the age of chivalry isn't dead.'

'What?'

'I was hoping to take the weight off myself.' Anna lifted a stilettoed foot.

He beckoned her closer. 'Come and sit on my lap, then.'

She wriggled onto his thighs, trying to get comfortable, then paused and turned to face him. 'Well, well, you *are* pleased to see me.'

His hands encircled her waist. 'I'm always pleased to see you.'

Anna leant in to kiss his neck. After ages of sneaking around, speaking to each other in public in tones of sarky derision and never leaving anywhere at the same time… *finally*, she thought, *finally…*

Behind her, she could hear the raised voices of Sally, Phil and Julian as they returned from the dance floor, and she felt Dan's body stiffen. His jaw was moving against her cheek, but she couldn't hear any words. She sat up, turning.

'Come on, Dan!' said Sally briskly. 'Fancy a dance?'

THEN

He extended his hand towards hers and she pulled him up towards her as Anna staggered to her feet. They disappeared into the next room.

Dan hated dancing.

Anna turned to Phil. 'What was Dan mouthing to you?'

'What do you mean?'

'He was saying something.'

Phil's eyes dropped to the floor.

Julian cleared his throat. 'Get me out of this,' Julian said. 'He was mouthing, "Get me out of this".'

Phil, ever tactful and kind, attempted to soften the blow. 'We assumed you'd had a row or something.'

Anna's face set, hard. 'No, Phil. We were not having a row.'

She bent down to retrieve her bag, threw it onto her shoulder and made her way through the crowd. She bit the corner of her lip. She wouldn't let herself cry.

She'd just reached the archway when she felt a hand on her shoulder. She spun round, arm half raised to deliver a slap, but it wasn't Dan.

'I saw your man back there.'

The guy spoke with a soft, Irish lilt. He pushed back his wavy blond hair. His eyes were a startlingly intense shade of blue.

'He's not *my* man,' Anna replied.

'Well, I should think you'd want to be feeling glad about that.'

She didn't answer.

'I'm Callum.'

'Anna.'

'Art student?'

'English teacher.'

He looked surprised. 'Out on a school night! I'm an architecture student, myself.'

She nodded, still fighting back waves of hurt and anger.

'You know, Anna, any man who'd treat a girl like that is a feckin' idiot. If you'll pardon the language.'

She bit her lip harder.

'Do you want to go on somewhere, for a drink or something?'

She unclamped her lip, suddenly decisive. 'Yeah. Let's go.'

Returning from the dance floor, Dan scanned the room for Anna.

Phil nodded his head towards the next room. 'I think she's left, mate.'

Through the archway, Dan could see a guy draping his arm around Anna's shoulders, steering her towards the stairs. She hadn't wasted much time.

Dan turned back, his face a wall of nonchalance. 'Another round?'

Phil and Sally exchanged a look, and Sally quietly despaired.

***

That autumn, Anna realised something that she had been too naïve – or romantically blind – to understand as an undergraduate: that all men want sex, and that it was

THEN

ridiculously easy to reduce them to a state of drooling lust. This belated realisation produced in her the heady excitement of a child standing in front of Woolworth's pick 'n' mix for the first time, except this time she could have whatever, and as much as, she wanted. Callum fizzled out by the end of the summer like the last, flat dregs from a Coke bottle and was replaced by a rapidly changing assortment of men.

There was dark, curly haired Reuben, the ridiculously wealthy heir to a high street chain of shops. 'Look at those legs!' he'd sighed to Phil as Anna walked past him in the bar one night. 'Can you just imagine those legs wrapped around you?' By the end of the evening, Phil had relented and introduced them. Back at his place, Reuben had covered her naked body in peach-flavoured yoghurt and slowly licked it all off, which was an interesting experience but left Anna, two showers later, still smelling vaguely of sour milk.

Then there was Jonny, a sweet and round-faced fresher, the Benjamin Braddock to her Mrs Robinson. He was hugely enthusiastic and, as a keen amateur rugby player, had the advantage of possessing great stamina. Anna finally had a reality check when she was going through exam entries one evening at school and realised that he was barely a year older than her A level students, after which she reluctantly called it a day.

After him came the darkly handsome medical student Sanjay, who looked like a Bollywood leading man. He was happy to share her bed but admitted that he found her self-confidence intimidating. Now that really made her laugh.

He was followed by shy Otto, who hailed from Germany, looked like Byron and whom she dropped because, although beautiful to look at, ultimately, he had no sense of humour.

She and Sally spent their weekends dancing to Deee-Lite in little black hot pants, competing with Phil, the Hulk and Julian to see who could drink the most pints (it was always the Hulk), passing around copies of Viz with the lads, laughing at Finbar Saunders and the Fat Slags, and eating hangover breakfasts of orange juice and fried egg sandwiches.

Anna hadn't seen Dan for ages. She'd heard that he'd moved back into Faraday Hall for his final year. Then, at a New Year's party, she saw him coming towards her down the stairwell. She lowered her eyes and picked up speed, taking the steps two at a time, determined to avoid him.

'Anna.'

She attempted to push past.

'Anna.' He held out his arm, blocking her path.

She looked up, and all the anger and hurt she'd felt came flooding back.

He felt her body against his arm, close enough to smell her perfume, and his mind was ambushed by the memory of her lips fluttering over his skin, the tips of her fingers tracing his cheekbone.

'Anna. Don't be like this.'

'Like what?'

He flung his arms wide, exasperated. 'Like…this!'

'Why? Afraid you'll need Sally to *get you out of this*?'

'For Christ's sake!'

Anna's mouth set firm.

THEN

'Look, I just thought we could talk. I'm not into anything heavy. I've got finals coming up in a few months.'

She stood silent, glaring.

He couldn't resist a parting shot. 'Anyway, from what I hear, you haven't exactly been short of male company.'

She shoved his arm, hard, and he let it drop.

'Go fuck yourself, Dan.' She pushed past him, not looking back.

As finals inched closer, the mid-week parties disappeared, then Saturday nights at the pub. Friday nights at the student union bar clung on for a while, like fingertips gripping a cliff edge, but there was a mood of unspoken anxiety in the air. Anna, who already had a BA (Hons) and a PGCE to her name, attempted to quell the rising tide of dread, but her platitudes fell on deaf ears and even Phil, who had dedicated most of the last three years to honing his pool-playing skills, picked up a textbook and started reading through his meagre lecture notes.

Anna had an Easter vacation job teaching English at a boarding-school exam crammer in the Home Counties, where she handed out fistfuls of revision notes on *Of Mice and Men* and *The Crucible* and spent evenings marking practice exam papers, trying not to wither away from boredom.

And then, almost as suddenly as it had begun, the exam period was over, and the short-lived relief was replaced by the agonising wait for results.

The phone was ringing as Anna entered her flat. It was Sally, breathless at the end of the line. 'Anna!'

'So, how did you do?'

'Upper second ! I can't believe it!'

Anna beamed. 'Oh, Sal! Well done! How did the others do?'

'The Hulk got an upper second, so did Julian. Stav and Jenny got Desmonds, and Phil got a third.'

'Ouch!'

'I know. But he's just been playing pool and drinking beer for the last three years, so…'

Anna hesitated but couldn't help herself. 'And Dan? How did he do?'

She could hear Sally shrieking with laughter at the other end of the line.

'You're not going to believe this!' she exclaimed and continued laughing. 'He only went and got a First!'

Anna wasn't entirely surprised. No one had seen him for ages. Clearly, he had been studying hard. 'Well, that's fantastic news!'

'Anyway,' said Sally. 'You'll have to come up to the bar after graduation. Everyone will be there. We can celebrate!'

Anna put down her bag of marking and switched the receiver to the other hand. 'Don't worry, I'll be there! Give my congratulations to everybody.'

'Will do! See you soon!' Anna heard a glass smash in the background followed by a loud cheer and then the click of the receiver, and the line went dead.

On graduation day, the student union bar looked like it had fallen victim to a takeover by a corporate bank, filled as it was with people in suits and ties and sensible shoes.

THEN

Sally had replaced her customary hotpants with a knee-length polka-dot shift dress and a smart navy jacket. Even Phil, whose entire wardrobe of two pairs of jeans and four T-shirts had been on rotation for the last three years, had scrubbed up well in a navy suit and blue tie. Proud parents had dispersed to their homes or hotel rooms, and everyone had congregated to get hammered together one last time.

Anna felt extravagant. She was, after all, the only one of them currently in gainful employment.

'A bottle of your finest champagne!' she commanded.

The barman looked at her, his face expressionless. 'This is a student union bar.'

'Yes, I know that.' Anna pulled some notes from her purse. 'I've been coming here for the last few years.'

'Well, then you'll know that we don't have much call for *champagne*.'

There was no need for that tone.

'But this is *graduation day*, a day of *celebration*,' Anna said with emphasis, like she was explaining something simple to a particularly dim student. 'Might you have anticipated a *call for champagne*, do you think?'

He stared back at her and shrugged his shoulders.

Her exasperation was increasing. 'Well, what have you got?'

His hand swept along the optics and the beer taps.

She gave him a steely look.

'There might be a few bottles of cava out the back left over from Christmas,' he relented. 'If you want me to have a look.'

'That would be *wonderful*. Thank you.'

And so they toasted each other in the finest, lukewarm cava, poured into wine glasses in the absence of champagne flutes.

'Just in time!' the Hulk announced his arrival, claiming the last dregs at the bottom of the bottle.

They held their glasses aloft and clinked them in unison. 'Cheers!'

Conversation centred on life after university – job interviews in the offing, who was staying in London, who was moving elsewhere. There was a heady mixture of excitement and trepidation: their whole lives lay ahead of them, to shape at their will. But Anna, a few years ahead of them down that road, didn't feel like she was shaping anything.

'Here comes Einstein,' muttered the Hulk. They all followed his gaze: Dan was hugging Jenny, who was congratulating him, and he was shaking hands with Stav and Julian, a wide grin illuminating his face. He looked over at the bar and began walking towards them.

Anna, who had only ever seen him in jeans, T-shirts and trainers, had to admit that Dan looked good in a suit.

Phil stood up to bear-hug him. 'Congratulations, mate,' he said, slapping a hand on his back.

'Yeah, congratulations,' added the Hulk, extending a hand.

Dan shook it politely. 'Thanks, mate.'

Sally flung her arms around him, squealing. 'You dark horse!' And she kissed him on the cheek.

'Yeah.' Phil laughed. 'How do you spend two-thirds of your degree course pissed and still come out with a first?'

THEN

Dan shrugged, smugly. 'Coffee, Pro Plus and natural genius, I guess.'

Anna watched him. He was deliberately ignoring her presence, and she wasn't going to let him get away with it. She extended her hand and smiled.

'Congratulations, Dan,' she said, a little too brightly.

Dan's hand remained by his side. For a few seconds, her hand stayed suspended in the air, before eventually retreating to her lap. The mirthful creases around his eyes had disappeared and when he finally looked at her, it was with an expression so cold, so dead, that it chilled her to the bone. She looked away and drained her glass.

The Hulk touched her hand gently. 'Another one?' he asked, glancing at her empty glass. She nodded.

Dan began to move off. 'I'll see you around, then!'

Sally and Phil yelled, 'Stay in touch!'

He disappeared into the crowd.

All too soon, the early evening sun began to fade, and the ghostly eye of the moon appeared behind Big Ben.

Anna finished the last of her drink and stood up. 'I think I'll be getting off.' It was a school night; she had a busy day ahead tomorrow.

Sally looked towards the bar. 'I think the Hulk's getting you another one.'

'You have it. I'm tired. Anyway, congratulations and all that.' She ruffled Phil's hair and gave Sally a peck on the cheek. 'I'll give you a call at the weekend, yeah?'

'Alright. Speak to you then.'

By the time the Hulk turned around, glasses in hand,

Anna had disappeared. Sally pushed the empty glasses to one side of the table.

'Where's Anna?'

'Gone home. She said she's tired. It's a school night.'

The Hulk put down the glasses and pushed his way towards the stairwell; he sprinted down the steps and began jogging along the Strand, sweating slightly under his suit jacket. She'd be heading towards Charing Cross. His eyes scanned the pavement ahead, and he increased his pace from a jog to a run, his new shoes rubbing uncomfortably against his heels. Finally, he made it into the station and paused to catch his breath. He had to find her before she got on the train. This was his last full day in London. At last, he saw her, holding up her travel card to the station attendant, walking towards Platform One.

He barrelled across the concourse towards her.

'Anna!'

She hadn't heard him.

'Anna!' he bellowed, desperate.

She turned.

He stopped before her, red-faced and panting.

'Hey!' She smiled, then, frowning, checked her bag. 'Did I leave my purse in the bar?'

No, he wanted to say. You left *me* in the bar.

She located her purse and looked up, her forehead still furrowed. 'Look, I'm sorry about the drink. I'm just a bit tired. It's been a busy week.'

'I don't care about the drink.'

'OK.'

Anna looked down the platform at the train and slowly,

THEN

they began to walk towards it. She stopped opposite an open carriage door.

He placed a hand on her shoulder. 'I'm still in love with you, Anna. For what it's worth.' He gave a small shrug. 'I just wanted you to know. Before we go our separate ways.'

He's in love with an idealised version of me, thought Anna. She wondered if he'd still love her if she snored all night, or after passive-aggressive conversations about whose turn it was to put out the bins.

'You don't always look happy,' he continued.

That's a ridiculous thing to say, she thought. *It's impossible always to be happy.*

'I just…I think I could make you happy.'

Anna wanted to cry. She didn't doubt for one minute that he was willing to spend the rest of his life trying to make her happy, which was precisely why she couldn't let him.

The whistle blew. Anna put her hand on the train door and placed one foot inside the carriage. He fumbled in his jacket pocket, pulling out a small, folded square of paper, and pushed it into her hand.

The whistle blew again.

Anna stepped inside the train and turned to him. 'I'm sorry. I've got to go.'

He leant in and kissed her, and then the carriage door shut.

Anna took a seat next to the window. The Hulk stood motionless as the train pulled away. She raised her hand, placing her palm against the glass.

The woman opposite her smiled. 'That was so romantic!'

Anna smiled weakly and unfolded the square of paper. On it was printed a new address, in Newcastle. She looked up. The Hulk was still there at the far end of the platform, watching her go. She looked out of the window at the figure shrinking into the distance and felt a heaviness descending.

And then the train left the station, and he was gone.

NOW

Dan and Anna blinked as they emerged into the bright sunlight. It was a swelteringly hot day. The university had attempted to transform the central courtyard into a leisurely chill-out space. Faux rattan sofas were grouped underneath canvas gazebos; there were tropical palms positioned incongruously in huge pots and the air was filled with the aromas of pulled pork wraps and jambalaya from catering stands. A trio of black-clad music students in the corner offered a slow, mournful rendition of 'Wonderwall'.

Anna made a beeline for an empty sofa. Dan veered off to the drinks stand. 'I'm getting a coffee,' he said. 'Do you want anything?'

She looked over at the chalked menu. 'An orange and mango smoothie please.'

She sat back and watched people milling about: self-important fathers glancing at expensive watches; mothers fussing with furrowed brows; awkward teenagers who exuded the impression that they had been dragged from Call of Duty and Snapchat against their will.

Two families sat across from her gripping lattes, the fathers absorbed in the site map, the teenagers absorbed in their phones.

'It was a fascinating lecture, wasn't it?' exclaimed one of the mothers in the kind of posh Home Counties voice that carries for miles. 'I didn't know that artificial intelligence could be so clever!'

Her son visibly cringed.

The other woman gave a high laugh. 'Of course, the younger generation are more *au fait* with the latest developments than our *analogue* generation. Giles has been writing code since he was knee-high.' She gestured halfway up her leg with the flat of her hand.

The first mother turned to address her son. 'And what did you think, Angus?'

Angus clearly didn't think much at all. He shrugged, his eyes never leaving the screen of his phone.

'I think this will be a good insurance choice,' she announced, adding conspiratorially, 'Angus's school has *insisted* that he applies to Cambridge.'

Dan caught the end of the conversation as he weaved around the faux rattan towards her and raised his eyebrows.

'Pretentious, middle-class twat,' Anna said under her breath.

'Pardon?' Dan said, looking affronted.

'Not you. Her.'

'Ah.' He thrust a plastic cup at her face. 'I got you strawberry and kiwi. They'd run out of orange and mango.'

'Thanks.' Anna gratefully took a long draught of the ice-cold liquid. 'Changed a bit since our day.'

NOW

Dan nodded towards the musicians. 'Except for "Wonderwall".'

They laughed.

Dan leant back, face upturned towards the sun, coffee balanced precariously on his stomach, and closed his eyes.

Anna watched as the two families began to gather their things and move off. She took another cold mouthful and swished the crushed ice around her mouth, wincing as it hit a sensitive tooth. She looked over at Dan as he attempted to doze.

'Can you remember the first time you met me?'

She remembered vividly the first time she had met him – the battered leather jacket, the way he had secretly checked her out, how handsome he had been.

Dan ignored her. He didn't know why women felt the need to ask questions like that. He wondered, not for the first time, why she always seemed compelled to fill the air with words.

She nudged his ankle bone with her toes and, reluctantly, he opened one eye.

'Can you remember when you first met me?' she repeated.

He shrugged. 'I dunno.'

'Charming! There must be some memories that have survived the alcohol-fuelled mists of time.'

He opened the other eye and looked into the middle distance, as if conjuring an image.

'Well, you had great legs, for one thing,' he began, 'and you've always had a cracking pair of tits.'

'Tits?' cried Anna. A startled father walking past spilt

coffee down his corduroys. 'Really?' She looked down at her modest cleavage. 'I've always thought they're a bit on the small side.'

Dan shook his head. 'There's nothing wrong with smaller tits. You don't want to wake up one morning and find yourself with a pair like bloodhounds sniffing a trail.'

She gave him a look. 'Eloquently put, as always.'

'Well, you did ask.' He lunged at her, squeezing her left breast.

'Get off!' She looked around them, embarrassed.

'Still nice and firm.' He grinned, then leant back once more, attempting repose.

The music students thanked their largely inattentive audience, pausing awkwardly in the absence of any applause, and then sloped off for a coffee break. Dan's upturned face smiled into the sun.

'Have you put some factor 50 on your head?'

'Uh huh.'

A police siren sounded on the street outside.

'It's funny, isn't it?' Anna began.

Dan's eyes remained firmly closed.

'All those random events, or those quirks of fate if you like, that kind of solidify into your life without you being really aware of it.' She felt for the sunglasses on her head and settled them on the bridge of her nose. 'I mean, if Mae hadn't fallen out with the boys and we'd had to move into halls, you and I would never have met. It's like those quizzes you get in magazines where there's a question and the options branch out like the legs of a man on a toilet sign...'

NOW

Dan's brow furrowed.

'...and you answer yes or no and yes or no until you arrive at the final answer.' She paused. 'I mean, if my mother and my father hadn't met, if it had been a no, there would be no me, and if your mother and father hadn't met, there would be no you, and if you and I hadn't met, there would be no Jack.' She imagined them all dangling from the legs of the toilet sign man, disappearing from existence in puffs of smoke.

Dan sighed loudly. 'Yeah, yeah, I get the idea. But they did and we did, so there you go.' Abandoning any hope of relaxation, he sat up, downed his coffee and resolved to change the subject to something more practical. 'So, what's next after the lecture? Accommodation tour?'

And they passed the rest of the hour thumbing through the accommodation brochure, exclaiming, 'How much?' at the eye-watering cost of the rent and wondering how they had ever managed to afford existing as students in London.

Their own halls had long since been demolished.

THEN

Anna met Tom in a bar in the City. It wasn't her usual stomping ground, but Sally had a job in an office nearby, so it was convenient for after-work drinks. Anyway, they – together with Jenny – were celebrating; Anna had just been accepted as a part-time doctoral student at their old university, and she was ebullient.

'Rather you than me,' Sally said, pulling a face. 'I couldn't wait to get shot of studying.'

Anna laughed. 'Uh, just reminding you, the purpose of this evening is *celebration* not *commiseration*?'

'No, I mean congratulations and all that.' Sally raised her wine glass, as if about to propose a toast.

'Thanks!'

'It's just,' she continued, 'it's going to be a *lot* of hard work.'

Jenny took a handful of peanuts from the complimentary bowl on their table. 'Yeah,' she agreed, her mouth full, 'how are you going to fit it around school?'

'I've got weekends,' said Anna airily, 'and all the school holidays. I'll make it work.'

THEN

The truth was, she'd felt increasingly directionless over the last few months. Many of the old gang had dispersed – she conjured a mental map of the UK, marked with little red dots: Newcastle, Cardiff, Surrey, Derby – and her colleagues at school, whilst lovely, had sensible mortgages and led sensible lives. She'd begun to feel like she was living in a loop: teach, eat, sleep, repeat. She loved her job but, increasingly, she also felt a sense of underlying panic that her life was running away like sand through an hourglass – one that she could never upend to buy herself more time. The doctorate, she decided, would give her some direction and purpose.

Jenny nudged Sally. 'They're looking over at us again.'

At the end of the bar, a couple of likely lads in flash suits nodded their heads in their direction and grinned. Sally looked at Anna apologetically. 'It doesn't look like they've got a third mate.' She had been single since her break-up with Kris a few months earlier, and Anna was quite willing to take a back seat on this one – neither of them was her type.

'You go ahead,' Anna urged. 'Really, I'm not interested.'

'Sure?' Jenny asked.

Anna nodded.

'OK, then.' Sally and Jenny exchanged smiles and made their way along the bar.

As she watched them, Anna thought it would be interesting to have a career as a behavioural psychologist: she observed the men suddenly standing taller as the girls approached, squaring their shoulders, and her otherwise perfectly sane and intelligent friends transform themselves into a pair of giggling coquettes. She turned around in her seat, reaching for the drink on her table, only to come face-to-face with a man sitting opposite her. He looked smart – his crisp Friday shirt unbuttoned at the neck, mother-of-pearl cufflinks at his wrists, dark hair, dark eyes.

'Sorry, is this seat taken?' His accent was pure South London. A City boy.

'No, feel free.' Anna gestured towards Sally and Jenny. 'My friends are otherwise engaged.'

'So I see.' He gave her a winning smile and looked at her glass. 'Can I get you a drink? I'm Tom, by the way.'

'Anna.' She looked at him. He was good-looking. Fanciable. She ran her index finger around the rim of her wine glass, then answered. 'Sure. Thanks. Dry white wine, please.'

He half stood to remove his wallet from his trouser pocket.

Don't be short, Anna thought. *Please don't be short.* She tapped one high heel against the other, self-consciously. He stood. He was a little shorter than her, she noted with disappointment, but not comically so.

They spent the rest of the evening deep in conversation, sharing their lives thus far. There was no banter, no cringeworthy sexual innuendo, no verbal sparring. It felt easy. And then it was last orders, and Sally and Jenny returned to the table with the flash suits in tow.

'You've not been lonely, then!' Sally exclaimed.

Anna glanced at Tom and smiled.

'We're off to a club. You two fancy joining us?'

Tom looked down at the table.

THEN

'Maybe not tonight,' Anna said. 'Another time?'

'OK, well I'll give you a ring in the week. Enjoy the rest of your evening.'

Jenny raised a hand in farewell and shrugged on her coat. The flash suit's hand steered her bottom towards the door.

'So...'

'So!'

They looked at each other.

'I'm going to get off home, I think,' Anna said.

'I'll walk you to the station.'

At the station they stood, looking at each other. He thrust his hands deep into his coat pockets. 'I've really enjoyed talking to you tonight.'

'Me too.'

'Can I see you again?'

Anna wanted to laugh. It was such a clichéd phrase, like something from a teen movie. Anna had only ever dated fellow students, who were linked by an extended network of friends and friends-of-friends, and both parties knew exactly where they would eventually find each other: the student union bar. It wasn't a question you ever had to ask.

'Yeah, OK.'

She fumbled in her bag for a pen, tore off the edge of an envelope and wrote down her number. He read it, then folded it carefully and stowed it deep in his wallet.

'So, I'll see you soon.' He leant forwards to kiss her, his lips brushing hers.

'See you soon.'

SOMETHING CHANGED

They went their separate ways, him towards the Northern line, her towards the Circle, each turning back briefly towards the other before disappearing into the labyrinthine tunnels.

He waited a few days before calling her, just long enough not to appear tragically keen. He invited her out to dinner at a little restaurant he knew behind Regent Street.

To Anna, everything about dating Tom was a novel experience. For a start, he'd never been to university, having left school at sixteen and gone straight to work in the City. For him, a career wasn't about trying to make a contribution to society, but simply a means of making as much money as possible. He was truly – if not literally – Thatcher's child.

Anna was also excited about the prospect of dressing up for a proper date at a restaurant – not a Pizza Hut with everyone arguing about who had ordered the extra garlic bread – a proper restaurant! When she pulled out her purse at the end of the meal to split the bill, he looked astonished and wouldn't hear of it. When they made their way back to the station at the end of the evening, he walked on the side of the pavement nearest the road because, he told her, that's what gentlemen do. Despite her oft-declared feminist principles, Anna discovered that she loved being so cosseted. She felt special; she felt valued. At the station, he kissed her goodnight but, to Anna's surprise, he made no move to invite himself back to her place. That was a novel experience indeed.

On their second date, he stood waiting for her on the station platform clutching a carrier bag. Later, in the

THEN

restaurant, he pushed it shyly towards her under the table. Inside was the dress she had admired in a shop window on their first date. She looked at the label. Size 10. She smiled up at him, taken aback by his thoughtfulness.

'It's even the right size,' she said. 'It's perfect.'

For their next date, Tom took her to a play she had wanted to see but which had sold out. Somehow, he had managed to get the best seats in the house. This was followed by another restaurant, a swanky cocktail bar, a champagne bar. After every date, he walked her back to the station and kissed her goodnight.

By the end of their sixth date, Anna began to wonder if he really was heterosexual, or if, perhaps, he didn't find her sexually attractive.

'He's been holding out for a while, that's for sure,' Sally declared, thoughtfully.

'Maybe he's just being a gentleman?'

'Maybe. Or maybe he's the shy type. How does he kiss you?'

'What do you mean?'

'Well, is it like a peck on the lips or a proper kiss?'

'No, he's a good kisser.'

'Well, I don't know, then. Why don't you invite him to yours and see what happens?'

'Good idea.'

The following Saturday, Anna spent the entire day holed up in her tiny kitchen, irritably making potatoes dauphinoise, an au poivre sauce for the fillet steaks, and a pear tart. She didn't know why some people found cooking relaxing. As the kitchen steamed up like a Burmese jungle and the windows dripped with condensation, she didn't feel like a domestic goddess, or even Delia Smith. She just felt hot and grumpy. She looked at her watch: he'd be here in half an hour. Time for a quick shower, to put on the dress he'd bought her, her best underwear and some red lippy.

He rang the bell five minutes early, as she was still tracing her lips with lipstick. She quickly brushed the damp tendrils of hair from the nape of her neck and sprayed herself with a cloud of Obsession perfume.

Tom stood in the doorway, preppy in a checked shirt and chinos, clutching an enormous bouquet of flowers in one hand and a bottle of champagne in the other. He leant in to kiss her. 'Mmm! Something smells nice!'

Anna laughed. 'Me or the food?'

'Both!' He smiled and held the champagne bottle aloft. 'This needs to be chilled.'

'Come on through.'

They squeezed into her tiny kitchen and Anna stowed the champagne in the fridge. Apologetically, she pulled out a bog-standard bottle of white.

'Sorry. It's not exactly premier cru.'

He smiled. 'It's fine. Let me pour you a glass.'

As Tom unscrewed the bottle cap, Anna – unaccustomed to receiving flowers and not in possession of a vase – resorted to filling a plastic jug with water and attempting an artistic arrangement of the blooms, which stubbornly persisted in listing to one side.

That evening, over candles and champagne, he pronounced her to be a wonderful cook (it was a lie: the

THEN

steak was overcooked, and the pears had made the pastry soggy) and told her how beautiful she looked in the dress he had bought her.

'I'm a lucky man. I have to keep pinching myself,' he said, as she led him to the sofa.

And you're about to get even luckier, thought Anna.

Thirty amorous minutes later, Anna rose, intent on leading him to the bedroom.

'Where are you going?'

Anna looked down at his upturned face. 'I thought we could go to the bedroom.'

He removed his hand from hers like she had the plague.

'It's OK if you don't want to,' Anna said quickly. 'I mean, if you don't fancy me or anything.' Never in her life had Anna imagined herself uttering the words she had heard so many times from the mouths of men. It was an unexpected role-reversal.

'It's not that I don't fancy you,' Tom began. 'You know I do, very much. But it's too important. I think I'm falling in love with you. It's not just about sex. It needs to be special. It needs to be right. Do you understand?'

Anna blinked at him. 'Yes – yes, of course.' She felt wrong-footed. She felt like the Whore of Babylon. He was the respectful, romantic hero she'd waited for her whole life. Of course, Tom was right: this was different – it was a serious, grown-up relationship, not a quick bunk-up after a night of knocking back the booze.

Tom looked at his watch. 'It's getting late. I'd better be going.' He made his way into the hall and picked up his coat, Anna trailing after him. At the door, he turned back to kiss her. 'Thank you, gorgeous girl, for a wonderful evening. I'll call you in the week.'

She watched him go, standing barefoot in her new dress. He hadn't even seen her best underwear.

It would be another two weeks before Tom decided the time was right. Not knowing when he might decide this, Anna had had to resort to hand-washing her one set of best underwear after each date, so that she wouldn't be caught unprepared in her sensible T-shirt bra and plain knickers. She slathered herself with Immac at the first sign of any hair growth and touched up her toenails in pillar-box red, considerations she had not always shown previous lovers – not, she reflected, that they'd appeared to mind, or even noticed.

Anna felt a now-familiar flutter of anxiety in her stomach as they stood together once again at Charing Cross station. Would he be coming back to hers tonight or going home? As if he knew what she was thinking, Tom took her hand firmly, announcing, 'Back to yours?'

Twenty-three minutes, Anna thought as the train departed. *In twenty-three minutes – or thereabouts – we will actually be in bed together.* As Tom squeezed her hand, she turned to smile at him nervously. It was an unfamiliar sensation. Suddenly, something that had always been so spontaneous had become a premeditated act that would take place in twenty-three – no, twenty-two minutes' time. She felt like someone had tipped a bucket of cold water over her head: stone-cold sober and gripped by panic.

THEN

She was consumed by questions that had never previously occurred to her: would they undress themselves? Each other? Was it possible to remove twenty-denier tights seductively? Why had she worn the dress with the sticky zip?

Back at the flat, it took her three attempts to get the key in the lock. She thought of how Dan had once made some crappy joke about the need for a firm thrust in the hole and she had rolled her eyes and they'd both fallen into bed with each other.

Tom placed his hand over hers. 'Let me help.' He grasped the key firmly and turned it in the lock. They stood together in the hall, the bedroom door lying open to their right. Anna was so nervous she felt sick. Tom kissed her and led her into the bedroom. She began tugging at the sticky zip at the nape of her neck.

'No,' said Tom firmly. 'Let me do it.' He expertly unzipped her dress and unhooked her bra. Anna stood self-consciously in her tights as he slid them, and her knickers, down her thighs. She lifted her feet obediently, like a Labrador having its paws wiped after a muddy walk. Finally, he sat on the edge of the bed, surveying the naked results of his handiwork as if admiring a Greek statue, before undressing himself. There were no giggles as buttons pinged off, no drunken pratfalls with pants around ankles, no heads wedged in too-tight tops, arms raised as if in surrender.

It was all very grown-up. And very quiet.

Anna was reminded of a school trip to a local cathedral when she was ten. They'd been given some black paper and gold crayons to make brass rubbings, and every time someone had tried to talk, the teacher had admonished them in a stage whisper: 'Ssh! This is a cathedral. Have some respect. Be quiet!' and they'd lowered their heads, silenced.

Afterwards, he cradled her head between his arm and his chest and stroked her skin and told her how beautiful she was and how much he loved her.

Their relationship was so grown-up that, just before Christmas, instead of dodging sarcastic questions about boyfriends, Anna took Tom home to meet her parents. Laden with chocolates and flowers, he'd charmed her mother, her sister and even her father, who was secretly relieved that she hadn't brought home some poetry-wielding socialist but a sensible man with good prospects in the financial services sector. His parents loved Anna too: who wouldn't be charmed by a sweet, intelligent girl who had dedicated her life to teaching children?

It all felt too good to be true.

'I keep feeling that something has to go wrong somewhere,' Anna told Sally, reaching for the last slice of garlic bread. She hadn't been in a Pizza Hut for ages, but it was nice to slum it for a change.

Sally adopted a brisk, no-nonsense tone. 'Don't talk rubbish! You've spent the last few years shagging a bunch of complete losers and dickheads—'

'Thanks very much!'

'Well, it's not like you haven't had fun, but it's true. The point I'm making,' she continued, waving a pizza crust in the air, 'is that Tom isn't like them, is he?'

THEN

Anna lifted the wine bottle on their table, realised it was empty, and felt despondent.

'It's like you feel you don't deserve to be treated well – you know, flowers, champagne, fancy restaurants…'

Anna frowned.

'But you do. And he does. He's a keeper, Anna, and I think he thinks you're a keeper, too.'

'Really?'

Sally leant back; her arms folded. 'Just enjoy it. Stop worrying. Stop overthinking everything.'

Anna bit her bottom lip.

'Jesus, Anna!' She laughed. 'I love you dearly, but you do drive me mad sometimes.' And then she uttered the ultimate rallying cry: 'Come on. Let's go and get bladdered!'

***

It was February, Anna's second most hated month after January. No fireworks, no Christmas lights, no warmth or sunlight, just short, dark days and the annual disappointment that was Valentine's Day. But this Valentine's Day was different; this year, she had higher expectations. She had Tom.

Things had moved fast after Christmas, and Tom had suggested buying a place together, reminding her that renting was wasted money. It all felt like an exhilarating whirlwind, in the midst of which they had spent their evenings following glib estate agents around flats near her school. The apartment with 'delightfully airy, open-plan living' materialised as a draughty room with a run of sticky avocado-green kitchen cabinets leaning along one wall; the flat that was 'close to all local amenities' turned out to be above the local chip shop, with the vague odour of fish rising through the floorboards and windows that shook every time the (frequent) commuter trains rushed past.

Tom had noticed her glum expression and squeezed her hand reassuringly. 'I know it's not easy getting a foot on the property ladder,' he said, 'but we'll find a place in the end. Trust me.'

And they had, sooner than they thought. It was two miles from her school – a bit further than she would have liked, given that she had no car – but as soon as they'd walked through the door, they'd turned to each other and knew that it was The One. A ground-floor flat, it had the luxury of its own front door, a Victorian fireplace, ceiling roses, a brand-new, white kitchen and bathroom, and a little garden. And it was just within budget. They'd put in an offer immediately.

Anna stared out of her classroom window at three o'clock that Valentine's Day, her pupils behind her intent on writing Carrie Willow's diary entry. It had been a cloudy day, and the light was already fading. *This is it*, she thought. *Miss Thompson, in your sensible skirt and blouse from Next, you've become a fully paid-up adult. You have a Significant Other, an arranged mortgage and a handful of Dulux colour charts.* She picked at the peeling paint on the windowsill and wondered why contentment still felt so elusive.

In the distance, the phallic monolith of One Canada Square was rising from Canary Wharf, surrounded by a

THEN

swoop of cranes. *Now that's a building designed by a man*, she thought, *probably one with an inferiority complex about the size of his penis.* She wondered if she should be thinking about penises in a classroom full of impressionable eleven-year-olds.

She felt a touch on her elbow and turned, startled from her thoughts. Niamh Mahoney was leaning back in her chair, trying to attract her attention. 'Miss, Miss…'

Why did they always say that twice?

'…there's someone at the door.'

The face of Mrs Scott, the school receptionist, was blinking through the rectangle of safety glass like a myopic owl. Anna beckoned her in. As she entered the room, her face almost entirely obscured by an enormous bouquet of pink roses, excitement rippled around the classroom.

Anna turned to face her charges, suddenly stern. 'Thank you, girls! Settle down. We still have another twenty minutes before the bell.'

'Somebody loves you!' whispered Mrs Scott excitedly, thrusting the bouquet at Anna's chest. 'Isn't it romantic? I thought I'd bring them down before they start to wilt.'

Anna took the flowers and placed them carefully on her desk. 'Thank you.'

'Oh, there's also a card,' added Mrs Scott over her shoulder as she left the room.

Anna opened the envelope as twenty-five pairs of eyes, no longer interested in chronicling the inner feelings of Carrie Willow, watched in excited anticipation. The little card was written in the florist's handwriting. Tom must have dictated the message over the phone. *See you at your flat at 4.15pm. Pack an overnight bag and a passport. I love you.*

'Is it a romantic message, Miss?' piped Kelly Flynn from the back row.

Anna smiled. 'Yes, Kelly, I suppose it is.'

'Is he good-looking, Miss? Have you got a photograph?'

Anna laughed. They'd all downed tools now, arms folded over closed books, waiting for an answer.

Anna conceded defeat. 'Alright, girls. We'll have a quick game of hangman and then you can pack up early.'

They cheered.

She was a master at deflection.

Just a few hours later, Anna slid forwards in her seat as the taxi driver hit the brakes and Tom put out his arm to stop her falling. She tilted her head against the window, looking up at the illuminated obelisk that punctured the night sky. The taxi smelt of Gauloises.

'Paris traffic!' Tom sighed, glancing at his watch. 'I thought we'd be well past rush hour by now.'

Anna stifled a yawn. It had been a long day. The bed had looked inviting, in the boutique hotel just off the Place de la Concorde, but it appeared that it was not to be their destination that evening. Tom had stood over her as she had collapsed into a mountain of pillows, still wearing the sensible skirt and blouse. She'd not had time to change after work.

He frowned. 'Did you bring a dress or anything?'

Anna glanced at her overnight bag. 'Yeah. Why?'

'OK, get changed. We're going out.' He'd removed his

THEN

jacket and tie and had begun to change his shirt. She'd leant over the bed and begun stroking the inside of his thigh.

'I thought maybe we could stay in tonight – you know, make the most of Valentine's Day.' She'd tried to sound seductive.

Tom removed her hand. 'Maybe later. Go and get your dress on.' He glanced at his watch. 'I'll call for a taxi.'

'Where are we going?'

He winked at her. 'Ah, now that's a surprise.'

The taxi lurched forwards again, and Anna's forehead collided with the window.

'Careful!' Tom cautioned, as if she was some mental headbanger who needed to practise restraint. The traffic eased slightly, and they moved smoothly onto the Cours la Reine. Anna watched hand-holding couples boarding the Bateaux-Mouches along the Seine.

'Are we going on a boat ride?' she asked, playing the guessing game.

'Nope.'

To her left, the Eiffel Tower came into view, sparkling with a million lights.

'Are we going to the Eiffel Tower?'

Tom smiled at her indulgently. 'Maybe.'

'We are!' she exclaimed excitedly, and he laughed.

'Gorgeous girl, you're too clever!'

Why did he make her feel like she was six years old?

The taxi driver swerved, uttered some swear words in French and accelerated like a maniac over the Pont d'Iena before slamming on the brakes.

SOMETHING CHANGED

'Looks like we've arrived.' Anna opened the car door as Tom paid the driver, wrapping her winter coat around her body tightly. She wished she'd brought a scarf. A bitter, biting wind tore down the Champ de Mars. She shivered.

But the view from the top was spectacular. Anna huddled into Tom as they tried to spot the landmarks illuminated in the distance: the Arc de Triomphe, the dome of the Sacre Coeur.

Tom undid the top button of his coat and slipped his hand inside, searching for something in the breast pocket. Then, in one swift movement, he presented a small, dark blue box with a flourish as he fell on one knee.

'Anna, will you marry me?'

He looked at her with the expression of a man who is absolutely certain of the answer.

A woman next to them raised her hand to her mouth and nudged her husband. Around her, the few remaining late-night tourists turned to watch, their expressions resembling a collective 'Ahh'.

Tom opened the box, revealing a diamond solitaire which he removed, ready to place on her finger.

Anna looked down at him. His face was set in an uncomfortable, fixed smile that was aware both of the occasion and the gathering audience.

'Say yes!'

She was in the most romantic city in the world, on the most romantic day in the world, with a man who had made the most romantic proposal in the world. What other response could she make than to say yes?

THEN

Anna glanced at her audience, who watched them from a respectful distance. She didn't want to disappoint them.

'Yes.'

She felt the cold metal sliding onto her finger. Tom stood to kiss her as the crowd broke into spontaneous applause. Anna pulled her coat tighter as Tom beamed like the cat that got the cream.

For some reason, she couldn't stop shivering.

***

Shortly after her return from Paris, she had become ill with the flu, so it was a few weeks before she managed to meet up with Sally.

'Let's have a look, then!'

'Can I get through the door first?'

Anna stepped into the hallway, shrugged off her coat and removed her left glove, extending her hand towards Sally.

'Ooh, it's a right little bobby dazzler,' said Sally, who had a penchant for such phrases. She tilted Anna's hand first to one side and then the other, so the diamond flashed in the light. 'How does it feel?'

'A little bit tight, to be honest.'

'No, I mean, how does it feel to be engaged?'

Anna shrugged.

'Well, have you set a date for the wedding? Can I be a bridesmaid?'

'No, and yes. Though probably next year, in the summer holidays.'

SOMETHING CHANGED

Sally clapped her hands together. 'Oh, it's so exciting! Have you thought about wedding dresses? A-line or straight?'

Anna removed her other glove and shoved it in her coat pocket. 'I haven't really given it much thought.' She followed Sally into the kitchen.

'Tea?' Sally held up a box of Yorkshire teabags.

Anna nodded and threw her coat over the back of a chair, watching Sally busy herself with mugs and milk. Sally flicked the switch on the kettle and turned to face her, arms folded beneath her bosom. 'I must say, you seem very calm.'

'I've not returned from a war zone,' Anna laughed, 'I've only got engaged.'

Sally narrowed her eyes slightly, scrutinising her friend's face, and then turned again, pouring water and stirring the tea loudly with a teaspoon. 'Well, I got a copy of *Brides* magazine on my way home from work,' she announced, 'so we'll look through that over a brew and a packet of Hobnobs, shall we?'

'Sounds great.'

Anna sat sipping her tea as Sally turned the pages of the magazine: plain dresses; lace dresses; sleeveless dresses; dresses with sleeves; big, ruffled, puffy dresses; straight dresses. *All those brides*, Anna thought, *all those dresses, and yet absent from every single image was the groom. Even the name of the magazine erased his presence.* She reached for a Hobnob and sighed.

'I wonder, who are weddings actually for?'

'What do you mean?'

Anna waved her hand over the magazine. 'All this. Not a bloke in sight.'

THEN

'Well, the bloke isn't the one wearing the dress.'

Anna had a sudden image of Tom in a puffy, crinoline number, with his dark, hairy arms poking out and his face shadowed with morning stubble, and stifled a laugh.

'What?'

Anna shook her head. 'Nothing.'

Sally frowned and then folded down a page. 'Anyway, I think you'd look lovely in that one.'

Anna looked down at the image of a bride standing in front of a stately home, head turned towards someone out of shot – presumably the groom – wearing a long, fitted lace dress. She flipped the magazine closed.

Sally shoved the packet of Hobnobs across the table. 'Another one?'

Anna shook her head.

'Are you doing anything the last Friday of this month?'

'Dunno. No plans at the moment.'

'Great, 'cos Phil and Julian will be in town, and Dan's coming up, too.'

Anna's stomach lurched. 'Dan?'

Dan had been off the radar for a long time.

'Yeah, he called me up out of the blue.'

'Right.'

'So, are you free? Do you think Tom will mind? I would invite him but, you know, I don't really think it would be his thing.'

'No, I'm sure he'll be fine.' She and Tom had always maintained very separate social circles. They were like a Venn diagram that only marginally overlapped.

'You'll be there, then? I'll phone Jenny too.'

SOMETHING CHANGED

Anna drank the last of her tea and brushed biscuit crumbs from her lap. 'Yeah, I'll be there.'

It was agreed that they would all meet in a pub near Bayswater tube station at 7.30pm. That Friday, Anna had got home from school and had taken a long shower. She'd bought some new leather trousers and squeezed herself into them, turning to the mirror to check the rear view. She slipped a black chiffon blouse over her head and half tucked it into the waistband. Finally, she slid her feet into some high heeled ankle boots. She felt good.

She wandered through the new flat, over the floorboards she and Tom had just sanded and varnished, past the tastefully fashionable furniture they had bought from Habitat and the arty architectural prints that lined the walls. The flat was spotlessly clean and tidy. *It's like a show home*, she thought.

As she leant to close the bathroom window, Anna heard the key in the lock and her stomach tightened. Work had not been going well for Tom; he'd been passed over for promotion in favour of someone who had only recently joined the company and each night, when he entered the flat, she was never quite sure what mood he would be in. Increasingly, she visualised him as a man perpetually followed by a dark cloud, like that character in Charlie Brown. She listened carefully to the door: if it closed with a click, it had been an OK day; if it slammed, it had been a bad one.

The door slammed.

Anna moved to the kitchen and began spooning ground coffee into the cafetiere. She heard the keys clatter loudly on the dining table and arranged her features into a bright, cheery smile before turning around to face him. She knew better than to ask how his day had been.

'Coffee?' she said brightly, like an over-eager waitress.

He shook his head and took a beer from the fridge, hitting the edge of the bottle top against the worktop to remove it. A shard of worktop fell to the floor. She wanted to remind him that they had a bottle opener in the drawer but thought better of it. Tom leant against the fridge-freezer and looked at her.

'Off out?'

'Yes, I mentioned it last week.'

He shrugged.

'I'm meeting up with Sally and some old university pals.'

'Ah, *university* pals,' Tom echoed.

She nodded, fingering the chipped edge of the worktop.

Tom raised the bottle to his mouth and downed half of its contents. He looked at her trousers and frowned. 'I've not seen those before.'

'They're new.'

'S&M club, is it?'

'What?'

'Are you going to an S&M club?' he said slowly, like she was hard of hearing. 'You know, rubber, leather...' He pointed to her trousers.

'No. Just a pub.' She touched her trousers self-consciously. Suddenly, they felt a bit much.

'Well, if the pub's in Soho, it could be a profitable evening.'

Anna chewed the corner of her bottom lip and looked at the kitchen clock. It was 6.30 and she needed to catch the 6.45 train. She smiled at Tom.

'I've got to go. I'll be late.' She watched him take another swig from the bottle and made her way into the hall.

'If they want you to whip them, charge extra,' he called as she shut the front door behind her.

Dan hadn't been in London since the day after his graduation. He'd been hired by an up-and-coming tech start-up full of young graduates like him. They hot-desked around a central atrium in which there was a tube slide, two tyre swings and an assortment of primary-coloured beanbags, which was supposed to facilitate Blue Sky Thinking. Dan hated it. He was forced to socialise with computer nerds – most of whom were men – at a succession of team-building events where he collaborated in building rafts from lengths of rope and a pile of logs, scrambled over assault courses in damp woodland being yelled at by ex-army types, and aimed a paintball gun at colleagues he especially hated for their unceasing fucking optimism.

A month into his new job, he'd caught the eye of one of the few passably attractive women in the company over a BLT in the staff canteen and had invited her out for a drink. After a series of awkward dates, when they had exhausted all the pubs in that godforsaken town at the furthest reaches of the commuter belt, they'd had disappointing sex in his half-furnished studio flat, after which they had determinedly avoided each other. One night, returning home alone with yet another beef madras from his local takeaway, he had

THEN

rifled through a box containing old university stuff and found Sally's number. A night with friends in the city was just what he needed to nourish his empty soul.

Anna was late. She hated being late. Every train and tube had seemed to conspire against her that evening. She burst through the pub doors, flustered, scanning the room for familiar faces. Finally, she saw them squeezed around a table in the corner.

'Sorry I'm late,' she said, pushing her fringe out of her eyes. She looked at the table of drinks. 'Anyone want another?' They shook their heads. At the bar, she took a deep breath and closed her eyes. Her entire body felt tense. She'd spent most of the journey replaying the conversation with Tom in her head like some hideous earworm. Then she felt a body close to hers and, as she turned, Phil pecked her on the cheek.

'Can I help carry your nuts?'

Anna laughed. 'I haven't even ordered a drink yet! D'you want some nuts?'

He gave her a cheeky grin. 'I'll take whatever you're offering.'

She caught the eye of the barman. 'Large dry white and a packet of nuts, please.'

Phil turned to her. 'So, I hear congratulations are in order.'

'Mmm?'

'The engagement.'

'Oh, yeah, thanks.' She took the wine glass from the barman and drained half the glass.

'Blimey, you're thirsty.'

'Yeah.' She smiled. 'Don't forget your nuts.'

Dan looked towards the bar. He wasn't the only man in the pub staring at her in those leather trousers. He felt a surge of the old desire and yanked his shirt out of his jeans, scooting his chair close to the table. He noticed the easiness between her and Phil; it had somehow never been like that between them.

Sally squeezed up so Anna could perch on the edge of her chair and raised her glass. 'Well, now we're all here, cheers everyone, here's to the old gang!'

As they all raised their glasses and drank, Dan completely missed his mouth. Beer dripped over his chin and neck and down his shirt towards his groin. He swore under his breath, though at least it had solved his burgeoning erection problem.

Anna raised an eyebrow in mock surprise. 'Missed your mouth, Dan? You should try taking your foot out of it occasionally.'

He felt them occupying their old positions. He wiped the beer from his chin with the back of his hand. 'At least I know when not to open mine.'

Julian gave a snort. 'Touché!'

'Right,' Sally cut in. 'I've booked a table at an Indian up the road in ten minutes, so we'll need to drink up.'

Dan wandered with Phil up the road towards the restaurant. Sally and Anna were chatting, arm-in-arm, ahead of them.

'Bit of a surprise about Anna's engagement,' said Phil.

THEN

'Yeah, how long has she known him?'

'I don't know, not that long.'

Dan blew air loudly out of his mouth. 'Not a man who hangs about, then.'

'Well, would you?'

It was a stupid question, given that Dan and Anna had spent years like a pair of bumper cars, occasionally heading straight for thrilling collisions, but mostly skirting around the periphery and swerving to avoid each other,

In the restaurant, over the Cobra beers and the wine bottles, Dan watched Anna as she reached for a shard of poppadum and dipped it into the mango chutney. She was left-handed, and every time she tore off a piece of naan bread or spooned rice onto her plate, the diamond flashed on her ring finger.

Sally ting-tinged the edge of her glass with the side of her fork. 'Now I'm sure we'd all like to say congratulations to Anna on her engagement.' She looked across at Anna and grinned. 'Just promise you'll put me in a *hot* bridesmaid's dress.' She raised her glass. 'Congratulations!'

Dan raised his glass with the others as they all yelled, 'Congratulations!'

But although Anna was smiling, he noticed a certain tightness to her smile, her lips still covering her teeth. He noticed the way that she lowered her eyes, the way she twisted her engagement ring compulsively around her finger. She didn't look like a woman who was excited to be engaged. She looked ill at ease. Tense.

Sally turned to Dan. 'And I think Dan has some news for us...'

'You're pregnant!' shouted Phil from the other end of the table. Dan aimed a piece of naan bread at his head and missed.

He paused. 'I've just got funding for a doctorate. At our old university, in fact. I'm moving back to London.'

Amidst the whoops and cheers, Sally looked over at Anna. 'So you'll both be studying at the same place. What are the odds?'

Anna fixed her smile firmly in place, but inside she felt consumed by a sudden and irrational fury. How dare he, how dare he come striding back onto her turf, into her life? She wanted him to fuck off back to outermost Surrey, or wherever he had come from. She rummaged in her bag for her purse and stood up, placing some notes on the table.

'Sorry, guys, I'm heading off. Lots to do tomorrow.'

Sally looked at her watch in surprise. 'Anna, it's not even ten o'clock yet. Stay a bit longer.'

Anna shook her head. 'Sorry, but thanks. It's been great to see you all.' She raised her hand in a gesture of farewell.

Dan watched her go and caught Sally's eye, giving her a look that said, *What's her problem?*

Sally shrugged.

Anna was nearly at the tube station when she heard footsteps thudding behind her. She gripped her bag more tightly, braced for a mugger, but it was Dan, panting, with her coat draped over his arm.

'You left your coat.'

She reached to take it from him.

'Thanks.'

THEN

They stood, looking at each other for a moment.

'Right, well I'd better get back.' He gestured up the road towards the restaurant.

'Yeah.' She looked down at the coat. 'Thanks anyway.'

'No problem.'

They turned away, Anna to the station, Dan back to the restaurant, where they'd ordered in another round of beer. They were talking about Anna's engagement. Dan took his seat next to Sally and thought of Anna twisting the ring around her finger, the tight-lipped smile.

'It won't last,' he said prophetically, as if casting a fairy-tale curse, but Sally just shook her head at him, smiled and continued the conversation.

On the tube station platform, Anna slid her arms into her coat as the train emerged from the tunnel. Mindlessly, she stepped forwards as the doors hissed open and took the nearest seat. She looked at the reflection in the opposite window, an image on a screen. The face looked tired, drawn. She lifted her hand to her cheek and realised she had been clenching her jaw. Slowly, she let her jaw fall slack and placed her ring finger to her lips, absent-mindedly nibbling at the gold band. She hoped that Tom would be asleep when she got home.

At Embankment, she got up to change trains and shoved her hand into her coat pocket. She felt some sort of receipt crackle against her fingers and frowned. She always kept receipts in her purse. She pulled it from the pocket. It was from W.H. Smith. On the back, in his instantly recognisable, terrible handwriting, Dan had printed an address and phone number. She felt a prod in the small of her back.

'Are you getting off, love?'

The doors had slid open. People were trying to get past.

'Sorry.'

Anna stepped off the train and walked towards Charing Cross. She boarded the train and buried the receipt with the others, deep in her purse. Later, she turned the key silently in the front door, removed her shoes and clothes in the hall so as not to disturb Tom and slipped like a ghost into their bed. She lay rigid for a moment, holding her breath, listening to his breathing, checking he was asleep. She exhaled silently.

Tom didn't even stir.

Dan lay, five miles away, under a blanket on Sally's sofa, cursing himself for placing his number in Anna's pocket. What had he been thinking? He'd been a bit drunk, that was for sure. In truth, he'd been lonely stuck in the furthest reaches of Surrey and, although he was reluctant to admit it, there was also a fair amount of egotism involved. In the past, he'd always been able to give Anna *that* look and know that they'd end up spending the night together. Part of him wanted to see if he could still exert that power over her. He knew that he was asking for trouble – she was engaged to be married to another man, for a start – yet he also knew that Anna wasn't the type to settle down. Everything about her was unsettling; she was provocative – verbally, sexually; she was a quick, sharp-tongued sparring partner.

THEN

He found it arousing but also exhausting. After spending any length of time in her company, he felt physically and mentally drained. He literally needed to retreat and recover. He turned on his side, on the verge of sleep, and hoped that Anna had reached into her pocket, found an old receipt and crumpled it in her hand, throwing it into the nearest bin along with all the other rubbish.

NOW

The sunlight glittered on the water as they drove across Waterloo Bridge. The car felt like a furnace and Anna adjusted the air conditioning to full blast, ineffectually fanning herself with the accommodation brochure.

Jack pulled up his T-shirt, baring his white, skinny torso. He had his father's broad shoulders but her slender build.

'I'm not getting much cold air back here,' he complained.

Anna rummaged in the cool bag at her feet and pulled out a carton of juice. 'Here, have this.'

Jack reached forwards, extracted a blue cool pack from the bag and raised it to his forehead like a frail Victorian lady on the verge of fainting. With his other hand, he pulled at the damp fabric clinging to his armpits.

'Sweaty bugger!' She laughed.

He threw the cool pack at her in response and turned to look out of the window.

'Your destination is on the left,' announced a female voice, helpfully.

'Ah, satnav lady,' sighed Dan, as if fondly recollecting a teenage crush. 'She's never wrong.' He indicated to pull over.

NOW

Anna reflected that, strictly, that wasn't true. Dan's unwavering devotion to satnav lady had, in the past, led them up a two-mile farm track with no turning space at the end and once – memorably – the back yard of an undertaker. She felt an itch of irritation that Dan, who had spent his entire life believing that he was always right, could demonstrate such public devotion to a disembodied female who he believed could do no wrong and with whom, unlike her, he never argued the toss.

Dan parked up in a side street, pulled the key from the ignition and addressed the rear-view mirror. 'Everyone out!'

Anna prised apart her thighs, which had stuck together in a revolting manner during the ten-minute car journey, and opened the door, only to be hit by a wall of heat.

'Can I just stay in the car with the air con on?' Jack pleaded, remaining resolutely immobile.

'No,' Anna replied. 'You most certainly cannot. Out you get. Let's have a look around where you might be living.'

They sought out the shady side of the street.

Dan pointed to their left at a Tesco Express. 'Shop!' he announced, like a toddler trying out a new word. 'Useful for food shopping.'

'No shit, Sherlock!' replied Anna.

'I'm just trying to make conversation.'

'Conversation is an art, Dan,' she corrected. 'You're just uttering words.'

They arrived at the halls of residence, a featureless orange-brick building that looked like it had been thrown up in the eighties.

'Hello!' yelled a stout redhead wearing a yellow

'Welcome' T-Shirt and a lanyard, at the end of which dangled the words 'Student Guide'. 'I'm Becky, and I'll be your accommodation guide today.' She beamed brightly. 'Please feel free to ask me any questions about the accommodation during your tour.' She nodded towards a table containing a jug of orange squash, a stack of plastic cups and some cardboard bowls filled with crisps. 'Help yourself to refreshments.'

After imbibing an array of E-numbers in an attempt to slake their thirst, they trudged up a staircase and along a corridor where one door was held open by a rubber wedge, as if saying: 'Ta-da!'

'So this is, like, a typical room,' announced Becky. They entered in single file. 'Desk, shelves, bed.'

It was a hard sell.

'Any original features?' Anna laughed.

Becky stared at her blankly. 'Sorry?'

Anna shook her head. 'Never mind. So, is that a *three-quarter* bed?'

'Yes, it's a small double.' Becky recited her well-rehearsed lines. 'The university has been engaged in an extensive programme of accommodation refurbishment over the last eighteen months. All single beds will be replaced with small doubles by September.'

'And what's behind this door?' enquired Dan, pushing the handle. He whistled through his teeth. 'An en-suite bathroom!' he exclaimed in wonder, as if he'd just found the Holy Grail.

'All rooms are en-suite in these halls,' announced Becky proudly.

NOW

'A bit different to our day!' said Dan, impressed.

Becky feigned interest. 'Oh, so were you, like, students here?'

'Yeah. In those days, bathrooms were shared and unisex.'

'Unisex?' exclaimed Becky, clearly horrified at the thought.

'Yeah,' Anna said. 'You learnt pretty quickly not to drape your towel over the door of the shower cubicle.'

She saw Jack cringe in embarrassment. Becky smiled politely.

'So, shall I take you to, like, the recreation area? It's downstairs.'

'We'd *like* that very much, Becky,' said Anna.

They trooped back down the stairs and across an inner courtyard containing some spindly trees encased in concrete and a few wooden benches.

'So, this is the area where, like, you can hang out,' Becky gestured, striding towards the other side of the building, 'and this is where we have the pool tables and a bar.' They surveyed a sad-looking, institutional room with peeling posters issued by Mind and the local STD clinic. Anna tried to imagine it buzzing with vibrant life and failed.

'And how have you found living here, Becky?' enquired Anna. 'Have you enjoyed it?'

'Oh, I don't live here,' replied Becky, fingering her lanyard. 'My parents live in, like, Surrey, so I commute in. It's, like, so much cheaper.'

Dan flashed a look at Anna.

She didn't say a word.

THEN

Anna and Tom stood on the platform at their local train station. Anna had a medium-sized black suitcase at her side. She and her colleague Claire were off to Italy for a week, travelling between Rome, Florence and Venice by train.

Tom's expression was closed, his jaw set. He didn't want her to go. She had explained to him that it was a holiday she and Claire had begun planning long before she met him, that she didn't want to let her friend down. It was the holidays and she'd only be hanging around the house, bored, whilst he was at work.

They saw the train approaching in the distance. Tom turned to look at her. 'Well, enjoy your *girls*' holiday.' He was aware that Claire was single. 'What's the plan? See great works of art, eat pasta, get seduced by an Italian?'

Anna's patience snapped. She raised her voice over the sound of the train pulling into the station. 'Yeah, Tom, that's exactly what I'm going to do. I'm going to fuck every man who looks at me and says, "*Ciao, bella!*"'

She turned her back on him, exasperated, and

attempted to heave the suitcase onto the train. Tom made no move to help her. Finally, a fellow passenger took pity on her and lifted it up, placing it next to an empty seat. She mouthed 'Thank you' and moved across to the far side of the train, away from the platform, and stared out of the window across the tracks. The train pulled away.

Tom went back to their flat and lay on their bed. He found her slip underneath the pillow and pressed it to his face, inhaling the scent of her. Later that evening, he found himself a few miles away on his parents' doorstep. As his mother opened the door, he told her that it was all over, that Anna didn't love him anymore, and he collapsed into her astonished arms, sobbing like a child.

And afterwards, he despised himself for his weakness.

By day five of their holiday, Anna and Claire had arrived in Venice. In Florence, they had admired Michelangelo's *David* and thoroughly approved of Botticelli's celebration of small-breasted, pear-shaped women in *The Birth of Venus*.

'It's good to know that, back then, I would literally have been regarded as a goddess,' Claire said, hands on her hips as she regarded the painting. 'Clearly, I was born a few centuries too late.'

'I think she looks a bit bored,' said Anna. 'She's probably fed up with people ogling at her.'

Claire tilted her head to one side, thoughtfully. 'I see what you mean.'

Now, lying parallel on their twin beds in the hotel in Venice, looking up at the candy cane twists of the Venetian glass chandelier suspended above their heads, Anna turned to look at the phone on the bedside table. She sat up.

'I'd better call Tom,' she said. 'Hopefully he's in a better mood by now and he's stopped sulking.'

As she dialled, Claire tactfully made herself scarce in the bathroom.

Anna listened to the phone ringing, imagining the sound echoing through their empty flat. She'd misjudged the time; perhaps he wasn't home from work yet. Finally, just as she was about to hang up, he picked up the phone.

'Hi, it's me.' There was a long pause. Anna waited. 'Are you still there?'

'Yeah, I'm still here.' His tone was frosty. Evidently, he was still in a bad mood.

She attempted to assuage his fears. 'You'll be glad to know that no Italian gigolos have attempted to seduce me. Just a few wolf-whistles. Claire's a bit disappointed, though.' She gave a little laugh.

Silence.

'So, I'll see you when I get home, then.'

'Yeah.'

She heard the phone click and the line went dead.

Claire emerged from the bathroom, her hair damp from the shower.

'Everything all right?' she asked.

'Yeah,' said Anna, rolling her eyes. 'He's still in a mood, but he'll get over it.'

The plane home had been delayed by two hours, and it was nearly 9pm by the time Anna turned the key in the lock.

THEN

The light wasn't on in the living room, but the TV screen flashed like sheet lightning through the open door and onto the walls of the hall. She staggered through to the bedroom with her case and unzipped it. She removed a slender bottle wrapped in two T-shirts and retraced her steps.

'I'm home!' she announced, stating the obvious in an attempt to break the silence.

Tom sat in the darkness watching MTV.

'I got you this.' She held out a bottle of limoncello.

He continued staring at the TV screen, his expression hard and unresponsive.

'I'll just put it down there.' She placed the bottle on the coffee table and stood for a minute, staring at the screen, then turned towards the bedroom. 'I might as well unpack, then.' She returned to the bedroom and began sorting clothes for the laundry basket; she removed her make-up bag and placed it on the dressing table. Then she saw him standing in the doorway.

'You're expecting *me* to move out, then?' Tom said quietly, his voice loaded with suppressed anger.

'What?'

'You heard.'

She frowned. 'Why would I want you to move out?'

'Isn't that usually what happens at the end of a relationship?' he said coldly. 'One person moves out?'

'What are you talking about?' Anna pulled some sandals from the side pocket of her case.

'You left me, Anna,' he said slowly. 'You left me to go and fuck around in Italy. Your words. You didn't even look back or say goodbye.'

Anna laughed. 'I was being sarcastic. I told you, I haven't slept with anybody.'

He advanced towards the bed and hurled the suitcase against the wall. 'Don't fucking laugh at me.'

Anna stood very still. Fear began to stir in the pit of her stomach.

Tom seized her slip from the bed and clenched it in his fist. 'I slept with this every night you were away just because it smells of you,' he said, in a voice full of self-loathing.

Her expression softened. She'd had no idea that he'd been this upset. 'Tom, I'm so sorry.'

'I don't need your fucking pity.'

'It's not pity,' she said carefully. 'It was just a misunderstanding. I say stupid things sometimes.'

He dropped the slip to the floor. 'I really loved you, Anna.'

She noted his use of the past tense.

'And I love you.'

He laughed – a hard, brittle laugh. 'I think it's best if we call off the wedding, don't you?'

Anna felt a rising sense of panic then, like she was trapped underwater and was fighting to reach the surface. Her chest tightened. A flurry of thoughts entered her mind: sitting hand in hand at their meeting with the vicar; the deposit her parents had paid to secure the country house reception; the wedding dress she'd placed on reservation at a boutique off Kensington High Street. After careering about like a pinball for years from one man to another, her relationship with Tom had made her feel grounded, a proper adult rather than someone who was playing at it. She had a future mapped out for her that involved the well-trodden path of marriage and children. For once in her life, she'd had the reassurance of knowing exactly where she was going.

Anna heard the words coming from her mouth like the voice of a dybbuk. 'Don't leave me.'

There was a shift in the dynamic as she said those words, a shift in the balance of power.

He looked directly at her. 'If you mean it, get down on your knees and say it.'

Anna looked at him in disbelief. He was deadly serious. She hesitated for a moment and then felt herself fall to her knees like a penitent in prayer.

He looked down at her. 'Say it.'

The voice spoke again, barely audible. 'Please don't leave me.'

'I didn't hear you.'

She closed her eyes and swallowed hard. 'Please don't leave me.'

He looked down at her and smiled. She smiled back, relieved. She'd played along, humoured him. She was forgiven.

'You know, Anna,' he said, the smile still on his face, 'you really don't have any self-respect, do you?'

He kicked the edge of the suitcase as he left the room. Anna knelt, staring blankly at the wall, before slowly standing and picking up her clothes from the floor.

That summer, after school ended, Anna threw herself into her doctoral studies with renewed vigour. Armed with a spiral-bound notebook and pencil, she would take the train to the library each day where she would read through books, photocopy articles from journals and make bullet point notes in her neat, upright handwriting. She often became so absorbed that when she looked up, rubbing at her dry eyes, she would find that five or six hours had elapsed and she suddenly became aware that she was hungry, or desperately thirsty. She liked the routine of being at the library; she liked the structure that it gave her. She liked the way that her research elbowed aside any other thoughts.

At the end of each day, she would walk along the Strand to Charing Cross station where Tom would meet her en route from the City, and they would travel home together. Since her return from Italy, she and Tom had not spoken about what had taken place between them that night. As if nothing had happened, he continued to kiss her each morning before he left for work; he held her hand in the street; he made love to her gently. There was an unspoken acknowledgement that Anna had hurt him deeply and that she somehow needed to atone for this. She cooked him elaborate meals, surprised him with little treats, dressed up in new lingerie, but each time, she sensed that whatever she offered him fell short in a way that she couldn't identify or define. The date for their wedding was still set for the following summer, but Anna had quietly phoned the boutique off Kensington High Street and cancelled the reservation on the dress.

At the start of the new school year, Tom told her one evening that he'd booked a lads' holiday to Greece with

THEN

some friends she had vague recollections of having met once or twice.

'That'll be nice,' she said.

'I'll miss you,' he said, squeezing her hand.

She smiled. 'I'll miss you, too.'

On Fridays, after late-afternoon meetings with her tutor, Anna would take herself to the library. In moments of mental tiredness, she would stretch her arms above her head, stand up from her carrell and wander amongst the bookshelves. Once she saw a figure with dark hair and broad shoulders wearing the same pale-blue denim shirt Dan used to wear, but as he turned, she realised it wasn't him. She supposed that there wasn't a great demand for books in his line of research. She imagined him staring at a computer screen full of indecipherable, mathematical hieroglyphics.

Then one Friday, as she was about to cross the inner courtyard, she saw him walking towards her, his eyes cast to the ground. She slowed slightly, waiting for him to look up. When he did, he was almost in front of her. He raised his eyes, and she watched as his expression changed. His mouth curled instantly upwards in a broad smile. He seemed genuinely pleased to see her.

'Hi,' she said.

'Hi.'

They stood smiling at each other.

He scratched his head, above his left ear. 'So, have you been studying?'

She raised an eyebrow at the stupidity of his question. 'No, I've been posing as a live, naked art installation in the centre of the library.'

He laughed. 'Well, I'll bet there are guys in there grateful for the distraction. Anyone mistaken your nipple for a light switch yet?'

'Not yet. Maybe when it's darker and the clocks go back.'

He grinned. 'So, where are you headed?'

'Home.'

'Fancy stopping off for a pint?'

'But you're on your way in.'

'It's nothing urgent. It can wait until tomorrow.'

'Maybe another time,' she said apologetically. 'Tom will be expecting me.'

'Right.' He looked away, over her shoulder. 'Well, do you have my number?'

He wasn't sure if she'd found it.

'Yeah. I'd offer to give you mine, but, you know, it might be a bit awkward.' She tried not to imagine how Tom would react if he answered the phone and Dan was at the other end of the line.

He nodded. They stood for another few seconds and then Anna shrugged her bag further up her shoulder, and he said, 'Well, see you around.'

'Yeah,' she said. 'See you around.'

A few weeks later, when she got home from work, Anna found she couldn't open her front door. It would only open a few centimetres before stopping. She pushed harder but doing so just created friction with whatever was behind it, making a noise like someone blowing a raspberry.

That morning, she had kissed Tom goodbye before she

THEN

had left for work, telling him to have a good time. He was catching an afternoon flight from Gatwick.

'I'll be back before you know it,' he said.

She tried the door one last time, taking a few steps backwards and hurling her whole body at it, right shoulder first. To her surprise and relief, it finally gave way, catapulting her inside.

The door had been blocked by not one, but tens of multicoloured balloons floating in the air. Along the wall in the hallway Tom had stuck a succession of brightly coloured Post-it notes leading to the kitchen. She followed the trail: *I. Love. You. Truly. Madly. Deeply.* They had watched the film together and she had cried, and Tom had gently teased her for being so sentimental.

In the bedroom, the bed was strewn with red rose petals. On one pillow lay a neat pile of blue envelopes secured with a ribbon. She sat down on the edge of the bed and pulled at the bow. On the front of each envelope was written *Open me on...* labelled with the date of each day that they would be apart. She opened the first envelope.

> *By the time you read this, I will be high in the air over central Europe. I miss you already and wish you were next to me. I'll be home soon, but in the meantime, solve the clue to discover something from me to you: I lie beneath hollow footsteps, waiting in the dark.*

She went instantly to the hallway cupboard that lay beneath the stairs to the first floor flat above them. Feeling behind the vacuum cleaner and the ironing board, she found a small box wrapped in coloured paper and ribbon. Inside was a pair of silver teardrop earrings. She removed her hoops and put them on.

The phone trilled and Anna jumped, startled. For a moment, she thought it was Tom, then remembered that Sally was coming over that evening. She picked up the receiver.

'Hiya.'

'Hiya,' Sally said. 'I'll be with you in about half an hour.'

'No problem, I've just got to take Tom's suits to the dry cleaner up the road before they close.'

'OK, see you soon.'

After she'd hung up, Anna went to the bedroom and picked up the two suits Tom had left thrown over the chair. A clinking sound came from one of the trouser pockets. She thrust her hand inside, pulling out some small change. Methodically, she checked the other pockets, finally sliding her hand into the inner breast pocket of the second jacket. She felt a small piece of paper and pulled it out. On it, in handwriting she didn't recognise, was a name – Elena – and a telephone number. She felt a jolt of shock, sensing instinctively that it wasn't a professional contact. She steadied herself, then placed the piece of paper in the pocket of her trousers.

She left the flat with the two suits folded over her arm and walked to the dry cleaner's shop at the end of the road. There, she handed over the garments, smiled politely, paid and collected her receipt. Then she walked back to the flat, turned her key in the door, and fought through the

THEN

balloons to the bedroom, where she lay on top of the rose petals and stared at the ceiling. She couldn't seem to think. Her mind was like a skating rink and thoughts kept sliding off before she could grasp them.

Eventually, the doorbell rang. Sally stood on the doorstep with a bottle of wine and looked over Anna's shoulder at the hallway full of balloons.

'Wow!' she exclaimed. 'Have I missed something? Someone's birthday?' She entered the hall, turning her head to read the Post-it notes on the wall. 'Is this Tom's doing?'

Anna nodded.

'Jeez!' Sally shrieked as she passed the open bedroom door. 'Are those rose petals on the bed?'

'Yeah. He's left me a letter for each day he's away. The first one was a clue.' She fingered her earrings. 'Leading to these.'

Sally stowed the wine bottle in the fridge. 'Well, I'm seriously impressed. He must be the most romantic man ever. I wish Kris was even half as romantic.'

Sally and Kris had recently got back together; he was practically living at her place and Sally seemed pretty happy about it.

'You are so jammy!' She gave Anna a fond hug.

Anna had not told her – had not told anyone – about what had happened on her return from Italy. She was unsure of what the reaction would be.

'Well, unless you want to spend the next hour popping balloons, I think we'll go *out* for a drink,' said Anna. She suddenly felt that she would rather be anywhere else.

'OK, whatever you like.'

SOMETHING CHANGED

In the pub, Anna tried very hard to concentrate on Sally's conversation, as if she would have to take an exam afterwards, but her mind kept drifting back to the piece of paper in her pocket.

'So, Kris has booked us a last-minute deal to Majorca. I can't wait to get some sun and escape this crappy weather.'

Anna nodded. *Just because Tom has a girl's phone number in his pocket, it doesn't mean anything*, she thought. It could have been an unwanted advance, pocketed and forgotten. He was an attractive guy. It would be naïve to think he never got offers.

'I'm not sure whether to take a bikini or a swimsuit,' Sally continued.

Anna nodded. 'Yes.'

'Yes, what?'

'Sorry?'

'Swimsuit or bikini?'

Anna decided to hedge her bets. 'Both.'

But why leave it in his jacket? Was he just forgetful or had he secretly wanted her to find it? After all, he was the one who had asked her to get his suits dry cleaned whilst he was on holiday.

Anna drifted in and out of Sally's monologue. Yes, she agreed, two pairs of sandals of different heel heights were plenty. Absolutely, she should buy a new suitcase with wheels, so she didn't break her back lugging it through the airport.

Anna could feel the paper crackling in her trouser pocket as she crossed her legs. Sally was staring at her.

'You're not really with me tonight, are you?'

THEN

Anna smiled. 'Just tired.'

'OK.'

'Would it be really inconvenient if you didn't stay over tonight? It would take us ages to get rid of all those balloons and rose petals, anyway.'

'You won't be lonely?'

Anna shook her head. She realised that she was actually looking forward to having the flat to herself for a while.

'OK then.'

Anna bade farewell to Sally outside the pub, wished her a happy holiday and walked home. It was 9pm. She removed the piece of paper from her pocket. Before she could change her mind, she picked up the receiver and dialled the number. She could hear her heart pounding as the telephone rang. After a long time, someone picked up. There was an echo: the sound of a phone in the communal hallway of a shared house.

'Hello,' Anna said. Blood was rushing to her ears, making a sound like breaking waves. 'Can I speak to Elena please?'

'One minute,' said the voice. She heard someone calling Elena's name and then footsteps coming closer.

'Hello?'

'Is that Elena?'

'Yes, who is this?' The voice sounded Eastern European.

Anna adopted an efficient, professional voice. 'My name is Susan Cross. I work at a sexual health clinic in south-east London dealing with sexually transmitted diseases.'

There was silence, and then Elena said nervously, 'Yes?'

'A Mr Tom Matthews passed on your details as a possible sexual contact.'

'Yes?' The pitch of her voice was higher now, more anxious.

'You know him?'

There was a pause. 'Tom? Yes.'

Anna took a silent, deep breath. 'And have you had any sexual contact with Mr Matthews?'

Silence.

'I apologise for the personal nature of the question, but it is my job to follow up possible contacts. Mr Matthews has been diagnosed with genital herpes.'

There was a long pause. 'We go together a few times to bars. He's on business trip now, I think.'

Like hell he was.

Anna continued, briskly: 'Well, should you discover any blisters or any unusual discharge, please do contact your GP or local clinic.'

'God,' replied Elena. She pronounced the word like the German 'Gott'. She sounded horrified. Anna imagined her rushing to the bathroom to examine herself for nasty little growths.

'Thank you for your time,' said Anna, and put down the receiver. Clearly the girl wasn't very bright if she believed a clinic would contact her this late in the evening. Anna knew that she hadn't done much for the sisterhood. What she had done didn't make her a very nice person, either.

But it made her feel *so* much better.

THEN

The next morning, Anna got out of bed, tore a black bin bag from the roll in the kitchen drawer and looked out of the window. The sky was a uniform, pearlescent grey. There was no breeze and the trees at the bottom of the garden looked like painted stage flats. The only sign of life was a single magpie strutting across the grass. One for sorrow. A sinking feeling began to develop deep in her stomach as she remembered the phone number. Removing the scissors from the knife block, she walked around the flat, stabbing balloons and picking up the shrivelled pieces of rubber that fell to the floor like used condoms. She gathered up the rose petals and removed the Post-it notes from the wall. She picked up the pile of letters and the ribbon. She held Elena's number between thumb and forefinger before crumpling it. It was all deposited in the bin bag and unceremoniously dumped in the bin. Finally, she went to her purse and sorted through all the receipts that had accumulated there. She found the old W.H Smith receipt with the terrible handwriting and then she picked up the phone and punched the number.

'Hello?' Dan's voice sounded breathless and slightly irritable, like he'd been interrupted in the middle of something important.

'Hi.'

He recognised her voice. 'Hi.'

It wasn't quite the enthusiastic response she had been hoping for.

'So, I wondered what you're up to this weekend,' she ventured.

'Uh...' There was a pause, as if Dan was consulting a very busy social calendar. 'I've got some stuff to do.'

'Right.' She guessed he had nothing to do. 'So, I don't know, are you free tonight or tomorrow?'

'Uh, possibly.'

'Well, I wouldn't want you to cancel anything *important*.'

'No, no, it's fine.'

Another pause. Dan really needed to learn the art of conversation.

'So,' she pressed on. 'Tonight, maybe? Where do you want to meet?'

'Yeah, OK. Uh, I don't know. How about the Lyceum? 7.30?'

It was a pub they had both frequented as students.

'OK, see you then.'

'See you then.'

Anna wondered what she was doing. She'd just behaved like a complete lunatic after discovering a phone number in Tom's pocket and now here she was doing practically the same thing. Except, she told herself, it wasn't quite the same thing because she and Dan had known each other for years. And, she reminded herself, they were just friends, of sorts. It definitely wasn't about sex. Definitely not.

Dan put down the receiver. He wondered why Anna had suddenly decided to phone him and why, of all things, she had asked to meet him on a Saturday night when she should have been cosying up in front of the TV with Lover Boy and a nice mug of Horlicks. He suspected that they'd had some sort of argument and hoped that he wouldn't

THEN

have to spend all evening listening to an 'I said, he said' saga of epic proportions. On the other hand, he'd been genuinely pleased to see her that day in the courtyard. Anna could be brutally funny, and besides that, he fancied her, and he had absolutely nothing else going on except his research.

That evening, Anna sprinted up the stairs to the first floor of the Lyceum. With its dark-wood panelling and dim wall lights, it was a cosy and intimate space. Dan had spread out on a low leather sofa near the window, pint in hand. She saw that he'd already ordered her a pint of cider. She hadn't drunk a pint in ages; Tom said that it wasn't very ladylike and ordered her white wine spritzers instead.

Dan looked up, saw her and smiled. 'Got you a pint in.'
'Thanks. Next round's on me.'
She was wearing a red minidress and black knee boots.
'You look good in red. You ought to wear it more often.'
'Thanks.'
She picked up the broadsheet newspaper that lay to his side and slid onto the sofa beside him. A few wonky capitalised letters had been filled in on the Quick Crossword.

'Fancy a go?' Dan said. 'You should be good at it, being an English teacher.'

She squinted in the dim light. 'Let's have a look. One down. The weapon of a dominant woman, six–three.' She thought for a few seconds. 'Clever wit?'

Dan shook his head. 'No, the first letter across has to be a 'B', because the resting place of Brunel's ship is Bristol.'

His lips moved, trying out alternatives, and then he said: 'Got it! Battleaxe.'

'Battleaxe? That's bloody sexist!'

Dan rolled his eyes. 'Calm down, Germaine Greer.'

Anna was defiant. 'Well, it is. Anyway, I think mine's a better answer. Never underestimate the power of the female intellect.'

'That's not *quite* how it works,' Dan said slowly, in a deliberately patronising tone. 'See, the whole point of a crossword is that you have to *guess* the word the crossword setter's come up with.'

She gave him the finger.

Dan raised an eyebrow. 'Not like you to run out of words.'

'Fuck off.'

'That's what I most admire about you, Anna. You have such an extensive vocabulary!'

'It's a word of Anglo-Saxon origin, actually.'

He ignored her. 'Right, twelve across. Exclaim suddenly, ten letters.'

'Ejaculate!' cried Anna.

Dan began sniggering and Anna kicked his shin. 'Alright, Finbar, don't wet yourself.'

Dan looked at her and they both burst out laughing.

The man opposite them, an office drone in a sad grey suit that had become shiny with wear, sniffed loudly several times.

'See that man opposite?' said Anna.

Dan looked over at him. 'The one constantly sniffing?'

'That's the one. He spends half his day at the photocopier and the other half at the water cooler hoping that Helen from Accounts might get dehydrated so he can ogle her tits. At the Christmas party, he found Jason from Mergers cutting a line and now spends his weekends snorting up the Big C in the Big City in a vain attempt to escape the tedium of his sad life whilst his wife thinks he's working overtime.'

Dan laughed. 'Fuck, I hope my life doesn't get that boring.'

'Ah, well,' said Anna, 'it's too late for you. Your life's already indescribably dull.' She nudged him affectionately. 'Except when you're with me.'

There was a truth in her statement that rankled and, true to previous form, he made a retaliatory strike. 'Yeah, because it's not like you're chained down with anything dull like a mortgage and an M&S wedding list or something.'

Her smile snapped shut. She reached for her pint and took a long draught. *Inviting him for a drink was a mistake*, she thought, *a stupid attempt to get even with Tom*. If they weren't having sex, she and Dan would just end up sniping at each other all evening, so what was the point?

He squeezed her hand, quickly, and laughed. 'Hey! I'm joking! The wedding list would be with John Lewis at least.'

He noticed the trace of a smile playing at the corners of her mouth. Their faces were very close together now and he wanted to kiss her. She turned to face him.

'So, how is domestic life, then?' he asked.

'It genuinely fulfils me as a woman,' Anna said, deadpan. 'I get up every morning, apply a full face of make-up before he wakes in fear that he might flee in horror from what I actually look like, cook him eggs over easy and kiss him off to work. There is no higher calling. I've got the frilly apron and everything.'

'Hey, less of the frilly aprons,' Dan protested. 'You'll get me going.'

'It doesn't take much to get you going, as I recall.'

He looked at her. 'It doesn't take much for *you* to get me going,' he said. 'And anyway, as I recall, you looked beautiful in the morning.'

Anna blinked, taken aback by the unexpected tenderness of his words. She laughed and turned away.

'I think you're confusing me with someone else. I was the one drooling on my pillow with panda eyes and my hair stuck to my face.'

He watched her trace her finger through the condensation on the pint glass. The diamond sparkled on her finger. He hated that fucking diamond. It was like a dog tag, reminding him that she belonged to someone else.

'Fancy another pint?' he said.

'Yeah.' She smiled. 'My round.'

NOW

'Free bench ahead! Jack, run ahead and get it!' Anna called, the side of the cool bag bumping against her calves.

Dan grabbed the handles. 'Give it here. You need to use the shoulder strap.' He hoisted the bag over his shoulder. 'Like this.'

'Thank you for the demonstration.'

'Good God!' He leant slightly to his left to offset the weight. 'What have you got in here?'

'Twenty kilos of cocaine. I thought I'd try a more urban market.'

Dan rolled his eyes. 'I hope you've got some pork pies.'

'I've got some sausage rolls.'

His face fell. 'What? No pork pies?'

'What is your obsession with pork pies?'

They reached the bench where Jack sat, legs extended, scrolling on his phone. Behind him, skateboarders rumbled beneath the concrete structures of the South Bank, flipping and twisting and tumbling.

SOMETHING CHANGED

Anna sat, unloading tuna wraps, a tub of houmous, homemade brownies and bags of crisps.

Jack looked up from his phone and laughed. 'I don't know why we always have to take a cool bag everywhere.' He gestured towards the colourful food stalls dotted along the riverside, offering the exotic delights of Wagyu burgers, sushi and paella. 'Because we don't appear to be stuck in the middle of Dartmoor.'

Anna threw a bag of salt and vinegar crisps in his lap. 'Because they charge six quid for a tiny bowl of rice with some bits in it.' She nudged him. 'As you will learn when you're living on a student budget.'

She suddenly heard herself, like someone had played back a recording, and wondered when she had become so terribly sensible, when she had finally turned into her mother.

Dan rummaged to the bottom of the cool bag, failed to find any pork pies, and made do with the consolation prize of a sausage roll. He leant over to look his son's screen. 'What's that?'

'A list of first- and second-year modules.'

Anna dipped a carrot stick in the pot of houmous balanced on her lap and lifted her face to the sun.

'Anything interesting?'

'Thatcher's Final Year. That sounds interesting, from a historical perspective.'

Dan turned to look at him. 'A *historical* perspective? More like current affairs.'

'Dad, it was nearly three decades ago.'

'God, that makes me feel old.'

NOW

Anna paused for thought, a carrot halfway to her mouth. 'I can remember that like it was yesterday. And after that was the Queen's *Annus Horribilis*. The Conservatives won another bloody election, the IRA were detonating devices all over London, and you daren't put a bag down in a train station for fear that it would be cordoned off as a suspected IRA bomb.'

Jack looked up from his phone, incredulous. 'What, and you still travelled on public transport?'

'How else do you think I got home? People just had to get on with their lives.'

Dan brushed pastry flakes from his lap. 'Cheery stuff, Anna.'

'Well,' she said, 'it was a memorable time, all things considered.'

THEN

It was the opening night of Sacred Heart school's production of *Bugsy Malone* – a bold choice for an all-girls' school. Emotions were running high, and Tallulah had already had a meltdown in the toilets where Anna and Fat Sam, aka Sinead O'Riordan, were attempting to calm her down.

'The spot's not that big,' said Sinead. 'Honestly, nobody will notice it.'

'It's right on the side of my nose!' wailed Tallulah. 'It's the size of a third nostril!'

For fuck's sake, thought Anna.

The audience, mostly proud parents and grandparents, together with some long-suffering governors and a few nuns, had already started arriving. She'd lost six pounds in weight since she'd started this school play ball rolling, and it was too late to stop it now; she realised she'd only eaten a bag of Hula-Hoops since breakfast. Anna took Tallulah's hand.

'Now, listen to me,' she said. 'You're a leading actress in this production and the show must go on.' She paused,

THEN

before playing her trump card. 'Unless you want Karina Martin to step in?'

Karina Martin was Tallulah's arch-enemy and also the understudy. They had both auditioned for the part and there had been bitter comments and veiled threats exchanged in the corridors since Karina discovered that she hadn't been selected for the star role.

Aside from the fact that all the actors were female in a play that contained only two female leads, casting had been fraught with difficulties. Anna had perched uncomfortably on a plastic chair in the school hall, script in hand, looking up pensively at the stage as a succession of girls emoted their way through different parts.

Claire, perched on a similarly uncomfortable plastic chair, had come along to offer moral support.

'The only one who can really sing is Sinead,' sighed Anna.

'Well, cast her as Tallulah,' said Claire.

Anna turned to look at her friend. 'Are you serious? She's built like a Russian shot-putter. If she slinks provocatively around tables and sits on someone's lap, the only reputation Tallulah will leave behind her is one for ABH. That girl could crush a grown man.'

Claire pulled a face. 'A little harsh,' she said, 'but maybe, on reflection, she'd be better as Fat Sam.'

'We wouldn't need any padding,' added Anna.

Claire shook her head and laughed.

'Well, I'm just saying. It can get hot under those lights.'

Now, twenty minutes before curtain-up, Tallulah briefly considered her options. There was no way she was going to let Karina Martin push her out of the limelight.

'No, Miss, you're right. The show must go on,' she said, raising the tip of her carbuncled nose into the air in a melodramatic fashion.

Anna breathed a sigh of relief as her stomach rumbled. 'Good girl. Now, go to make-up, get a bit of concealer and get yourself backstage.'

Emerging from the toilets, she glanced at her watch as she crossed the cloakroom. She needed to check the stage manager was in place, that Claire was ready with the prompt script and that the first actors were made up and ready to go on. She switched on her walkie-talkie – on generous loan from the Geography Department – and it fizzed and crackled in her hand.

'All OK in sound and lighting?' she enquired.

'Roger that. All A-OK,' crackled the head of physics from the balcony, as if he was departing on an RAF bombing mission.

Anna looked over at Tom, sitting at the edge of the cloakroom next to the toilets as girls milled around him. He looked completely out of place in his corporate suit, sitting next to a sign reading: *Please do not flush sanitary towels down the toilet. Use the bins provided.*

'I'd like to help,' Tom had said when she'd first announced that rehearsals were under way, and she needed to work late.

'Really?' She was unconvinced.

'Absolutely!' he'd replied. 'Why wouldn't I want to support my future wife in her directorial debut?'

She could think of a lot of reasons but had the wisdom to keep her mouth shut. 'Well, it would be really helpful

THEN

if you could supervise the kids offstage,' she said. Those not immediately about to tread the boards were to be corralled in the cloakroom, down a narrow staircase from the main stage.

'Right, sure,' said Tom. He had never sounded less sure of anything in his life and had evidently been expecting to support her in a rather less active manner, as a member of the audience in the front row of the auditorium.

'Great!' said Anna. 'That's settled, then.'

Dan, on the other hand, had laughed hysterically when she'd told him that she was staging an all-female production of the play. Since that Saturday night, they had fallen into a routine of meeting each other every Friday after her tutorial. She'd told Tom that she was studying – which wasn't entirely untrue, she did occasionally pop into the library to pick up books and journal articles – but mostly she sat in the Lyceum bar with Dan.

'What fool teacher came up with that bright idea?' he'd asked.

'Me,' she said.

That made him laugh even harder.

The first half had gone well, all things considered. The speakeasy dancers had finally managed to coordinate their movements, and the spotlight had actually followed Bugsy instead of suddenly illuminating an alarmed Dandy Dan whilst he adjusted a wayward bra strap. The last-minute decision to use crazy string for the splurge guns rather than foam had proved a wise one. Unlike the dress rehearsal, no one had skidded on the slippery residue and ended up in the middle of the jazz band.

'Well done, girls!' said Anna, backstage at the interval. 'Off you go to the cloakroom. Second half in twenty minutes.'

The girls moved off, chattering excitedly, and Anna leant against the wall in the darkness, sipping from her bottle of water. She decided to take the opportunity to go for a pee. But as she made her way towards the cloakroom, she could hear all hell breaking loose. Reaching the bottom of the staircase, she saw Dandy Dan and Knuckles attempting to tear out chunks of each other's hair and screaming into each other's faces, surrounded by a goading crowd.

Tom hovered ineffectually a few feet away, saying: 'Come on, now, stop that, come on, now,' like he was the Invisible Man.

Anna stood at the bottom of the stairs and folded her arms. She boomed one word: 'GIRLS!', and within seconds, everyone in the room had frozen like a game of Grandmother's Footsteps.

'Dandy Dan and Knuckles, over here. The rest of you, have a drink, use the toilet and get in position for the second half.'

As the crowd silently dispersed, Tom flung his arms wide behind Dandy Dan and Knuckles as if to say, *What could I do?*

Anna stared disapprovingly at the girls. 'Right, we're in the middle of a play. What's this about? You have thirty seconds.'

THEN

Knuckles twirled her trilby. 'Maeve said Danny Connor fancies her and he's going to dump me.'

'Thank you, Knuckles – I mean, Nicola,' said Anna, thinking, *if only her written work was so concise*. 'Tell me, how long have you two been friends?'

They looked at each other. 'Five years,' they chorused.

'Five years,' repeated Anna. 'And you've known Danny Connor for – what?'

'Two months,' said Knuckles.

'Right. Two months. So you're willing to ruin a five-year friendship over a boy you've only known for a few weeks?'

The girls hung their heads.

'OK, so what are you going to do now?'

'Say sorry,' mumbled Dandy Dan.

'Correct.'

They muttered 'sorry' to each other.

'Trust me, girls, your friendship is a lot more important than Danny Connor. You'll still be friends long after he's a distant memory.'

'We're sorry, Miss,' they said, chastened.

'That's alright. Now get yourselves back upstairs.'

Tom watched from the corner of the cloakroom. Claire came up next to him, holding two cups of grey coffee in polystyrene cups, and handed him one.

'Milk and one sugar.'

'Thanks.' He took a tentative sip of the scalding liquid and turned to Claire. 'How does she do it?'

'The whole freezing a room thing?'

He nodded.

'They're shit scared of her,' said Claire, blowing over the surface of her drink. 'And that's just the staff.'

They saw Anna coming towards them, water bottle in hand. 'Everything alright?'

They both nodded.

Anna looked at her watch and Claire moved off.

'Well done,' said Tom. 'They were absolutely feral. I had no idea teenage girls could be so violent.'

Anna raised her eyes and looked at him. 'Well, you know what Kipling said…'

Tom shook his head.

Anna continued, looking directly into his eyes: 'The female of the species is deadlier than the male.'

He laughed, uneasily.

She smiled. 'Well, hang on in there. Only another hour to go.' And then, glancing at her watch again, she headed back up the stairs.

***

The row had started just before Christmas. For some time, she and Tom had led virtually separate social lives.

'You've got three parties coming up,' she said one night over dinner, 'and I'm not invited to any of them.'

'They're just work parties. You'd be bored out of your mind. Everybody just drinks too much and talks about work.'

She looked unconvinced.

'Anyway, you've got a Christmas party, and I'm not invited to that.'

THEN

'If you want to join me and the nuns for a sherry and a mince pie after the end-of-term church service, you're more than welcome,' she said.

'I'll give it a miss, thanks.'

'Well, at least I have offered,' she said, pointedly.

It wasn't that she actually wanted to spend more time in the company of Tom's friends and colleagues, it was more that, increasingly, she didn't trust him. When she'd asked to see photos of his holiday to Greece, he'd told her that the camera had jammed so he hadn't been able to take any. Yet days later, when she picked up the camera, it had worked perfectly. One night, he'd arrived home at three in the morning, drunk. She'd pretended to be asleep as he'd blundered around removing his clothes and had fallen into bed. As he curled up next to her, she could smell another woman's perfume on his skin. And, of course, there had been Elena's phone number, of which she had made no mention. Yet wasn't she a hypocrite? Didn't she spend Fridays in the pub with Dan when he thought she was studying in the library? Increasingly, she didn't see how they could ever function as a married couple.

***

In the Lyceum Tavern on the last Friday before Christmas, only one clue remained to be solved. An artificial Christmas tree flashed in the corner, and someone had decorated the window with fake, spray-on snow. The IRA had detonated bombs in London a few days earlier, and London's population was feeling on edge rather than festive.

'There were police all over the tube stations this morning,' said Dan.

Getting off her train that afternoon, Anna had been greeted by sniffer dogs. 'I know what you mean,' she said. 'I'm paranoid about putting my bag down for a second in case they detonate it in a controlled explosion and my tampons come shooting out like low-flying missiles.'

They sat in parallel, heads close together, looking down at the newspaper.

'Twelve down. Motley assortment. Seven letters,' said Dan, a stubby pencil poised in the air.

Anna frowned. She looked at the letters they had already filled in. 'I'm stumped,' she said. 'I think we may have to admit defeat.'

Dan turned his face towards hers in mock astonishment. 'Defeat? I don't think you've ever been defeated by anything in your life. You just keep arguing until the opposition capitulates.'

'You'd be surprised,' she said. 'But I'm impressed that you know what capitulate means.'

He put down the pencil and leant forwards so that his forehead was touching hers. She closed her eyes. She could feel his eyelashes fluttering against her skin like a butterfly's wings, smell the synthetic freshness of his deodorant and the musky sweat beneath. Then he reached for her hand. She felt him curl his little finger around hers and squeeze it tight. They sat like that for a while, silent, and then he felt her pull away.

'Farrago!' said Anna, triumphantly.

'What?'

THEN

'Motley assortment. Seven letters. Farrago.'

He looked down at the crossword. She was right. 'See? I told you. Undefeated.'

She laughed. 'Well, my brains are what you've always most admired about me.'

'Not true,' replied Dan, head down, pencilling in the letters. 'What I've always most admired about you is your legs and your arse. It wouldn't matter to me if you had an IQ of one.'

She shoved him.

'Anyway,' Dan continued, rummaging in the rucksack at his feet. 'I got you a Christmas present.'

She was astounded. Other than drinks and the odd packet of peanuts, Dan had never bought her anything in all the years they had known each other. She looked down at the badly wrapped rectangle he'd placed in her lap. Paper was bunched up at either end, and on it he'd written ANNA in biro in his customary capital letters.

She looked up. 'I'm sorry. I haven't got you anything.'

He shrugged. 'Doesn't matter. I just thought you'd like it.'

She sat, looking at the present.

'Well, aren't you going to open it?'

She slid her finger underneath the tangle of Sellotape at one end and a book fell out.

'*The Wasp Factory*,' she said.

Dan's literary choices consisted almost entirely of science fiction, but he had raved about *The Wasp Factory*.

'I can't believe you haven't read it yet,' he'd said one Friday night. 'It's a modern classic.'

'Well, it's a modern classic that must have passed me by.' Anna laughed.

She read the blurb on the back and grimaced. 'Three murders? Cheery festive fare. I'll look forward to reading that over a plate of mince pies and a glass of Bailey's.'

He looked wounded.

'Hey,' she nudged him and looked into his eyes, more serious now, 'I love it. Thank you.'

He smiled.

Anna flicked through the opening pages. Thankfully, there was no inscription. In the unlikely event that Tom noticed, she'd just say that she'd bought it in a bookshop. She tucked it between the library books in her bag and looked at her watch. It was 9.30.

Dan watched her. 'Time to go?'

She nodded. She was always very careful to be home by 10.30, so she was in the house before Tom arrived home from his Friday night out.

They walked under the clear night sky, huddling into their coats, hands deep in their pockets. Above them, sparkling fairy lights threaded their way across the Strand. A few shops were still open selling expensive handmade stationery and artisan soaps. The Pogues' *Fairytale of New York* blasted out onto the pavement before a door swung shut and silenced it. They stopped, as usual, outside McDonald's. She would head to the train station, and he, to the tube.

'So, what are your plans for Christmas?' he said. 'Home to your parents with your bloke?' He never referred to Tom by name; it was always 'your bloke' or 'lover boy'.

THEN

'I'm off home to see the folks. You?'

'Same. So is lover boy not coming with you, then?'

She parroted Tom's words: 'No, he's only got a couple of days off. It's not worth travelling all the way there and back.'

He made a mental note of that and nodded.

'Well, happy Christmas then.' She leant forwards and gave him a hug.

'Yeah, have a good one.'

He stood there and watched as the mouth of Charing Cross station swallowed her up.

***

When Anna returned to London in the New Year, Tom was in a conciliatory mood.

'How do you fancy a foursome?' he said.

This was a departure from his normally conservative sexual preferences, so she thought it best to seek clarification.

'How do you mean?'

'Well, Max has just got a new girlfriend, and you complain that we don't socialise enough together, so I thought we could have a double date.'

'Ah! Right. Yes, OK.'

'You could sound a bit more enthusiastic,' he said. 'I've gone to a lot of trouble to arrange this, just to make you happy.'

'Well, thank you,' she said. 'I'm very happy.'

The evening of the double date, Anna emerged from

the bedroom wearing dark jeans, a red top and high heeled ankle boots: smart-casual.

Tom perched on the arm of the sofa and wrinkled his nose slightly, as if he'd detected an unpleasant smell. 'Are you wearing jeans?'

She looked down at her legs.

'It's just that it's a smart bar. What about your little black dress?'

Wordlessly, she turned on her heel and removed the offending trousers, slipping her body into the tiny dress. Somehow, the dress had felt OK when she was a student, but now she was older, it made her feel like a hooker.

She stood in the doorway. Tom looked her up and down approvingly. 'Yeah, that's much better.'

As it turned out, the bar in which they met was not particularly smart. It was just an ordinary city bar. Max's girlfriend was wearing jeans and a smart top. Anna felt completely, self-consciously over-dressed. As Tom chivalrously removed her coat in the centre of the room, she could feel men's eyes moving over her body.

'Max, this is Anna. And this is Max's girlfriend, Sara.'

'It's lovely to meet you, Anna,' said Max, staring at her thighs. 'Tom, you never told me she was such a lovely creature.'

'Creature!' Anna laughed. Her tone was deliberately light-hearted. 'You make me sound like the bride of Frankenstein!'

'Ah, but Frankenstein could never create anything quite so lovely!'

Max's girlfriend sat opposite him, a polite smile fixed

THEN

to her face. Max patted the seat next to him. 'Come and sit next to me, Anna. I want to find out exactly how Tom managed to persuade you to marry him.'

Drinks ordered, Tom took a seat next to Sara, his face bent close to hers to better hear what she was saying over the noise of the bar.

'So, how did you two meet?' asked Max.

'In a bar very similar to this one,' she replied. She made polite small talk – amusing anecdotes about the pupils she taught, a little about her doctoral thesis.

'Tom!' Max boomed. Tom looked up from his conversation with Sara. 'You didn't tell me your fiancée has both beauty *and* brains!'

Tom looked at Anna and smiled.

'Another drink?' Max said, looking at her empty wine glass. He leant over her to reach the cocktail menu and she felt his hand on the inside of her thigh. She waited for him to remove it as he righted himself, but he left it there, sure of himself, brandishing the menu in his other hand. 'What do you fancy, Anna? Maybe Sex on the Beach?'

She cringed. She was aware that Max was senior to Tom; she was also aware that Tom had been passed over for promotion. She didn't want to cause a scene or say anything that might cause tension.

'Another glass of white, please,' she said. 'I'm just off to powder my nose.' As she stood, Max's hand slid down her thigh. She knew that Tom had seen it. Although he was still talking to Sara, his body had stiffened. As she moved away, Max's hand returned to his lap.

Anna stood in front of the mirror in the ladies' and

stared at her reflection. Mechanically, she removed a tube of lipstick from her handbag and applied it to her lips. She practised three different smiles, trying to find one that looked genuine, and then fixed the expression on her face.

'Here she is!' cried Max as she returned to the table and took her seat. 'So, where will you be going on your honeymoon, Anna?'

She looked over at Tom. 'I don't think we've decided yet.'

'Somewhere hot maybe? Ah, I'll bet you're a bikini girl, aren't you, Anna?' He patted her thigh and left his hand resting there. 'Sara's more of a swimsuit girl.'

Anna looked at Sara. 'I'm sure Sara looks lovely in a bikini,' she said, diplomatically.

Sara smiled politely.

Max slid his hand further up her thigh. She looked over at Tom. His jaw was set, his back ramrod straight. *In a minute*, she thought, *his fist is going to slam across the table and into Max's face.* But instead, Tom turned to Sara and resumed their conversation. Anna felt a queasiness in her stomach. In any other situation, she'd have seized Max's hand, held it aloft in the air and said: 'Anyone claiming this? I found it wandering on my thigh!' But she felt paralysed. If she embarrassed Max in public, she knew that Tom could wave goodbye to any possibility of climbing further up the corporate ladder. She daren't even contemplate the door-slamming and recriminations if that happened.

At 10pm, Anna reached for her handbag. 'You know,' she said, looking hard at Tom, 'we need to be getting back soon. I've got an INSET day at school tomorrow.'

THEN

Max leant towards her, reeking of beer and sweat. 'I'll bet you looked good in a school uniform,' he sniggered into her ear.

Anna stood. Tom stared up at her. 'It looks like Anna wants us to go,' he said slowly.

She willed him to move.

He turned to Sara. 'Sorry about this. Anna's a *teacher*.' He looked at Anna. 'She's not very good at staying up late, are you, Anna?'

'No,' she replied.

'Let me help you with your coat,' offered Max, standing.

'Thanks, but I'm fine.'

'I insist.'

As she extended an arm into her coat, he slid his hand onto her bottom and smiled. Anna felt her hand clenching into a fist. She was close to punching him herself. She pulled away and stood next to Tom. He rose slowly from his seat.

'Sorry about this,' he apologised again, pulling on his coat. 'It's been a lovely evening, hasn't it, Anna?'

'Lovely.'

'We must do it again,' Tom continued.

'I'll see you in the office tomorrow and we'll fix a date,' Max beamed. They slapped each other on the back.

Sara, an air-hostess smile still fixed to her face, nodded goodbye.

As Anna emerged onto the street, she heaved an audible sigh of relief and looked over at Tom. His jaw was still set in anger. They walked in silence to the station. Anna waited for him to calm down, her stomach churning.

Finally, looking up at the departures board, Tom said, 'Don't ever embarrass me like that again.'

'Sorry?' Anna thought that she must have misheard.

'Don't ever embarrass me like that again,' he repeated, still staring ahead at the departures board.

Her stomach was so tense now, she felt like she was going to throw up. 'You think *I'm* the embarrassment?'

He stood in silence.

'Your so-called friend spent the entire evening feeling me up.'

He wheeled around with terrifying speed and force, slamming the flat of his hand against her left shoulder. She staggered backwards, attempting to stay upright. He pushed his face close to hers, his expression contorted.

'I didn't see you complaining,' he spat. He shoved her shoulder again and pain shot through her body. 'I'll go into the office tomorrow,' he snarled, 'and they'll all be laughing behind my back, knowing my fiancée is a fucking cock-tease.'

Anna froze. Behind Tom, she became aware of people slowing and staring, unsure whether to intervene or continue walking.

Tom advanced towards her again, shoving her hard. 'You're a fucking embarrassment!'

On the last shove, she lost her balance and fell, smashing the side of her face against the corner of Tie Rack. He stood for a second, looking down at her, and then turned away from the station, moving towards the street.

Anna lay half-sprawled on the station floor, the contents of her handbag scattered around her. Above her,

THEN

she became aware of a middle-aged man in a trench-coat asking gently, 'Are you OK?' She stared up at him. She couldn't speak. The man was joined by a young couple.

'Is she alright?' the girl asked.

The man shrugged.

The girl knelt down next to her and began picking up Anna's possessions. When she had finished, she handed Anna the bag. 'Are you alright?' she asked.

Anna nodded slowly.

'Can you stand?'

Anna tried to put one hand behind herself and winced.

The girl looked up at her boyfriend and back to Anna. 'Are you OK if my boyfriend helps you up?'

Anna nodded.

They positioned themselves either side of her and lifted her to a standing position. The world around her shifted slightly and then slid back into place.

'Can we call anyone for you?' asked the middle-aged man.

Anna stared at him blankly.

'Do you want us to call the police?' the girl said.

Anna slowly shook her head.

'Can we get you an ambulance?'

Anna tried moving her jaw. One side of her face felt like it had when she'd had her wisdom teeth extracted.

Anna shook her head again. She became aware that she was shaking.

'Can I at least get you a cab?' said the middle-aged man.

Anna nodded.

All four of them made their way slowly to the taxi rank. People turned to stare as they passed. She watched as the middle-aged man exchanged some words with the taxi driver and handed him some folded notes. The couple helped her onto the back seat.

'You really ought to get a doctor to check you out,' said the young man. She nodded, and he closed the door. She flinched as it slammed shut.

The taxi driver cast a concerned look in his rear-view mirror. 'Where to, love?' he said gently. He waited patiently as she processed the question. Finally, Anna tried moving her mouth, to see if it would make a sound. She found her voice and told him her address.

The driver saw her to the door.

'Have you got your keys?' he asked.

She stared down at her bag, blankly, and the driver rummaged around, found them and unlocked the door.

'Do you want me to check everything's safe?' he asked. She looked at him and nodded. He moved through each room, switching on the lights, and came back to the doorway where she was still standing.

'No one home,' he said. He paused for a second, awkwardly. 'I'll be off, then. Look after yourself.'

Anna closed the front door, flipped the lock and pulled the chain across. She removed her shoes and slid, fully clothed, under the duvet. She was shaking uncontrollably, like she couldn't get warm. Finally, her body exhausted, she began to sob – hot, scalding tears that coursed down her cheeks, soaking the pillow beneath. Her chest heaved. In the distance, she could hear the sound of the last train

THEN

pulling away from her local station before she fell into a deep, black, dreamless sleep.

Anna was startled awake by the phone, its loud trill echoing in the next room. She lifted her head slightly and winced. One side of her face felt rigid and tender; her shoulder throbbed. Memories of the previous night came back to her like a still photo montage. She looked at the alarm clock: 6am. She lay still, looking up at the ceiling, and wished she'd bought a phone with an answering machine. It rang on and on, incessantly.

Cautiously, she extended one foot to the floor and slowly levered herself up. She padded to the living room, sat in the armchair and picked up the receiver.

'Anna?' Tom's voice sounded reedy, insubstantial. 'Anna, I'm so sorry...' On the last syllable, his voice broke, and he began to sob. She sat, numbly, the receiver to her ear, until, after a few minutes, his sobs began to subside.

'I love you *so* much.'

She listened, silent.

'It physically hurts how much I love you.'

Her shoulder throbbed.

'It's just... I can't... I can't bear it,' he continued, 'the way men look at you sometimes...'

She was still wearing the black dress he'd wanted her to wear.

'I'm not making excuses. What I said, the way I behaved. I'd had too much to drink. I can't remember half of what happened.' He paused. 'Are you still there?'

She made a 'mmm' sound.

'Anna, it will never happen again. I promise you.'
Silence.
'I understand if you need some space. I can stay at my parents' place.'
Silence.
'I love you, Anna.'
'Mmm,' she said, and replaced the receiver.

She stood up and caught sight of her reflection in the mirror over the fireplace. A bluish-purple bruise streaked across her cheekbone and extended, like a fat thumbprint, to her temple. One cheek pillowed out slightly, and she had a sudden memory of how her childhood hamster would pack his cheeks with nuts and seeds until they bulged.

She turned back to the phone and punched in the school's number, leaving a message that she had been involved in a minor accident and needed to get checked out at the hospital. Then she called for a cab.

Dan had a knack for choosing godawful places in which to live and this place was no exception.

'Nearly there, love,' said the cabbie. The cab driver had kept glancing in his rear-view mirror, looking at her face, too polite to question her about it.

Anna looked out of the window. They were entering one of those grim estates that town planners of the 1960s had described as 'modern homes of the future'. The grey sky bled into the damp concrete buildings until they became virtually indistinguishable. They passed a Spar with a boarded-up window. The black fingers of saplings

THEN

reached skyward, tiny islands surrounded by oceans of tarmac. National Front graffiti littered the walls.

'Here we are,' said the cab driver. The car stopped outside a low-rise block of flats.

Anna looked at the meter. It was a horrendous sum. She would never normally dream of taking a cab all the way across London, but the alternative – commuters staring at her face with roadkill curiosity – was unthinkable. She counted off an extra five-pound note as a tip and handed it over.

'Thanks,' he said. 'Have a good day.'

Anna removed the piece of paper from her purse and re-read the address. She'd never been here before. They had always met at the Lyceum and always on Fridays.

The foyer smelt vaguely of urine and bleach. White paint flaked off the spindly metal banister and black refuse sacks slumped in one corner. Institutional tiles covered the floor and stairs. There was no lift. She began climbing to the second floor.

Outside the door she looked again at the piece of paper, checking the number, then she knocked. She stood for a minute or so, listening for footsteps, but there was only silence. She didn't know why she hadn't called first before coming all this way; she hadn't been thinking straight. She looked at her watch – 7.25am – and knocked again, louder. Finally, she heard a sound on the other side of the door. It was Dan's voice.

'OK, OK,' she heard him say, irritably.

The door opened. Dan's expression was grumpy. He looked at her.

'Whoa! What happened to you? Was it a disgruntled pupil with a low-flying netball?' He realised instantly that he had misjudged the mood as her eyes began welling with tears. 'Hey, sorry, sorry.' He stood to one side. 'Come in.'

Anna slipped past him, head down.

'Are you alright?' Clearly, she wasn't.

A flatmate opened his bedroom door and poked his head into the hallway. His hair was still dishevelled from sleep. He stared at Anna for a second, then ducked his head back in, closing the door behind him.

'Have you had an accident?'

She didn't answer. Dan walked to the end of the hallway and opened a door to his left. 'Sorry, no living room,' he said.

The room was sparsely furnished: a single bed was pushed against one wall; there was a desk and chair, a chest of drawers. A Killing Joke poster hung on one wall at a slight angle.

Dan sat down on the edge of the bed and gestured for her to sit next to him. She realised she'd got him out of bed; he was wearing only boxer shorts and a T-shirt.

'What happened?'

'I fell.' She began crying and saw a panicked look flash across Dan's face. Dan couldn't cope with emotional women. 'Sorry,' she said, pulling herself together. She wiped her hand across the eye that hadn't swollen. 'I must look like crap.'

She looks terrible, Dan thought. He said, 'Do you need to see a doctor?'

She shook her head.

THEN

Dan wondered why she'd turned up at his flat at this hour of the morning. She'd seemed to have had a bad fall and was clearly shaken up, but why wasn't she at home? Shouldn't it be lover boy offering to take her to the doctor?

'OK, so how did you fall?'

She sniffed. 'Tom was pushing me, and the last time he pushed me so hard, I fell and hit my head.'

'Pushing you? What, like larking about?' Even as he asked the question, he knew the answer.

'No,' she said.

Dan sat very still. He paused for a moment, thinking, and then turned to her. 'He hit you?'

'He pushed me.'

He looked at the swelling on her face, the bruise along her cheekbone. 'Because real men don't hit women, Anna.'

She looked at him. 'You sound like the slogan for a domestic abuse helpline.' She swallowed. 'He didn't hit me or anything. He pushed me.'

Dan frowned. 'Hitting, pushing, it doesn't matter. What matters is that he laid his hands on you, and he hurt you.' He could feel a swell of anger rising inside him. 'Where is he? Is he at your flat? I'll fucking kill him.'

Anna had come here on instinct, without thinking, but as he said those words, she realised that it was exactly what she had wanted to hear. She wanted him to take care of her and protect her and make it all go away.

She twisted the ring on her finger. 'No, I don't know, he's at his parents' place probably. I'm not sure if he really meant to hurt me. He was angry.'

'What about?'

She sat there for a while. Eventually, she said: 'We were on a double date. He said I was an embarrassment, a cock-tease.'

Dan raised his eyebrows. 'Why, what did you do?'

Anna's body stiffened defensively. 'What do you mean, what did I do?'

He shifted uncomfortably. 'Well, sometimes... well, you know, sometimes you can say things that can be a bit provocative...' Dan struggled to find the right words. 'Not intentionally but, well, a certain type of man might take some of those things the wrong way...'

Anna stared at him. 'You think I got what I deserved?'

'No!' Dan said, frustrated. 'That's not what I meant. He hit you, pushed you, whatever. The bastard hurt you. But, you know, he's obviously a man who's easily provoked.'

'I didn't *say* anything. His friend was feeling me up!'

'OK.'

They sat next to each other on the bed, looking at the floor. Eventually, Anna pulled at the hem of her dress. 'I'm still wearing yesterday's clothes.'

He turned to her. 'Do you want a shower or something?'

She nodded. 'Yeah, if that's alright.' She stood. 'My shoulder still hurts,' she said. 'Can you help me?'

Gently, he lifted the hem of her dress up towards her ribcage. She bit her lip as he eased the fabric up over her breasts and towards her neck.

'Every bloke's fantasy,' she said, her eyes narrowing with pain, 'being asked by a woman to strip her naked.'

'It's not a particular fantasy of mine at the moment.'

THEN

She looked down at her bra. 'Sorry. Can you undo the hooks at the back?'

Dan fiddled, trying to undo the bra. Eventually, the hooks gave way, and he eased the straps down her arms. She sat before him, virtually naked. A large bruise spread from her collarbone to her armpit. He was overcome by a terrible feeling of pity and anger. He wanted to take that bastard's head in his hands and smash it repeatedly against a wall. What kind of a lowlife would push a woman?

'I'll put the shower on.'

Dan's flatmate was brushing his teeth in the bathroom. Dan jerked his head towards the door and his flatmate nodded, spat in the sink, rinsed and left. He switched on the shower and placed his hand under the water to check the temperature.

'Shower's running,' he said, returning to the room. He rummaged through some drawers for a clean towel, failed to find one, and handed her the towel draped over the back of the chair.

Anna stood under the warm shower, lifting her face to the water. She was washing off the impression of Max's hand on her thigh, the beery breath, the spittle, the dirt of the station floor. She let the water cascade over her body and emptied her mind. Finally, she twisted her hair into a slick, dark rope, squeezed it, and wrapped the towel around her body.

Dan was lying on the single bed, his back against the wall to make room for her. Swaddled in the towel, she lay down next to him. Carefully, so as not to hurt her, he placed his arm around her and kissed the top of her head.

She smelt of damp hair and Imperial Leather soap. He felt her body relax and her breathing become slow and even. He watched the clouds scudding past through the window. After some time, he felt Anna stir.

'Why do I fuck everything up?' she said, her words muffled against his chest.

He bent his head down towards her face. 'You don't fuck everything up.'

'Sometimes I think there's something inside me that just makes things go wrong.'

'There's nothing wrong with you.'

He saw her eyelids flicker and close, and they lay like that, his arm going numb, until the light faded, and the grey landscape darkened to an inky mass.

***

'What do you think of these?' Sally picked up a pair of white jeans from the rack.

'Yeah,' said Anna. 'Try them on. I think they'll suit you.' Sally added them to the other three items she had draped over her arm and wandered to the changing room. Anna sat on the other side of the changing-room door.

'We really need to look at some bridesmaid's dresses today,' called Sally. 'It's time to make a decision.' She emerged from the changing room in the white jeans.

Anna nodded approvingly. 'They suit you. Get them.'

'You're not secretly planning to put me in some hideous lampshade dress, are you?'

Anna laughed. 'No!'

THEN

'Well, we need to choose something today, then.'

Anna inhaled sharply through her nose. 'The thing is, Sally, we've decided to postpone the wedding.'

Sally stared down at her. 'Postpone it?'

'Yeah.'

'Why?'

'Lots of reasons. At the beginning, we got engaged and moved in together really quickly. We just want to take a bit more time to get to know each other…'

Those were exactly the words she had used to her parents. Her father had sat, stony-faced.

'We'll lose the deposit for the reception.'

'I'll pay you back.'

'And the wedding car.'

'Let me know what it all comes to, and I'll pay you back.'

'What about the guests?' her mother had said, anxiously. 'They'll need to be told.'

Anna's sister had cut in. 'I'll do it,' she'd said. 'I'll let everyone know.'

She had turned to Jess in relief. 'Thank you, sis.'

For all their history of petty childhood squabbles, Anna had never in her life been as grateful to have a sister as she was at that moment.

Sally stood in her white jeans, looking entirely unconvinced by her friend's explanation.

'O-K,' she said, slowly. She sensed that Anna was not telling her the whole story but now was not the time.

'I'll try the top on then, shall I?'

'Yes.' Anna smiled. 'You do that.'

SOMETHING CHANGED

***

Dan sat in the Lyceum bar, pint in hand, waiting for Anna. Since that day at his flat, he'd felt a growing unease about Anna's situation. He'd offered to accompany her home, but she had simply shaken her head and asked him to call her a taxi. He'd offered to get someone to change the locks, but she'd replied that she couldn't lock Tom out of his own home – he was, after all, paying half the mortgage. Over the last few months, from what he could gather, Tom had showered her with tears of remorse, bouquets of flowers and protestations of love.

'He had too much to drink, gave me a push and I fell over,' she told Dan. 'He's not some gorilla with "Love" and "Hate" tattooed on his knuckles who's beating me black and blue every night. It was an accident. A one-off. To be honest, I'm embarrassed I made such a fuss about it.'

He was finding it increasingly difficult to reconcile the woman he thought he knew – feisty, clever, independent – with the woman who could make such a statement.

After 'giving her some space' for a while, Tom had arranged one weekend to pick up some clothes and had managed to persuade her to let him move back in.

'Is he sharing your bed?' Dan had asked.

'It's *our* bed, and yes, he's sharing it. It's a one-bedroom flat. Where else would he sleep?'

'The sofa?'

He wondered if they were having sex, wondered what she was like in bed with Tom. He'd never met the bloke, which was just as well because if he ever did, he'd want

THEN

to punch him in the face. The only sensible decision that had been made, as far as he could tell, was postponing the wedding.

He looked up from his pint to see Anna entering the bar. She raised her hand in greeting. She had become so thin; her face had taken on a gaunt, slightly hollow look.

'Hello, you,' she said, pecking him on the cheek. 'How's your week been?'

'Yeah, OK. Same old, same old. You?'

'Ah!' she said. 'The annual Thorpe Park school trip.'

She began regaling him with the tale of her Year Ten trip. 'All that oestrogen packed into two fifty-six-seater coaches,' she said. 'You cannot imagine. We were awash with lip gloss, mascara and Impulse body spray. And then we got to the coach park and who should be pulling in next to us but St Thomas's boys' school.'

'Is that a good thing?'

'Depends on your perspective. For St Thomas's boys, it was definitely a good thing, because Erin Doherty was flashing her tits through the back-seat window. I soon put a stop to that.'

'Killjoy.'

'So, most of the trip, when I wasn't trying to prise gargantuan bags of sweets out of Louise Connor's hands—'

'What are you, the Child Catcher from *Chitty Chitty Bang Bang*?'

'He didn't *steal* kids' sweets, you idiot, he *lured* them with lollipops! Anyway, she's got ADHD. The additives send her hyper. No, I was mostly focused on trying to prevent another sort of bang-bang situation from arising.

I told the girls they weren't allowed to go on any of the rides with a boy. Or, indeed, to ride any boy. It was like being the sex police.'

A slow smile spread over Dan's face.

'Yeah, and you can get that image out of your head,' said Anna. 'I know exactly what you're thinking, and I'm definitely not doing that with your imaginary truncheon.'

He laughed. 'So, a successful trip, then?'

'Yeah, no pregnancies yet. Fingers crossed.'

This was more like the Anna he knew.

He held up a newspaper, folded to the crossword page. 'Shall we?'

'You've already filled two in!' she exclaimed, biffing him on the arm. 'You could have waited for me.'

'OK, three across. Union. Eight letters.'

'Marriage,' they said, simultaneously.

They sat in awkward silence for a few minutes, neither looking at the other, and then Anna gave a tight-lipped smile. 'You know, in a few weeks, it would have been my wedding day.'

'Yeah,' he said, privately thinking that she'd dodged a bullet.

She sighed heavily. 'I don't want to be at home in the flat on the day I should have been getting married,' she continued. 'Are Tom and I just supposed to pretend it's a normal Saturday and push a trolley around Tesco?'

'Well, if you like, I could take you away for the weekend.'

The words had just come out of his mouth, he didn't know where from, and now he couldn't retract them.

THEN

'*You and me?*'

He looked at her.

She thought for a minute. 'No funny business?'

'Spoilsport… OK, no funny business.'

'Where would we go?'

'I'll think of somewhere.'

'I'm not spending the weekend at some binary code convention in Cleethorpes.'

He laughed. 'Binary code convention? What the hell is that? And anyway, what have you got against Cleethorpes?'

'Well, it's not my idea of fun being surrounded by a load of geeks and nerds. Spending a weekend with you will be quite enough.'

'Hey! Anyway, I see myself more as a suave, sophisticated man about town.'

'You keep telling yourself that.' Her face fell as reality hit. A weekend away was a ridiculous suggestion. 'It's a lovely thought,' she said, 'but I can't really spend a weekend away with another man.'

He'd been reprieved at the eleventh hour.

Dan shrugged. 'OK.'

Anna thought about her relationship with Tom. Increasingly, she felt like one of those soap actresses who get typecast and become trapped, forever playing the same part. She suddenly looked up, defiant.

'You know what?' she said. 'Life's short. I've changed my mind. Let's do it. I'll work something out.'

'Right,' he said, gulping his beer. 'I'd better get something booked then.'

When the weekend arrived, Anna found herself outside Dan's flat staring at a battered Ford Escort.

'D'you think it'll get us there?' she said, doubtfully.

'Of course it'll get us there. Stop worrying.' Dan's flatmate had lent him his car in exchange for Dan fixing his computer.

'And you're definitely insured?'

'Yes!'

She checked the tax disc on the windscreen wasn't out of date and then threw her bag on the back seat. 'Why are there bungee cords on the passenger door?'

'Oh, sometimes it doesn't shut properly. It's just to hold the door closed.'

'That fills me with confidence.'

'Hop in, then.'

She sat in the passenger seat whilst he secured the bungee cord, attaching it to the seat. Dan started the car. The engine noise was followed by a hideous, metallic scraping sound.

'Sorry, wrong gear.' He shoved the gear stick into position, and they pulled away.

'Where *are* we going exactly?' asked Anna. She's imagined it would be somewhere like Brighton or Whitstable. Somewhere within easy reach of London.

'Blackpool!' announced Dan triumphantly.

'Blackpool?'

'Yeah, I haven't been there since I was a kid.'

She looked nervously at the bungee cord to her left and hoped fervently that it wouldn't give out halfway up the M1.

THEN

The light was starting to fade by the time they reached the hotel in a little street off the seafront. Above the plate-glass doors, an illuminated sign proclaimed that it was 'The Regency' despite the fact that the entire hotel appeared to have been constructed in the 1950s. The letter 'C' blinked like a nervous twitch.

Anna emerged from the car like an unoiled Tin Man, legs stiff. She rubbed her backside and turned to Dan.

'My bum's gone numb!'

'I think I can help with that,' Dan said, extending his hand towards her bottom.

Anna dodged sideways. 'Hands off, Lothario! Let's get our bags. I'm knackered.'

The hotel reception was like something from a mid-twentieth century photograph, and not in a kitsch or ironic way. It was all teak, Formica and curlicued wrought iron. On the wall, a Spanish flamenco dancer swirled her scarlet skirts in a white frame. A vase of faded plastic flowers gathered dust amongst a motley collection of Venetian glass animals. Anna had no idea what they – or the flamenco dancer – were doing in Blackpool, so far from home.

She began to wonder what *she* was doing in Blackpool, so far from home.

'Welcome to the Regency,' said the receptionist without breaking into a smile. 'Do you have a reservation?'

Anna looked at the deserted lounge to her left.

Dan told the receptionist his name and she consulted a typed list, down which she slid a scarlet talon. Her hair had been permed, bleached and backcombed to within an inch of its life sometime in the early eighties. It was an impressively permanent structure held in place with industrial quantities of hairspray.

'Double room,' she confirmed, still looking at the list.

'Double room with twin beds,' Anna said quickly.

The receptionist glanced up briefly at the engagement ring on Anna's finger. Clearly under the impression that they were a couple intent on preserving their virginity until the big day, she nodded and turned to remove a key from one of the hooks behind her. That anyone would think she and Dan were a pair of earnest virgins amused Anna so much that she began to giggle.

'What are you laughing at?' asked Dan as they made their way up the stairs.

'Just this place,' she laughed, 'it's hilarious. I keep expecting Basil Fawlty to come round the corner whacking Manuel over the head.'

Their room was similarly frozen in time: the modern innovation of the duvet had passed it by, and instead there were bed sheets, blankets and olive-green candlewick bedspreads.

'Candlewick bedspreads!' exclaimed Anna. 'My gran used to have those!'

She explored the bathroom: a pale-pink suite surrounded by white tiles shot through with a pattern like pink thread veins. On the cistern sat the piece de resistance: a plastic doll with a hypnotic stare, stretching her crocheted pink skirts over a spare toilet roll.

'Jesus! Is this for real?'

Dan looked over her shoulder at the doll. 'We're actually in an episode of the *Twilight Zone*,' he said, 'and in the middle of the night, she'll come alive and bludgeon us to death in our beds.'

Anna turned to him. 'Ah, you know how to show a girl a good time.'

'I aim to please.'

'Right, so, who's first to the bathroom?'

Dan let her go first. Anna took her weekend bag with her so she could change into her nightwear behind closed doors. *This is ridiculous*, she thought, as she stripped off her clothes. *How many times have we seen each other stark naked?*

She emerged from the bathroom damp-faced and minty-breathed in cotton pyjamas.

Dan was reclining on the bed, his arms folded behind his head and his eyes fixed on the bathroom door. Anna watched with amusement as his face fell in disappointment.

'Oh. Pyjamas,' he said, like a schoolboy who was hoping for a Scalextric set but had got a Matchbox car instead.

'Yeah, funnily enough I left the stockings and suspenders at home.'

'Shame.'

She shoved him. 'Go and get washed, you sweaty bugger. You smell like Arsenal's changing room at half time.'

'I won't ask how you know that.'

Anna lay on the bed poring over leaflets promoting local attractions, listening to the sloshing and gurgling of water on the other side of the bathroom door. Finally, Dan emerged, smelling more fragrant. He looked at the leaflets.

'What d'you fancy doing tomorrow, then?'

'I dunno. I thought you could take me up the tower and maybe down the pier.'

A larky smile spread across Dan's features. 'Hey, I'll take you up the tower anytime. And if you're very nice to me, I might take you down the pier, as well.'

It was like being in a *Carry On* film. She closed her eyes, despairingly. When she opened them again, Dan was in bed, pulling the candlewick bedspread over his boxers and T-shirt.

'Night, Dan,' she said.

'Night, Anna.' He clicked off the bedside light and they both lay, side by side in separate beds, listening to each other's breathing until sleep eventually washed over them.

Anna was woken the next morning by a shard of bright sunlight that had pierced through the curtains. She experienced that fleeting sensation upon waking when you orientate yourself, and realised she was not at home but in a hotel room. Squinting, she turned away from the light and towards Dan, who was still sleeping. One arm was lifted and curled around his head on the pillow, as if he was trying to protect himself from an avalanche. She had forgotten that he slept like that and felt a rush of affection. Then she remembered that today was supposed to have been her wedding day, and her stomach sank.

Knowing that the best lies are rooted in the truth, she'd explained to Tom that spending time with him on the weekend they were due to get married was just too difficult, and he had been understanding of her need to get

THEN

away with Sally for a girls' weekend. He had only met Sally a few times; he didn't have her number or know where she lived, so she thought she was safe. She knew that she should feel guilty spending the weekend with another man, even if it was just Dan, but in truth, she could summon up no feelings at all. Not for the first time, she wondered how everything had got so messed up. The straightforward lives that other people acquired so easily always seemed beyond her reach. Anna sighed and heard Dan stirring. He frowned, blinking, and then, as he registered her face in the next bed, he smiled and extended his hand towards hers.

'Morning.'

She reached out and felt her hand encased in his. 'To quote Billy Idol, it's a nice day for a white wedding,' she said flatly, nodding towards the sunlight.

Dan saw the sadness in her eyes. He knew it was not because she'd desperately wanted to marry the bloke, but rather because she felt she had failed in some way. Her hand was very still inside his.

'Fancy a hug?'

She nodded.

He slipped out from underneath the bedcovers and into her bed, curling his body around hers. After a minute, Anna half turned her head over her shoulder.

'Dan, are you hard?'

'What, like Ronnie Kray hard?'

'You know perfectly well what I mean.'

'I might be.'

Anna sighed. 'You are incorrigible.'

'I'll take that as a compliment.'

'Only because you're not sure what the word means.' She began giggling. 'It would be a good euphemism, though. "Eh, love, you've given me a massive Ronnie!"'

'I can't help it,' he protested. 'It's an automatic physical response, like when a ferret sees a rabbit hole.'

'Charming!'

He stifled a yawn. 'Come on, let's get up and get some breakfast.'

The breakfast room was set out in long rows of tables, presumably to accommodate coach parties. The Formica tops were partially covered with disposable paper tablecloths and at each place setting was a green, upended teacup on a saucer. Anna looked around for the buffet, but there wasn't one. They sat themselves at the other end of a long table from a gaggle of elderly ladies with blue rinses and waited. An old man shuffled past them clutching a Zimmer frame.

Anna could feel a giggle bubbling in her throat. 'Are you sure you booked us into a hotel and not a care home?'

'Very funny.'

Eventually, a waiter arrived with a rack of white toast and two pats of margarine. This was followed by watery instant coffee and two glasses of a startlingly orange liquid that had been squeezed from the imagination of a food scientist rather than any natural fruit.

'Blimey,' said Anna, holding up her glass. 'Forget sweets, if Louise Connor got her hands on a glass of this, I'd be coaxing her down off the ceiling.'

THEN

'Will it be a full *English* breakfast?' asked the waiter obsequiously, hovering above them.

'Are there any alternatives?' enquired Anna.

The waiter, who had clearly never been asked this question, stood smiling mutely.

Dan gave Anna a look. 'A full English will be fine,' he said, and the waiter departed, relieved.

That day, they skirted around the ballroom at Blackpool Tower on their way to the top, surrounded by geriatric dancing couples and a huge organ that rose, Hammer-horror style, from beneath the floor.

'Don't even think of making any jokes about large organs,' Anna warned.

At the top of the tower, they looked down at the ant people below as they strolled along the promenade. The sky was a cloudless blue; the sea glittered with diamond chips of light.

'What next?' asked Dan. 'Pier or Pleasure Beach?'

They bought themselves two cones of chips and walked along the pier, dodging kamikaze seagulls.

'Bastards!' cried Dan, clutching his cone as yet another gull made a bid for his chips, and Anna held her sides with laughter.

At the Pleasure Beach, they bought pink sticks of minty rock and Dan managed to get three darts to stick to a dartboard at his fourth attempt. He presented her with a small stuffed hippo like Raleigh returning from the Americas.

'Here you go. Reminds me of you.'

'Thanks a bunch!'

'I meant the brown eyes, obviously.'

She refused point-blank to go on the huge rollercoaster on the basis that she'd throw up, so they went on the bumper cars instead.

Dan was an absolute fiend on the bumper cars, stealthily skirting around the edges before darting in and causing multiple pile-ups. Anna covered her eyes with her hands, laughing and screaming.

As the light faded, they sat on the promenade munching steak pies. Lights flashed at the end of the pier, and they could hear the waves hushing onto the sand. Tinny music carried on the air, which wafted aromas of fried onions and hot oil. Anna tilted her head slowly to one side, then the other.

'I think I've got whiplash.'

'Miss Whiplash!' Dan grinned.

'Do you *ever* stop?' Anna licked the last few flakes of pastry from her fingers, crumpled up the paper bag and nudged his arm. 'You know, it's not been a bad wedding day,' she said, 'all things considered.'

Dan turned to her. 'Yeah?'

'Yeah.' She looked up at him. 'Thank you.'

He smiled at her. 'My pleasure.'

In fact, she couldn't remember the last time she'd laughed so much. A sudden image of Dan being attacked by gulls came into her mind and she erupted with laughter.

'What?'

'You and those gulls!'

'It was like a scene from that Hitchcock film…'

THEN

'*The Birds*!' She laughed.

'Yeah,' he said, vengefully. 'Bloody bastards nicked my chips.'

Anna bent double, gripping her sides, tears of laughter streaming down her face. No, it hadn't been a bad wedding day after all.

***

But as the heat of summer faded, so did her memories of gulls and chips and pies on the seafront and hotels frozen in time. That night, Tom was taking her to a dining club. Anna had never been to a dining club before. In her imagination, a dining club consisted of wood-panelled rooms with tobacco-coloured leather chairs and creaking waiters wheeling laden dessert trolleys. This place, however, was a series of slick, white, modern rooms full of glass and chrome and modern art.

'It's the future of dining,' said Tom as they descended the steps into the basement just off Gower Street. He had a vested interest, given that it was he who had brokered investment in the venture. She suspected he may have invested some of his own money, too.

She'd dressed simply, in a cream silk shirt, black palazzo pants and high heels. Tom kissed her, smudging her lipstick.

'You look very chic,' he said. 'What's that perfume you're wearing?'

'Coco,' she said. 'You bought it for me last Christmas.'

'So I did. I'd forgotten.'

A waiter took her coat, and they sat down to a succession of exquisitely presented plates of food in tiny portions; food accompanied by 'foam' and 'jus'. Anna poked at her coriander foam. It reminded her of sputum. She felt a sudden wave of nausea and pushed her food to one side. Tom looked pointedly at her virtually untouched plate as the waiter asked if she had finished but said nothing.

At the pudding course, the waiter lifted the dome above her plate and what appeared to be dry ice snaked into the air before her. She pushed an edible flower from the top of her dessert with the side of her spoon.

'Are you anorexic or something?'

Anna had become very thin. She looked like one of those size zero actresses that now populated Hollywood, or the models that promoted Heroin Chic.

'No,' she said. 'I'm just not very hungry.'

'You could have told me that before I brought you here.'

She said nothing and watched him eat a tiny sliver of chocolate truffle cake. Raspberry coulis had been swirled artfully around the edge of the plate.

That night, she let him undress her. He didn't like her to undress herself before sex. He kissed her, leaning her body backwards onto the bed, and slid inside her. As he moved, silently, she felt his chest hair brush against her skin and moved outside of herself, viewing them from above. She watched his thrusting, hairy buttocks, her spread legs, her impassive face looking up from the pillow. She was reminded of a documentary she'd watched one night about the lives of primates and how the alpha male, having seen off his rivals, had mated with the fertile female. *Human beings have created this cultural concept of romantic love*, she thought, and it wasn't that she didn't believe in love – she did; the kind of love she imagined a mother might feel for her child – but what *romantic* love really amounted to was sex: two primates ensuring the continuation of their species. She looked down once more on her impassive face, as if through the lens of a camera, and directed herself into expressions of passion. She parted her lips, threw back her head on the pillow, quickened her breathing. His thrusts came more quickly then, and she dug her fingernails into his flesh, experimented with some tiny moans. He thrust hard, came, and collapsed onto her, burying his face in her hair.

'God, that felt good,' he said. He never asked whether it felt good for her. Either he was convinced by her modest pantomimes, which depressed her, or he didn't care, and that depressed her even more. She felt him kiss her neck.

'I love you,' he said.

'I love you, too,' she replied, and turned to face the wall.

A few miles away, Dan sat in front of the computer screen in the university room he shared with two other doctoral students, both of whom were Greek and who spent all day speaking to each other in their native language. He'd reached a sticking point in his research. He took another mouthful of instant coffee, made with two teaspoons not one, and hoped that the caffeine would kick-start his brain into action. His mind drifted back to the summer and the weekend he'd spent with Anna in Blackpool. He smiled at the memory. He pictured her sitting on a bench on the promenade, doubled with laughter, tears rolling down her face. In truth, he'd been dreading the weekend, fearing that he had condemned himself to forty-eight hours of listening to the tearful musings of an emotional woman on what was supposed to be her wedding day, but it hadn't been like that. They'd had a good laugh. The only thing he hadn't managed to do was seduce her. An even earlier image entered his mind of Anna lying naked on her bed in halls, her skin slicked with his sweat, her dark hair fanned across the pillow, and he felt a dull ache of desire. He wondered if she'd noticed his visits to the pink bathroom in order to relieve the sexual pressure under the unflinching gaze of the toilet-roll doll or whether she'd just assumed he had a urinary tract infection. He was not sure which was worse.

'Are you coming for something to eat?' The two Greeks stood over his desk.

'No, I'll go later,' he said. Dinner could wait. He closed his eyes and leant back in his swivel chair. He was going to hold on to that image of Anna for just a little while longer.

***

Despite evidence of winter on the other side of the plate-glass window, Sally and Anna had decided to meet in a fashionable ice-cream parlour on the edge of Leicester Square.

'We're a greedy pair of buggers,' said Sally, staring

THEN

at the sundae glass containing a mountain of ice-cream scoops in various flavours.

'So, how does it feel to be engaged?' asked Anna, looking down at the sapphire on her friend's finger.

'I can remember asking you that, once.'

'Yeah, the irony hasn't escaped me.'

Sally looked at her friend's bare finger. There was still a slight depression in the flesh from where the ring had once been. 'Sorry, is this just really awkward?'

'No.' Anna smiled. 'Not at all. I'm delighted for you and Kris.' She meant it.

Sally placed a spoonful of ice cream in her mouth and let it melt slowly. 'It's such a shame,' she sighed. 'Tom was such a romantic guy. Remember those balloons?'

Anna licked chocolate sauce from the corner of her mouth.

'And he took you to the top of the Eiffel Tower to propose. Kris proposed to me over a pie and a pint after Newcastle won a match.'

'Yeah, well, romance isn't all it's cracked up to be. And it's obvious to everyone how much Kris loves you.' She dug her spoon deeper into her ice cream.

'So what happened, then? Did you just drift apart?'

'Yeah.' Anna's tone was matter of fact. 'And I think he was probably seeing other women.'

Sally looked shocked. She reached over to take her friend's hand in hers. 'Anna, that's awful. Why didn't you say anything?'

'Oh, it was nothing I could pin down. And to be honest, in the end I realised I just didn't care.'

Sally stared at her friend and realised that she was telling the truth. She began excavating a brownie chunk with her spoon, wondering how to change the subject.

'I hear you and Dan have been spending some time together.'

Anna sat up straighter and put down her spoon. 'Who told you that?'

'Jenny bumped into Dan on Tottenham Court Road, and they went for a drink. She said you'd been to Blackpool or something.'

Clearly, the grapevine was still thriving.

'He was just trying to cheer me up. It was the weekend I was supposed to get married. I couldn't face spending it with Tom.'

'Well, that's understandable.' Sally sat back in her chair and looked at her friend. 'Of course, we all knew you and Dan were shagging each other.'

Anna blinked.

'Years back when we were at university.' Sally laughed. 'I could never understand why you two went to such lengths to pretend it wasn't happening.'

Anna couldn't answer that.

'So, what's the score now, then?'

'Well, we're friends.'

'Just friends?'

'Just friends. Nothing more interesting to report.'

'That's a shame.'

'Why?'

'I always thought that if you two ever stopped fannying about, you might actually be good together.'

THEN

Anna decided to change the subject and placed a finger on Sally's engagement ring. 'Promise me one thing.'

'What?'

'Don't make me a bridesmaid.'

'O-K,' said Sally, as she scraped the last vestiges of sauce from the bottom of the sundae dish, 'whatever you want.'

***

In the Lyceum bar, the crossword had been completed, and eight pint glasses stood empty on the table.

'Fancy another?' He'd had five pints to her three and was well on the way to inebriation.

'No, I'm good thanks.'

Dan held up one finger to the barman, who knew them by now as regulars. The barman nodded and brought him another pint. He knocked back a mouthful of beer and turned to look at her, his face lurching closer until his forehead was touching hers. She could smell the beer on his breath as he curled his little finger around hers.

'Why do you do that?'

'What?'

'Curling your little finger around mine.'

He looked down at their hands. 'I dunno.' Abruptly, he sat upright and removed his finger.

'I don't dislike it,' she said, quickly. 'I just wondered why you do it.'

He shrugged. After a while, he said, 'Well, I can't exactly kiss you, can I?'

'Can't you?'

He laughed uneasily, unsure if she was teasing him.

'Well, you've not been too keen. Twin beds in Blackpool and all that.'

She rubbed her ring finger. 'Yeah, well, in case you've forgotten, I was engaged at the time.'

'Yeah, well. I'm just saying.'

When Anna had told him that Tom had moved out, Dan hadn't initially paid much attention. Lover boy had moved out before, only to sweet-talk her into moving back in. It was only when she had mentioned legal paperwork transferring the flat into her name that he'd realised it was final. Since then, she had been more distant somehow, like she had constructed some sort of protective carapace, and occasionally her anecdotes and jokes had taken on a bitter, cynical quality that didn't suit her.

He looked at her. 'Do you *want* me to kiss you?'

'Do *you* want to?'

He moved his mouth towards hers, brushing her lips tentatively. It had been years since he had given her more than a peck on the cheek. As she parted her lips, he kissed her more deeply. He had a powerful memory of how it felt to be inside her.

Eventually, he broke away. Neither of them spoke. They knew they would be spending the night together. The tension stretched taut between them, and she attempted to ease it.

'Get your coat, love,' she joked, nudging his arm. 'You've pulled.'

THEN

Later, they lay in the double bed in her flat, arms draped around each other.

'Blimey!' he'd said when he entered the flat. 'It's properly grown-up!'

She supposed it was, to someone still living the life of a full-time student. 'Yeah,' she said. 'I've got a cafetiere and everything.' She locked the front door behind her and slid the chain across.

Dan turned. 'Has Tom still got a key?' He imagined Tom lurking in the wardrobe like Kato in the *Pink Panther* films, leaping out to attack him before he'd got his boxer shorts off.

'No, I got the keys back. I just use the chain for extra security. Just in case he got a replica key cut.'

'You need to change the locks.'

'Yeah, I'll get round to it.'

He touched her shoulder. 'I mean it.'

Her relationship with Tom had, in fact, ended with a whimper, not a bang. For the umpteenth time, he had accused her of being unfaithful – an accusation that had now been thrown at her so many times, she had given up trying to defend herself. She'd carefully positioned herself in the narrow hallway, away from objects that could be hurled, and next to the front door to facilitate escape.

'Whatever you say, Tom.'

He turned towards her, and she braced herself.

'What's that supposed to mean?'

'It means it doesn't matter whether I have been seeing someone else or I haven't. It doesn't matter anymore.' She spoke from a weariness that came from deep within her bones, within every fibre of her being.

Tom stared at her belligerently. 'If I go this time, I'm going for good. And I won't be paying the mortgage.'

Part of him evidently thought that still mattered; that somehow money gave him some leverage, some power over her. She was exhausted. 'OK, whatever,' she said.

He stood, staring at her, waiting for her to capitulate, but she remained motionless, looking at the floor. Eventually, he moved into the bedroom, and she retreated to the living room, closing the door. She listened as he filled bags with clothes and personal possessions, as he called a taxi; she heard the dull thunk of the taxi door in the street outside as he closed it behind him.

Finally, he had left.

But despite her initial relief, in the days and weeks after he had gone, amidst the solicitors' letters and financial transactions, she had sometimes experienced the sensation that she was at the top of a skyscraper in an elevator plummeting uncontrollably to the ground. As the palpable sense of panic rose, squeezing at her throat, she knew that all she could do was extend her arms to brace herself, hoping that something or someone would stop it before it hit the ground and destroyed her.

Now, lying next to her in the double bed, Dan traced a fingertip over Anna's skin and felt goosebumps form on her arm. He touched his lips to her shoulder and felt her shiver. Every inch of her body was hyper-responsive, like there was an electrical current moving through it. It had never been like that with anyone else. He wasn't sure what

THEN

tonight was – some kind of belated rebound sex, or the need for a comforting shoulder to lean on – but he didn't care. To his surprise, what he did care about, what kept tugging at the edges of his consciousness, was the fact that they were in the bed she had once shared with Tom.

'Does it feel strange?' he said, stroking her arm. 'Me being in this bed?'

'No.'

He felt her yawn before settling back into his arms. He wondered if she was tired or just bored.

'So, tonight – it was OK, then?' God, that made him sound needy.

She looked up at him. 'Dan Randall, are you fishing for compliments?'

'No.'

They both knew it had been better than OK.

Anna waited. She sensed what was coming next. He was a male on what had been another man's turf and – metaphorically, she hoped – he needed to mark out his territory.

He affected a jokey, laddish tone, the one he always used in the belief that it would conceal his feelings. 'So, lover boy, did he have a big dick, then?'

She sighed. 'Yeah, enormous.'

His hand momentarily stopped stroking her skin.

'It was the size of the Eiffel Tower. Even Linda Lovelace would've struggled.'

He realised with relief that she was joking. 'He was good in the sack, then?'

They lay in silence for a while.

'It was different,' she said at last.

He resumed stroking her arm. 'Yeah?' Despite himself, his tone invited elaboration.

Eventually, she said: 'It was quiet.'

She could feel the laughter rumbling in his chest. 'What, you? Quiet? You're never...'

She lay still as the implication of what she had said dawned on him. Looking up, she saw Dan's mouth stretch into a smug grin. She shoved him, hard.

'OK, Casanova, don't get too big-headed.'

He laughed and held her tighter, reassured. 'God,' he said, 'and you were actually going to marry the bloke.'

'Well, I didn't.'

He squeezed her arm, suddenly reflective. 'We're pretty compatible,' he said, 'in that way.'

She thought about that for a moment. 'Like two interlocking pieces of a jigsaw.' She brushed strands of hair from her face. 'Maybe some people just fit together.'

He bent his head to look at her. The conversation had taken a dangerously serious turn. He slid his hand between her thighs and felt himself stiffen.

'So,' he murmured in her ear, 'ready to go again?'

***

Ofsted was coming: an acronym that struck dread in the hearts of every teacher in the land. To make matters worse, they had been given weeks of notice to prepare. Instead of a short, sharp plaster rip, it would be a slow, prolonged agony, culminating in five whole days during which they would be observed by stony-faced suits with clipboards in deadened classrooms suddenly devoid of all the normal banter that oils the wheels between students and teachers. Stress was a palpable presence in the staffroom, lurking in their peripheral vision like an uninvited guest. Colleagues who had once strolled together to the local deli at lunchtime now hunched over their desks, buried in paperwork or chasing up missing homework they'd let slide. Friday lunchtimes at the wine bar down the road ceased by unspoken consensus. Formerly convivial types suddenly developed frown lines and snapped irritably.

Anna sat before her Year 7 class, a copy of *The Demon Headmaster* in her hands, and imagined the Demon Inspector, a terrifying, humourless figure designed to judge, measure and categorise all the things that can't be measured and categorised: the subtle shifts in tone or body language designed to encourage or cajole; the borderline politically incorrect in-jokes that kept the disaffected engaged. Anna sighed.

'OK, homework tonight.'

The whole class groaned.

'Yes, I know how you feel. It's homework for me, too; I've got to mark it. OK, a short article, please, on the five qualities you feel a good headteacher should possess.'

A small girl with plaits raised her hand. 'Miss, does the headteacher have to be a nun?'

'No, it's not a Department for Education requirement that a headteacher must be a nun.'

'But our headteacher is a nun.'

'Yes, that's because we are a Catholic school.'

The irony of her employment by a convent school full of nuns had not escaped her, given her agnosticism and previous history of sexual incontinence, nor the fact that she had been put in charge of Year 10 PSHE, which included sex education. *It's like putting a crack cocaine addict in charge of a drugs rehabilitation programme*, she thought. After the third teenage pregnancy at school in the space of eighteen months, she had smuggled in condoms from her personal supply like a furtive dealer and demonstrated how to unroll them properly on a Fairtrade banana she'd brought in for her lunch.

'Not a word to anyone, girls,' she said. 'The nuns would have a fit.'

The pupils nodded silently, their expressions serious, their eyes fixed on the banana held aloft before them.

Anna pinched the teat at the top. 'Expel the air so the condom doesn't burst,' she demonstrated, 'and then roll it down the shaft this way around, like so.'

At the word 'shaft', one of the pupils began to snigger, sending a ripple-effect around the room. Anna looked up, fixing them with a steely stare, and the laughter subsided.

'In the interests of not raising your expectations,' she said, looking at the object in her hand, 'I think it's only fair to point out that this is a very *large* banana. I wouldn't want to be responsible for any future disappointment.'

It was a good job Ofsted hadn't been there when she had delivered *that le*sson.

'It's like knowing exactly when the Grim Reaper will

THEN

come calling,' she told Sally. 'It's horrible. I just want to press the fast-forward button and for it to be over.'

Sally nodded sympathetically and Anna watched as she stuffed another piece of battered saveloy in her mouth. They were squeezed together on Sally's tiny IKEA sofa-bed in the equally tiny attic flat she shared with Kris, polystyrene containers of food on their laps. The whole flat reeked of chips and vinegar.

'I don't know how you eat those. Do you eat battered Mars bars as well?'

Sally dug a small wooden fork into a chip and shook her head. 'No, that's the Scots not Geordies.'

'Close enough,' said Anna.

'*Southerner!*' It was Sally's ultimate insult. She wiped her mouth. 'Seen Dan recently?' she asked, casually.

'No, not for ages. He's got higher things on his mind. He's focusing on finishing his doctorate at the moment and apparently that means avoiding *distractions*.'

'Ah.'

The brakes had been applied to her own research the moment the Ofsted announcement had been made. In all honesty, she envied the way Dan was able to work with a singular focus, not having to juggle study with a full-time job. But his funding was about to end, and he was under pressure to complete.

Since that night in the Lyceum, they had continued to see each other every Friday, although now he came back to her flat at the end of the evening instead of bidding her farewell at Charing Cross. At first, it was a novelty waking up next to each other on Saturday mornings, pottering around the kitchen scrambling eggs for brunch after lazy, morning sex. Sometimes they would stroll around the local market or walk by the lake in the park. But, without fail, by late afternoon, Dan would be checking the time and inching his way towards the train station.

'Do you want to go to the cinema tonight? See what's on?' she'd say.

Dan would shake his head. 'No, I've got stuff to do.'

'What stuff?'

'Just stuff,' he'd say, closing the conversation down.

Sometimes she wondered if he'd been head-hunted by the secret service to work on some cyber-security issue of national importance, or whether he was leading a different sort of double life, with a wife and two kids secreted away in another part of London. She wondered, in the parlance of Hollywood romcoms, 'where it was going' and whether 'it' actually needed to be going anywhere. And then, one day, his mouth half-full of toast, Dan announced that he had an interview for a research post in Leeds.

'Leeds?' Anna repeated, taken aback. 'I didn't know you were thinking of leaving London.'

He shrugged. 'No point in telling you till I knew I'd got an interview.'

'Right.'

She tried to visualise where Leeds was, loathe to admit that her knowledge of the geography of her own nation was limited to the bottom half between Land's End and Birmingham.

'If I get it, you're welcome to come and visit. I could

give you a guided tour of the land of flat caps and whippets, and all that.'

She turned his words over in her head: 'Visit.' He clearly envisaged her as an occasional visitor, a guest – nothing more. She felt that old, familiar stab of hurt deep in her guts.

'You know what?' she said. 'I think I'll give the land of flat caps and whippets a miss.'

He shrugged. 'Whatever,' he said, and reached for his coffee. She'd made it clear that she wasn't that bothered about seeing him. Maybe moving to Leeds wasn't such a bad idea after all.

The week of the Ofsted inspection finally arrived. Staff began arriving at 7am, checking resources and equipment, that no one had drawn a cock and balls of anatomically inaccurate proportions in Tippex on any of the seats. Anna felt nausea sloshing in her stomach. She just wanted to get it over with. Five days. It was just five days of her life. Five days and it would be over, and she could begin to live life normally again. Whatever normal was.

Sure enough, at the beginning of the first lesson, an inspector walked in, taking a seat at the back of the classroom. She attempted to continue as normal, directing questions at pupils who had suddenly become very quiet and robotically well-behaved. For forty-five minutes, he sat there, making notes, observing interactions, peering at their written work. And then, five minutes before the bell, he was gone. Anna heaved a sigh of relief. Her formerly quiet pupils began chattering nervously.

'Did we do OK, Miss?'

'You were brilliant,' Anna told them, 'as you always are.'

And so the week wore on and the inspector paid Anna four more visits. At lunchtimes, the staff would congregate, discussing who'd had a visit from an inspector and who hadn't – a science experiment that had gone spectacularly wrong; a history discussion that had been unexpectedly thoughtful.

As she entered her empty flat each night, she had a powerful impulse to pick up the phone and call Dan. She wanted to tell him how her day had been, how she felt permanently sick with nerves. She wanted him to reassure her that she was a wonderful teacher, and it would all be OK. Then she realised how needy she would sound; needy and pathetic. Anyway, she told herself, in a few months, he would be living at the other end of the country, making a new life for himself. Some things were better left alone.

By 4pm on Friday, the inspectors were gone, and the staffroom was rammed. Those who couldn't find seats perched on the edges of tables or leant against the walls. At last, Sister Agnes entered, her habit billowing behind her, followed by the deputy head.

'Good afternoon, everyone,' she began, quietly, and a hushed silence descended. All eyes were watching her for clues to the verdict. She surveyed the room, serious and straight-lipped, relishing the moment, and then began to smile despite herself. 'Congratulations on an *outstanding* inspection!'

The room erupted. Hurried plans were made for a celebratory pub crawl as the deputy head, in a moment of

THEN

rare abandon, cried: 'Don't give them any homework next week!'

Anna and Claire hugged each other in relief.

'Thank fuck for that,' said Claire. 'Now we can go and get pissed.'

Anna froze. Sister Agnes had appeared behind Claire like a spectral vision. 'Ah! Just the two ladies I've been looking for.'

Claire looked at Anna, her eyes widening in alarm.

'My office? Five minutes.'

They nodded as Sister Agnes turned towards the door.

'Fuck,' said Claire when she was out of earshot.

'Can you stop saying fuck?'

'D'you think she's going to discipline us? I didn't think my lessons went that badly, all things considered.'

'Who knows what she's thinking?' said Anna. 'She's got one of those inscrutable faces. If she wasn't a nun, she'd make a killing as a professional poker player.'

They stood, shoulder to shoulder, outside the head's office like two naughty schoolgirls, staring at van Eyck's *Arnolfini Portrait* that hung on the opposite wall.

'Do you think she's pregnant?' said Claire.

Anna turned quickly to look at her. After realising Claire wasn't referring to Sister Agnes and an immaculate conception, she replied: 'Critical consensus is that it's a fashion statement. I think the husband is a cloth merchant. She's displaying his wealth.'

'Odd fashion statement. Does my bump look big in this…?' Claire's voice trailed off as Sister Agnes's door opened.

'Do come in, ladies.' Sister Agnes was poker-faced as usual. Anna wondered with sudden alarm if she'd found out about the banana and the condom.

'On my desk, I have two reports,' she announced weightily, placing a palm on each.

Anna imagined what such a report might contain. Statements like: 'must try harder' or 'Anna would make greater progress as a teacher if she didn't conduct lessons with raging hangovers'.

The poker face broke into a smile as Sister Agnes continued: 'Reports written by our inspectors, who have commended both of you on your consistently *outstanding* teaching. Congratulations. I am not in the least surprised.'

Anna was, and so was Claire, judging by the startled expression on her face.

Sister Agnes pushed the reports across her desk. 'Copies for you to keep,' she said. 'Now go and enjoy yourselves. You deserve it.'

Anna stood in the corridor and read the report: five separate lesson observations by an inspector named Mr Bold who was, comically enough, completely bald. Every single one had been judged 'outstanding'.

Claire looked up at Anna, grinning. 'Right,' she said. 'Now we have a bone-fide reason to get completely shit-faced.'

The staff pub crawl began in the pub down the road before moving on to a wine bar, shedding colleagues like loose hairs along the way. By the time they got to the fourth pub, someone had called a fleet of taxis for the hardcore drinkers, and they were heading towards Bar Madrid.

THEN

The bar was hot, dark, sweaty and packed. Below, down a staircase, lay the dance floor – a Dante's inferno of writhing bodies. Dance music was blasting from the speakers. Like Clark Kent, Anna stripped off the sensible jacket and shoes that defined her as Miss Thompson, stuffed them in her handbag and shoved it in the corner, taking to the dance floor in her black shift dress and bare feet. Arms above her head, eyes closed, she threw back her head and felt intoxicated not just by the copious amounts of alcohol flowing through her veins but also the possibility of existing purely in the moment.

As the evening wore on, Anna became aware of a man watching her from the opposite side of the room. She narrowed her eyes, attempting to stabilise his image: it continued to wobble alarmingly at the edges, like a cartoon character from *Roobarb and Custard*. Then, suddenly, he was standing in front of her. She looked up at him: dark blond hair, aquiline features. She could feel her hair sticking to her neck, the sweat beginning to crawl down the small of her back.

'How did you get here?' she asked.

'If you mean this evening, by tube. If you mean from there to here, I used these.' He pointed at his feet.

Anna looked down and the floor swung up to meet her. She took a deep breath and tried to steady herself.

He watched her, amused. 'Or maybe your question was more philosophical?' he teased. 'In which case, we could have an interesting conversation about the nature of existence.'

Anna stared at him. Debate was currently beyond her capabilities. She was getting to the point where even basic conversation was proving to be a challenge. She tried to read the caption on his T-shirt, but the words wouldn't stay still.

'Sorry,' she said, poking at his chest with a finger. 'I'm struggling to read what it says.'

'Ah, are you dyslexic?'

'No, I'm an English teacher.'

He stifled a laugh. 'Well, I'm Rory,' he said.

'Anna,' she said, addressing his chest.

'Do you fancy a drink, Anna?'

Unwisely, she nodded and, after having the remarkable presence of mind to collect her bag from the floor, she followed him upstairs to the bar, palming the wall for support like she'd suddenly been rendered blind. Halfway up, she met Claire coming down with two bottles of San Miguel. Claire stopped dead, holding up the human traffic behind her.

'Where are *you* going?'

Anna stabbed a finger at Rory's departing back. She looked at the two bottles in Claire's hand. 'You have mine,' she said, concentrating hard on articulating the words clearly, and then she continued her climb, palm sliding damply against the sticky plaster.

The following morning, Anna was awoken by a shower of kisses on her skin. Eyes still closed, half asleep, she turned, smiling.

'Dan...'

'Who's Dan?'

Anna opened her eyes. A complete stranger was lying in her bed. She gathered what was left of her wits and said: 'My parents' dog.'

THEN

He suppressed a smile. 'And your parents' dog normally wakes you like this in the morning, does he?'

She blinked. 'Sometimes. Obviously, he's a bit more slobbery.'

He fought back a laugh. 'A bit more slobbery. Right.'

She raised her body experimentally and the room began moving like she was on a rotating platform. She rested her head against the headboard, noting with relief that she wasn't completely naked.

'You had quite a lot to drink last night.'

Anna closed her eyes. 'How did we get back here?'

'A succession of buses. You seemed to know exactly where you were going, like a homing pigeon.'

Her mouth felt sandy and dry. She needed to get up; get a drink. She braced herself and swung her legs over the edge of the bed. Slowly, the rest of her body followed.

'It'll probably be another twelve hours before the alcohol's gone from your bloodstream,' he said.

Anna turned her head, slowly. 'What are you, a doctor?'

He laughed. 'Actually, yes.'

'So – uh, so...' She couldn't remember his name. 'Would you like some coffee? Tea?'

'Tea would be lovely. Milk, no sugar.'

Now upright, her head was pounding. The noise of the water filling the kettle was amplified to the sound of the Reichenbach Falls. She placed teabags gently in two mugs and winced as the kettle clicked off like a bullet entering her temple. Carefully, she poured milk into the mugs and padded back to the bedroom.

He was sitting upright, sickeningly bright and alert, flicking through the copy of Michel Foucault's *The History of Sexuality* that had been lying on her bedside table. She handed him a mug and took a mouthful of tea, wrinkling her eyes in pain as the liquid scalded her tongue. When she had recovered from this assault on her senses, she turned to him.

'So, Doctor, what do you prescribe for a hangover?'

He looked up from the book and said, 'Do you have any Dioralyte?'

'Uh – no.' Anna didn't know what Dioralyte was, but she made a mental note to get some.

'Well,' he said, turning the book face down on the duvet, 'any combination of fluids, salt and sugars will do. The salt will replace your electrolytes.'

Anna thought of contents of her kitchen cupboards. 'So, water, a packet of ready salted crisps and a Mars bar?'

'Yep. That'll do it.' He picked up the book. 'An interesting read.' He wasn't being sarcastic.

'I'm just reading it for research,' she said.

'A Masters?'

'Doctorate.'

He raised an eyebrow. 'So, we have *two* doctors.'

'I'm not a doctor yet.'

He continued to watch her in amusement.

At last, she said: 'Do I amuse you?'

He laughed. 'Yes.'

'Why?'

'Well, one minute you're giving me an introductory lecture on post-modernism, the next you're contemplating peeing behind the hedge of someone's front garden because you don't think you can hold out until you get home.'

Her head slumped into her hands.

'It was a memorable night.' He laughed, putting his arm around her and pulling her towards him. 'In a good way.'

'Did we...?'

'No,' he said. 'I don't take advantage of inebriated women.'

'It's probably part of the Hippocratic Oath.'

'Probably.'

He looked at her for a while, then he said: 'I don't think I've ever met anyone quite like you before.'

'What, a dipsomaniac with an interest in literary theory and poor bladder control?'

'Yes,' he laughed, 'I think you're fairly unique in that respect.' He smiled. 'So, can I see you again?'

Frankly, she was amazed he was still here. She shrugged nonchalantly.

'Do you have a paper and pen?'

Anna rummaged in her bedside drawer, pulling out the small spiral-bound notebook and pencil she kept for moments of late-night inspiration.

He scribbled onto the paper and handed it to her. 'I've got terrible handwriting,' he said, apologetically. 'It's a bit of a prerequisite if you're going into medicine.'

She looked at the piece of paper in her hand. 'Rory!' she exclaimed. Of course, his name was Rory.

'You forgot my name, didn't you?'

'No,' she lied.

'Look, I'd better be getting back. I'm staying with a friend. He'll be wondering where on earth I am.' He began plucking items of clothing from the bedroom floor and dressing himself. Finally, he stood in the doorway.

'I'll see you out,' she said.

At the front door, he hesitated and turned. 'So, you'll call me?' he said.

She smiled. 'I've got your number.'

He kissed her on the cheek and then he was gone.

Anna leant against the wall in the hallway. This guy had seen her at her very worst and, unbelievably, he had not run for the hills. That gained him some brownie points. In fact, that gained him quite a few brownie points indeed.

She left it a while before calling him. She didn't want to seem desperate. She'd imagined meeting for dinner or drinks in town, but he'd invited her for the weekend.

'Why don't you stay over, and I'll meet you at the station?'

Anna watched through the carriage window as the grimy congestion of London gave way to the leafy suburbs of the commuter belt. Her stomach fluttered with nerves, which were compounded by the realisation that she couldn't quite remember what he looked like. What if she didn't recognise him? What if he didn't recognise her? She removed a mirror from her handbag and stared at her reflection. With the tip of a finger, she removed a smudge of lipstick from her Cupid's bow. Eventually, the name of Rory's station was announced, and she took a deep breath. What was the worst that could happen?

THEN

She scanned the ticket hall: a father greeting his teenage daughter; a frazzled mum with two toddlers; an old lady and her Cairn terrier. He'd stood her up. She felt a mixture of anger and relief. Then, leaning against the wall in the corner, she saw a man smiling at her: dark blond hair, aquiline features.

Stone-cold sober, Anna realised that, physically, he wasn't her type at all. She swallowed hard and looked down at her overnight bag. It was too late to turn back: he'd seen her. There was nothing to do but put on a smile and make the best of it.

He walked towards her, still smiling, and kissed her cheek. 'Hello. Good journey?'

She registered for the first time that his voice was terribly posh.

'Oh, you know. The rail network is on its usual form. Sorry if I'm a bit late.'

'No problem. Can I take your bag?'

They walked to his car.

'It's not far. I just didn't know if you might bring a suitcase or something.'

'I travel pretty light.'

He threw her bag in the boot and opened the passenger door. 'I thought we could meet up with some friends tonight if that's OK with you?'

'Sure.'

'Just a local bar.'

He indicated to pull out and they drove past streets of red-brick Victorian terraces. Within minutes, the car had pulled up outside yet another Victorian terrace.

'This is me.'

It was a quirky little house, long and narrow, full of scrubbed pine and bookshelves.

'I'll take your bag upstairs. You can freshen up, if you like.'

She followed him up the stairs.

It was at this point that Anna realised she knew nothing about this man, aside from his phone number. She had accepted an invitation to spend a weekend in his house and, for all she knew, he could be a serial rapist or a murderer. She could see the tabloid headlines now: 'Young Teacher Missing After Weekend With Mystery Man'. There would be tearful statements from friends and appeals for witnesses. She tried to recall if she had told anyone of her plans: Claire, maybe Sally. But neither of them had a phone number, let alone an address. Her fears were not allayed when she passed the only other bedroom in the house: it was stripped bare, quite literally, with a wallpaper table in the middle of the room.

'Redecorating,' he said.

He stopped at the foot of a double bed. 'So, this is where you'll sleep.' He dropped her bag to the floor. 'I'll be on the sofa downstairs.'

'I don't mind taking the sofa,' she said with relief.

'Absolutely not. I'll leave you to freshen up. Are you hungry, thirsty? I've got some wine, and I make a mean spaghetti carbonara.'

He was trying so hard.

'Thanks. Sounds great.'

THEN

As he left, she sat down on the bed. She could smell the aroma of freshly laundered sheets. She sighed, removed her toiletries bag and locked herself in the bathroom. She brushed her teeth, combed her hair and reapplied her lipstick. Then she wandered downstairs.

He was standing at the hob in the kitchen, his back to her, stirring something with a wooden spoon. The appetising smell of garlic and smoked bacon filled the air, and it made her feel ravenously hungry. A large pot of water was coming to the boil, and a box of eggs was lying, opened, on the worktop.

'Smells wonderful,' she said, brightly.

Rory turned around. He had a sweet, tentative smile that was endearing.

'Glass of wine on the table.'

Two glasses of white stood on the kitchen table, the chilled contents beading the glasses with condensation. She took one and brought him the other.

'Thanks,' he said. 'Could you do me a favour and grate some parmesan?'

'Sure.'

Anna picked up the grater, unwrapped the cheese and recalibrated her thoughts. Making spaghetti carbonara together didn't seem like the normal prelude to a violent sexual assault. Maybe he wasn't a rapist after all.

He glanced across at her and smiled. They prepped the meal in companionable silence: stirring, chopping, grating. He dangled spaghetti above the pot.

'Want to test the pasta?'

She nodded, leaning in to take a bite. As she did so,

a few strands of hair fell forwards, and he reached out to tuck them gently behind her ear.

'Perfectly *al dente*,' she said.

As they sat eating, she watched him twist pasta expertly around his fork. 'This is delicious,' she said. 'Thank you.'

'Glad you like it. I enjoy cooking. I find it relaxing.'

Anna thought of Tom, who had never once cooked for her, and Dan, who lived on Super Noodles, chips and kebabs and insisted that Heinz tomato ketchup counted as a vegetable.

'It must be stressful sometimes,' she said, 'being a doctor.'

'I think I'd find controlling a classroom of stroppy teenagers way more stressful.' He laughed.

'Oh, they're all right,' she said, taking another forkful of pasta. 'And education's not a matter of life and death, is it? Although the way some of my pupils behave, you'd think it was, sometimes. I mean, you're trying to save lives.'

'Yeah, and sometimes you can't. Like yesterday, for example, I had to do open cardiac massage for the first time. Factory accident.' He gave a long sigh. 'Poor guy was never going to make it.'

'You must see some hilarious accidents as well,' she said, trying to lighten the mood.

His face brightened. 'Oh, yeah.'

'Such as?'

He thought for a minute. 'Well, a lady came into A and E a few weeks ago,' he said, 'very embarrassed. She'd inserted a light bulb deep into her vagina and couldn't get it out.'

THEN

'A *light bulb*?' Anna grimaced and instinctively pressed her thighs closer together, thinking: what's wrong with a vibrator, for god's sake?

'Of course,' he continued, 'what you do in those circumstances is say that you need to consult with colleagues, and they all come in and have a look. We're very professional. We never laugh out loud. Well, not in front of the patient, anyway.'

'So did you get it out?'

'Yes, eventually, but we had to be careful. I mean, it was glass.'

'I'll bet she won't be doing that again.'

Rory laughed. 'You'd hope not!' He stood up, gathered the pasta bowls and placed them in the sink.

'So, are you ready to meet my friends? They don't bite. Well, most of them don't.'

Anna looked at this tall, unflappable man with the endearing smile. He seemed reassuringly capable. She looked at the hands with which he saved lives. There was a certain aphrodisiac quality to that.

His friends were sitting around a table in the bar as they entered: two couples and a guy with dark, curly hair. She felt them watching her as Rory took her coat, sizing her up. Several bottles of wine were already open on the table. Rory made the introductions: pale, wan Alice and ruddy-faced boyfriend Will; Mike and his toothy girlfriend Rachel and, 'Andrew, my old pal from Radley.'

That explained the posh accent, then.

After making small talk for a while, Andrew, who was clearly on his second bottle, leant over towards Anna.

'You have a slight accent, Anna. I can't place it. Where are you from?'

She smiled politely. 'The West Country.'

'Ah! Zomerzet! Scrumpy! I've got a brand-new combine harvester and all that.'

What an absolute dick, she thought.

'Order the girl a cider, Rory!' he cried.

'I'm OK with wine, thanks,' she said quickly, and drained her glass. Rory, ever attentive, refilled it.

'We've been discussing the deplorable state of UK politics,' Andrew continued. 'The future for the Tory party.'

Anna looked directly at him. 'I'd suggest that, for the Tory party, the future's looking pretty bleak.'

Andrew sat upright. 'What do you mean, bleak?'

She looked at Rory. He had that bemused look on his face again, but he wasn't warning her off.

Fuck it, she thought. *His friend is an asshole.*

'Bleak as in self-destructive,' she said. 'Bleak, as in the Labour Party can afford to sit back and watch as they metaphorically knife each other in the back. Major should have known what he was getting into. I'm no fan of Thatcher but look what they did to her. *Et tu, Brute?*'

Andrew lifted his glass of red wine and drained it. 'That's one point of view,' he said. 'But the Tories will still defeat Labour in the next election.'

Anna raised her eyebrows. 'Really? Can you count? Have you seen the results of the local council elections?'

'Count?' Andrew spluttered. 'I'm an accountant!'

'Well, then you'll be able to count the fingers of both

THEN

your hands. And the Tories don't even control as many councils as you have digits.'

Rory stifled a laugh with one hand and poured himself another glass of wine. Will and Mike exchanged a look. Alice and Rachel began a quiet conversation about a mutual friend.

Andrew reached over for another bottle, nearly toppling it. 'What you don't seem to *understand…*' Her skin prickled at his patronising tone. 'Is that council election results don't equate to general election results. Nobody's going to vote for the Labour party. They remember the seventies when they called the three-day week.'

Anna sat back and narrowed her eyes. 'It was a *Conservative* government who called the three-day week.'

Rory cleared his throat. 'Andrew, didn't you say you were meeting Charles tonight?'

Andrew looked at his watch. 'Bugger. You're right.' He turned to grab his coat and stood unsteadily. 'Nice meeting you, Anna,' he said, tersely.

Anna stretched out a smile. 'It's been *delightful*.'

As he passed Rory, Andrew nudged his friend's shoulder. 'You need to keep an eye on that one, old friend.'

After he'd gone, Rory burst out laughing.

'Sorry,' said Will. 'Andrew can be a bit of an idiot when he's had a few to drink. But he's genuinely a nice guy.'

Anna doubted it, but at least Rory's other friends were more amiable.

'I'm sorry,' said Anna as they walked home. 'I know he's your friend, but…'

'He's an arrogant, patronising idiot?'
'Yes. How did you know I was going to say that?'
'I took a wild guess.'

Anna felt gripped by self-loathing. This poor guy had invited her to spend a weekend with him and the first thing she'd done was to start an argument with one of his oldest friends. What was the matter with her? 'Provocative' was the word Dan had once used; he said she could be provocative. Why couldn't she just behave like a normal person and make polite conversation? Looking at Rory, it suddenly occurred to her that she cared what he thought of her.

They had reached the house. Rory felt in his jeans pocket for his keys and unlocked the door.

'I hope your other friends liked me,' she said, desperately. They had certainly been friendly enough.

They were standing very close together in the doorway. He looked at her. 'If they feel the way I do, they'll probably worship the ground you walk on.'

Anna took a step back, defensively. The statement was so ridiculous, so hyperbolic, he was obviously mocking her. She looked at his face, but his expression was serious. She felt off-kilter, unable to read him or the situation.

Wordlessly, she followed him into the house. She watched as he poured the last half of a bottle of wine into two glasses and then followed him to the front room, where she sat cross-legged on one end of the sofa. He handed her the glass of wine, then rifled through some CDs and selected Radiohead's *The Bends*. She watched his fingers as he removed the CD from its case, pressed a button and

THEN

inserted the disc into the player. She had never found a man's hands erotic before. His fingers curled around the slender stem of the wine glass as he sat down next to her. The tips of their knees were touching.

Anna listened as Rory recounted an anecdote from his school days, one in which Andrew had behaved like an idiot. She realised that he was trying to make her feel better about the argument earlier that evening, a simple act of kindness that stirred in her a deep feeling of gratitude and affection. She became aware that he had stopped talking and was looking directly at her. Thom Yorke was singing the chorus to 'High and Dry'.

He leant forwards and brushed her cheek with the edge of his thumb. 'You're lovely,' he said.

Anna didn't feel lovely at all. Underneath all the feistiness and the smart comments, she felt like the world's biggest fuck-up.

He leant forwards and kissed her, at first gently and then more deeply. She uncurled her legs and pressed her body against his. And then they lay on the sofa in each other's arms, talking and listening to the music, until they fell asleep.

The following weekend was hot and sunny.

'I know a great beach,' Rory said. 'I'll drive and we can spend the day there.'

They walked down the long, steep cliff path towards the sand. The beach was virtually deserted. Removing their shoes, they walked hand in hand and barefoot through the waves as they lapped the sand, beachcombing for shells.

The sun was high in the sky. Anna lay between Rory's legs, her head resting on his lap, surrounded by their treasure. His body enclosed hers and a feeling of utter contentment washed over her. It felt like a release. Her mind was emptied of all thought except the hushing of the waves and the sound of gulls wheeling in the vast blue sky above her. They lay like that for a long time, until Anna felt strands of her hair blow into her mouth. A breeze was strengthening, coming in off the sea. Eventually, she felt Rory stir and sit upright. He leant over her, smoothed her hair away from her face and bent to kiss the sunburnt bridge of her nose. She smiled up at him, her eyes still closed.

'Hey,' he said, softly. 'Shall we head back?'

She lay, unmoving. She wanted to stay there for the rest of her life, right in this moment. She opened her eyes, raising her hand to shield them against the brightness of the sun. He took her hand in his and helped her up. They brushed the sand from their clothes and walked back to the path, swinging their shoes in their hands.

Driving home, they were overtaken by a black Audi which sped past them as they rounded a corner on the narrow road. Rory put his foot sharply on the brake.

'Jesus!' cried Anna. 'What's his problem?'

Two corners later, the road straightened. Anna could see distant, dark shapes hunched at the edge of the road. 'What is it?'

'I think someone's had an accident.'

He pulled over alongside the grass verge. A motorcyclist was splayed on the side of the road, blood pouring through the ripped thigh of his jeans, his motorbike on its side.

THEN

Kneeling beside him was a cyclist, who was attempting to remove the motorcycle helmet.

Rory leapt from the car and removed a first aid kit from the boot. He ran towards them.

'Don't move him!' he called. 'He may have a spinal injury!' The cyclist looked up as Rory knelt next to the injured man. 'I'm a doctor,' Rory said, examining the leg wound. 'What happened?'

'Bloody Audi,' said the cyclist. 'Driving like a maniac. This guy swerved to avoid him and came off his bike. Bloody driver didn't even stop.'

Rory was removing bandages and scissors from the First Aid kit. The flow of blood from the man's thigh was increasing.

'Are you local?' he asked the cyclist.

'Yes.'

'Is there a house near here? Anyone with a phone to call for an ambulance?'

'A few minutes up the road.'

'OK, go and get an ambulance.'

The cyclist mounted his bike and began speeding off the way he had come.

Anna got out of the car. She could hear Rory talking to the injured man. 'Is there anything I can do to help?' she said, hovering over them.

'Can you just apply some pressure here?' Rory said, indicating an area above the wound. Anna knelt next to him, trying not to look at the blood. She was squeamish. She placed her hand on the man's thigh, not wanting to hurt him.

'No, harder than that, Anna.'

She pressed harder as Rory bound and twisted gauze tightly above the wound. The motorcyclist groaned in pain and Anna flinched. After a time, the blood flow began to ease. She listened as Rory spoke to the man, calming and distracting him. Eventually, the cyclist appeared over the brow of the hill and skidded to a halt before them.

'An ambulance is on its way,' he panted. 'How is he?'

'He'll be fine,' said Rory. 'But he'll need a few stitches.'

After a while, they heard the ambulance siren in the distance, coming closer. The paramedics jumped out; she heard Rory briefing them on the man's condition and saw them nodding. She stood and walked back to the car. A few minutes later, Rory joined her. He looked over at her, smiled, and turned the key in the ignition. They drove in silence for a while.

At last, Anna said: 'That was impressive.'

He shrugged. 'Just doing my job.'

The countryside flashed by. She opened the window slightly, tilting her head to feel the warm air rush past her skin. Her dark fringe rippled and fluttered.

'It was quite a turn-on, actually.'

He looked over at her, incredulously, and laughed. 'A road accident? A turn-on?'

'No, you know what I mean. You were very calm. In control. Authoritative.'

'Well, they teach you that at medical school. Nobody wants a panicking doctor.'

A minute passed.

'Did you play doctors and nurses as a child, then?'

THEN

'I went to boys' schools,' he said. 'The only nurse was Matron and, believe me, you wouldn't want to mess with her.'

She slipped off her shoes, rested her feet on top of the glove box and smiled. 'Do you have a stethoscope?'

'Yeees,' he said slowly. 'Why... would you like me to wear it?'

She looked over at him. 'Do you think that's weird?'

'I don't know,' he laughed, 'maybe.'

Anna cursed her stupid mouth. Now he'd think she was some weird sexual fetishist. She was unsure if it was the thought of the stethoscope, or his hands, or his calm power over life and death, but despite him not being her 'type', she realised that she wanted to sleep with him. She sighed and decided the safest thing to do was to remain silent. She turned on the radio and closed her eyes.

That evening, they moved easily around each other as they prepared a meal. She discovered that his parents had retired to a chateau in France, and that he had four siblings, all of whom had been educated at top public schools. She thought of her own parents' three-bed semi and her comprehensive school education. They came from such different worlds. Rory was not arrogant, like his friend Andrew, but his privileged upbringing had given him the kind of self-assurance and inner confidence that she knew she would never possess.

Her fear that he thought she was a weird sexual fetishist dissipated later that evening when he kissed her.

'I'm afraid I don't have my stethoscope with me.' He smiled.

'That's OK,' she said, and they began to undress each other. He had beautiful hands. He was a gentle, attentive lover, and as he made love to her, her eyes began welling with tears. To her embarrassment, she felt a tear trickle down her cheek.

Rory, kissing her, felt the salt liquid on his lips and lifted himself to look at her.

'Hey,' he whispered. 'Are you OK?'

She nodded, passing the back of her hand over her eyes. 'I'm really sorry,' she said eventually. 'That's never happened before.'

'And... is it a good thing or a bad thing?'

'A good thing,' she said.

He smiled. 'Well, that's a relief. Usually, when a man reduces a woman to tears, it's never a good thing.'

At weekends, she and Rory would rattle up and down the train lines towards and then away from each other. One Friday, Anna was waiting for him outside her local train station as usual. She scanned the faces of the commuters as they poured through the exit and saw him at the back of the throng. She was struck anew by how unremarkable he looked and wondered how it was that she had become attracted to him. It occurred to her with an uncomfortable jolt of self-awareness that she had always been quite superficial in that respect. The men she had previously dated could all be described as good-looking; in fact, she had rejected the advances of some really lovely men without a second thought because they didn't quite fit her physical 'type'. Somehow, she thought, Rory had just crept up on her.

THEN

'Hello, you,' he said.

'Hello, you.'

He bent to kiss her.

'Pub?'

'I thought you'd never ask.'

They made their way into the courtyard garden at the back and sat at a rickety wooden picnic table. Anna held up her pint of cider.

'Here's to your dear friend Andrew,' she said. 'Cheers!'

'Cheers!' He took a mouthful of foamy beer, wiped his mouth and then fumbled in his jacket pocket. 'I have something for you.' He handed her a small, square package. It was the size and shape of a small jewellery box.

She froze in horror, immediately transported back to the night at the top of the Eiffel Tower.

He smiled at her. 'Well, open it!'

She looked at him. Her fingers pulled open the paper and she slowly lifted the lid, like it was Pandora's box. She wanted to cry with relief: it was a pair of earrings.

'Do you like them?'

'They're beautiful.' She kissed him. 'Thank you.'

The next morning, she was poaching eggs in the kitchen when she heard the rattle of the letterbox.

'Rory, can you get that?'

'Sure.'

The toast pinged up from the toaster and she began spreading the butter whilst the toast was still hot. She could hear Rory's footsteps coming towards her.

'You've got a postcard,' he said. 'From your parents' dog.'

'What?' She turned, laughing.

He handed her the postcard. On the front was a picture of the *Venus de 'Medici*. She flipped it over. The postmark was Florence. She immediately recognised the capitalised handwriting:

SAW THIS AND THOUGHT OF YOU. DAN.

She looked up, quickly. 'He's an old friend from university.' She smiled. 'A bit of a joker.'

Rory didn't say anything. His expression remained neutral. He just nodded.

Anna removed the eggs from the boiling water and placed them on the plates of toast. 'So, what shall we do today?' she said, kissing his cheek.

He smiled at her then, and everything fell back into its normal place.

Aside from the postcard, Anna hadn't heard from Dan for ages, so, when she heard the phone ringing as she got in from work one day, the last person she expected it to be was him.

The voice at the other end said: 'Sally's wedding. Have you seen the price of the hotel rooms?'

Dan always began telephone conversations like this. He never said: 'Hi, it's Dan,' or, 'Hi, how are you?' For him, telephones were simply devices through which he could convey information as efficiently as possible.

'I'm fine, Dan, thank you,' she said.

He took the hint. 'Did you get the postcard?'

'Yeah. What were you doing in Florence?'

'Conference. I was presenting a poster.'

'Lucky you.'

'So, have you seen the price of the hotel rooms?' he repeated.

'I can't say I've had much time to look, no.'

'Well, they're bloody expensive. Do you want to share a room? Split the cost?'

She remembered that he was still technically a student. 'All right.'

'Great. Do you want me to pick you up? I'm driving.'

'Uh...' she said, doubtfully. She remembered the dodgy door lock and the bungee cord.

'It's OK; the car door's been fixed,' he said, as if reading her mind.

'Alright, then,' she said. 'But we'll meet at yours. We'll have to set off early.'

On the morning of the wedding, Dan was up as soon as it was light. A garment bag hung on the back of the door containing his one and only suit. The last time he'd worn it was years before on graduation day. The waistband was tighter, but he was pleased to discover that it still fit; he could always undo the trouser button underneath the suit jacket. In the bathroom, he contorted his face into different expressions as he shaved off the previous day's stubble. The last six months had been bloody hard. His funding was about to end, which had given renewed impetus to his resolution to complete his thesis instead of dicking about playing computer games. He'd put in twelve-hour days – fourteen, sometimes – seven days a week. One of the first decisions he had made was to stop seeing Anna at weekends. Much as he enjoyed her company – and she made him laugh – she was also an unnecessary distraction. Anyway, Anna would still be there six months down the line. It wasn't like she was going anywhere.

Now, with his viva completed and a new job in Leeds, he felt a certain smug self-satisfaction. He'd had some minor changes to make but he'd got his PhD, and the rest of his life could now begin.

He heard a knock at the door.

Anna stood there, weighed down with a folded suit bag and an overnight case.

'Christ!' she said. 'Getting here is like some tortuous board game: a train, a tube and two buses.' She glanced at her watch. 'And all before 8am.'

'Good morning to you, too.'

Anna smiled at him. She looked different, somehow. Despite her moan about public transport, she looked… content. Glowing, even.

'You look well,' he said.

'Thanks. I'll just have a pee and then we'll get going, shall we? It's a long drive.'

The wedding was being held at a country house hotel just south of Newcastle at four o'clock in the afternoon. They had a five-hour drive ahead of them.

'Five hours!' exclaimed Anna. 'But at least we've got a lot to catch up on.'

Dan was uncharacteristically talkative as they made their way up the M1. She heard about his viva: 'The internal examiner was an absolute *bastard*,' he said. 'The

THEN

internal examiner, mind you. He's the one who wanted me to make those changes. It's taken me weeks. It's the *external* examiner who's supposed to be the bad cop.'

'Well, never mind,' said Anna, wondering if she'd remembered to pack spare tights. 'At least it's all over now.'

He talked about his research post in Leeds and how good it would be to earn a proper salary again and the project he would be working on. He talked about finding a place to live.

Anna let the words wash over her as the miles sped by, occasionally contributing an 'Oh' or an 'I see' or a 'Right'.

At one point, he looked over at her and said: 'Are you actually listening?'

'Yes,' she said, and mechanically repeated the last two sentences he'd spoken.

By the time she'd begun to tell him about the Ofsted inspection, they'd arrived at the end of a long drive lined with rhododendron bushes. The tyres crunched over the gravel. A sign read: *Kris and Sally's wedding - guest parking*, and they followed the arrows to the rear of the building. It was 1.30.

'Plenty of time to get showered and freshen up before the ceremony starts,' said Anna.

The foyer of the house was large with high ceilings. The flagstone floor shone, smoothed with years of use. At the centre was a round mahogany table on which sat an artful arrangement of flowers. The walls were panelled in dark oak, above which hung an elaborate chandelier. It smelled of furniture polish and potpourri.

'I'll get the room key,' said Dan, making his way to the

reception desk. Anna looked at the paintings that lined the walls: hunting scenes; a fleshy man in a tight waistcoat with a King Charles spaniel at his feet. She saw Dan waving the key at her and they climbed the curved staircase to the first floor.

Dan had splashed out on a garden-view room rather than the cheaper rooms that, he suspected, overlooked the bins at the back. He felt that he needed to make amends for the so-awful-you-have-to-laugh hotel room he'd booked that time in Blackpool, even though they were splitting the bill.

'Ooh, this is nice,' Anna said as she walked through the door. She ran her hand up one of the high, tapered bed posts. 'You could put your eye out on that.'

Dan's mouth began to move.

'Don't say it,' Anna warned him wearily. 'Just don't.' She kicked off her shoes and fell back against the rows of plump cushions and pillows that lined the headboard. Her T-shirt dress rucked up her thighs. Then she sat up abruptly like a woman who's just realised she's left her baby outside the post office.

'It's a double bed!' she said, stricken.

Dan looked at her. 'Yeah, I said did you want to share a room and split the cost, and you said yes.'

'You said share a *room*, Dan, not share a *bed*.'

He sighed. What was her problem? It wasn't like they hadn't shared a bed before, for Christ's sake. It wasn't like they'd never had sex. He hoped it wasn't going to be a repeat of their weekend in Blackpool when he'd felt almost ill with lust. The facial expression of that hideous

THEN

doll watching him every time he relieved himself in the bathroom was still indelibly imprinted upon his memory.

Anna gave him a look. 'Go to reception,' she said. 'See if they can swap us for a twin.'

He sighed irritably, put his shoes back on, grabbed the door key and let the door slam behind him.

Five minutes later, he was back.

'They said they're fully booked. *Apparently*, there's a wedding on.'

Anna gave a little huff. 'I suppose we'll just have to share, then.'

'I suppose we will.' He removed his shoes for the second time and lay on the bed next to her. 'So, you were telling me about the Ofsted inspection. How did it go?'

He listened as Anna described the inspectors and the tense wait outside Sister Agnes' office and the special report she had received for outstanding teaching. He turned to her and smiled.

'See? All that worry for nothing. I've always told you you're a great teacher.'

He'd never seen her in a classroom and, for all he knew, she could be a dreadful teacher, but she appreciated the sentiment. 'Thanks.'

'So, do you fancy celebrating the fact that you're officially *outstanding*?' He grinned, sliding his hand up her thigh as he turned to kiss her.

She pushed him away.

He looked at her, confused. 'What's the matter? Time of the month?'

'No, Dan! Believe it or not, the time of the month is

not the only reason a woman might have for rejecting your advances.'

He sighed. It *was* going to be like Blackpool all over again. He'd been really looking forward to this weekend but instead it seemed he was destined for twenty-four hours of sexual frustration.

'What is it, then?'

'I'm in a relationship, actually.'

He lay there next to her and looked up at the ceiling. How stupid of him. Of course she was. He hadn't seen her for most of the year, after all. Stupid to think she'd still be there, waiting to take up where they'd left off. He suddenly remembered university, and the thought that used to run through his head in every bar, at every party: why is she *never* alone?

'I met him in a bar the night the Ofsted inspectors left,' she said. 'He's a doctor – a medical one.'

'Right.'

'I've been seeing him ever since.'

He blew air through his lips. 'It's not serious.'

She didn't know whether it was a statement or a question.

'I don't know yet.'

'Right.'

They lay in silence for a few minutes, two parallel bodies staring up at the ceiling.

'Look, I said I'd phone him when I got here.'

'Don't mind me,' he said. He got up and began to take his suit out of its bag. Clearly, he wasn't going to leave the room.

She picked up the bedside phone, punched the button for an outside line and then pressed some numbers. After

THEN

a few seconds, Dan heard her say, 'Hel-lo.' Her voice was soft and gentle. He glanced over his shoulder. She was smiling at whatever he was saying to her.

'Yes,' she said. 'Just over five hours…'

He didn't consciously register his jealousy; he was just overcome by an overwhelming urge to sabotage the conversation.

Anna watched as Dan sat at the end of the bed and slid himself towards her.

'Yes,' she said, 'I think the hotel is the old family seat of a lord or something.'

To Anna's horror, Dan placed his head between her outstretched legs and began kissing her thighs. She pulled up her knees to try to kick him with her feet, but that just jammed him into position. He looked up, grinning.

She mouthed, 'Get off!'

Rory was asking her what time she thought she'd be back the next day. 'About 4pm,' she said, but the 'pm' came out as a tiny squeak as Dan reached the top of her thigh.

Dan began laughing softly. His head was now close enough for her to take a good swipe at it with her hand.

Bastard, she thought. *Bloody bastard.*

She could hear Rory saying, 'Is everything all right?'

'Yes.'

What was she supposed to say? 'Yes, everything's fine. Due to a misunderstanding, I'm sharing a bed with my on-off lover of many years, but don't let that bother you.' She'd felt awkward enough explaining that the wedding invitation wasn't a 'plus-one'.

She glared at Dan, mouthed, 'Fuck off!' and shoved her

hand against his head with full force. His mouth shaped into an "O" of pain.

'Is there someone there with you?'

'No, why?'

'I just thought I could hear someone.'

'It's probably the TV. I've got the volume on low.'

'OK,' he said. 'Well, have a good time. I'll see you when you get back. Miss you.'

'Miss you, too.'

Anna put the receiver down, furious.

Dan sat up, laughing, and mimicked her voice. '*Miss you too!*'

'What the *fuck* are you playing at?'

Dan laughed, but more sheepishly now. 'God, you've lost your sense of humour,' he said, defensively. 'I was just having a laugh.'

'Yeah, Dan, it's absolutely hilarious. Can you see me laughing?'

His face fell and he slid off the bed, mumbling grumpily about people with no sense of humour, and made his way to the bathroom.

'You're pathetic!' she yelled, as he slammed the bathroom door. 'And don't spend too long in there. I need a shower!'

Sally looked radiant in a white lace wedding dress, her hair artfully arranged on top of her head and threaded with little white flowers. Kris stood in front of the registrar looking effortlessly cool in a blue velvet suit, a yellow rose in his buttonhole. Anna watched him turn to look over

THEN

his shoulder as Sally entered the room. His face broke into a smile of such love and devotion that even Anna, for all her cynicism, felt her heart soften. She heard some sniffing and looked along the row of gold-coloured chairs: Jenny was searching in her handbag for a tissue. Next to her, Phil and Julian rolled their eyes at each other.

Dan stood stiffly next to her. Anna still hadn't forgiven him, but they were in the middle of their friend's wedding, so she'd had to smile, kiss cheeks and make small talk instead of doing what she really wanted to do, which was to give him a piece of her mind and make him offer her a grovelling apology.

The registrar asked the congregation to be seated. Anna noticed that Dan's knee was touching hers and turned her legs at a slight angle, away from him. He gave her a sideways glance, but she stared resolutely ahead, refusing to make eye contact.

As Kris and Sally exchanged vows, Anna reflected angrily on just how immature Dan was. Since she'd first met him, he'd been a perpetual student – the year at the tech start-up in Surrey didn't count – and he needed to bloody well grow up. He'd airbrushed her out of his life for months and months without a second thought. What did he expect her to do, put her life on hold until he was ready to pick things up again? And what was there to pick up anyway, if he was moving to Leeds? Despite herself, she couldn't help but compare him with Rory. If Rory wasn't too keen on doing something, like watching a French film with sub-titles, he'd say, 'Maybe another time,' rather than a derisory, 'Fuck off!' He'd say, 'Shall we make love?' rather than 'Fancy a shag?' She realised that her relationship with Dan – or whatever the hell it was – had got stuck somewhere in 1989, in sarky banter and puerile innuendo.

The registrar told the groom that he could kiss the bride. They all clapped dutifully as Kris held Sally in his arms and the newly married couple turned to walk down the aisle. Dan looked at Anna's knees, angled away from him. He noticed she was chewing her bottom lip furiously, a sure sign that she was still angry with him. He wanted to lie down on the floor and howl like a child. He'd fucked things up so badly, with someone he cared about – cared about deeply, he realised – and he didn't know what to do or say. The truth was, he'd been desperately jealous of the way she had spoken to the new man in her life. Just hearing Rory's voice, it seemed, was enough to make her smile. It was like she was a different person with him – softer, more gentle – not the sort of person who angrily yelled, 'Fuck off!' Anna had been the only woman in his life for years and, selfishly, he didn't want to share her with anyone else. But how could he tell her any of this? In a couple of months, they'd be living at opposite ends of the country, and she'd still be loved up with Doctor bloody Kildare.

People began shuffling out of their rows, heading towards the drinks reception. There was a table laden with filled champagne flutes and waiting staff circulating with platters of assorted canapes. Anna handed Jenny another tissue.

'Wasn't it beautiful?' Jenny said, dabbing at her eyes. 'It was so emotional.'

THEN

'It was lovely.'

'Has my mascara run? I should have worn waterproof.'

'No, you're fine.'

Jenny looked over at Dan and sniffed. 'You know, Dan's hairline is really starting to recede.'

Anna turned. Dan was deep in conversation with Julian and Phil. 'Yeah, well, none of us is getting any younger.'

'We're not that old.'

'Charlotte Lucas was considered an old spinster of the parish, and she was only twenty- seven,' Anna said. 'We've passed that milestone.'

'Who's Charlotte Lucas?' asked Jenny. 'Is she a friend?'

Anna sighed. 'Never mind.'

Jenny looked back towards Dan. 'So, are you two together then?'

'Well, we came up in the car together.'

'Anna...'

'No, we're *not* together.'

Jenny swiped a smoked salmon blini as it sailed past her at shoulder height. 'But aren't you sharing a room?'

'How do you know that?'

'Phil mentioned it.'

Bloody grapevine.

'It's purely a practical, cost-cutting exercise.'

'Right.'

Anna could see Sally walking towards them, champagne glass in hand.

'Here comes the bride!' said Anna. She kissed her friend's cheek and glanced at Jenny. 'You made Jenny cry.'

Sally pulled a sad face. 'Aww, Jen!'

'Sorry, it was just so emotional!'

'Anyway,' Anna said, 'you look absolutely beautiful.'

'Aww, thanks. Just don't let me get pissed on all this champagne, will you? I've spent a bloody fortune on bridal lingerie, and I don't want the memory of my wedding night to be a complete blank.'

Anna laughed. 'You and Kris found a house yet?'

'We saw a nice house last week. A third of the price of a house in London. It'll be good to have a job closer to home. See more of my mam and dad.'

Anna looked across the room at Sally's parents: her dad puffed with pride; her mum self-conscious in a small, jaunty hat.

'Well, I'm going to miss you, buddy.'

'It's Newcastle, pet, not Outer Mongolia.'

Anna raised an eyebrow.

'You're such a *southerner*! Anyway, you can visit any time.'

'I know.'

Anna thought of London without Sally and without Dan, and her heart sank a little. Soon, she'd be the only one of the old gang left. She could see Kris waving at Sally from the opposite side of the room.

'Better go!' said Sally. 'Duty calls! I'll see you for the dancing later.'

Jenny gave a series of short, sharp sniffs. 'It's the end of an era!'

Anna rolled her eyes. 'Come on,' she said. 'Pull yourself together and let's look at the seating plan.'

THEN

That evening, Anna stood beneath a gigantic mirror-ball as it scattered needles of light through the darkened room. An ageing DJ in red-framed spectacles swayed arthritically behind the decks, flanked by two enormous speakers and a rig of flashing lights, as Wet, Wet, Wet declared that 'Love Is All Around'.

'If Marti Pellow walked into this room now, I'd be tempted to punch him.'

Jenny looked at her. 'What's Marti Pellow ever done to you?'

'Let's just say that he and Richard Curtis have a lot to answer for.'

'Well, it's a wedding. They're hardly going to play "Anarchy in the U.K.".'

Phil laughed. 'I wouldn't mind seeing some of the old grannies moshing to that!'

Anna listened as Julian described his new marketing contract for a gambling company that was moving into the fledgling online gaming market. Her younger, student self would have started some heated discussion about the evils of capitalism and the immorality of enticing those who could least afford it into crippling debt, but the older Anna just nodded and smiled. Phil had morphed into grey-suit man and was working in insurance; Jenny was now managing a small chain of restaurants in the suburbs of Manchester. It all seemed very grown-up.

Anna met Phil's eye. 'Is the Hulk here?'

'No, he's swanning about in The Hague.'

That was a relief.

They all watched as two little girls in yellow

bridesmaids' dresses chased each other across the dance floor, which was otherwise empty.

They'd eaten their fill of salmon fillets and raspberry pavlova and clapped politely at the Best Man's speech, and now people had gathered in small groups waiting for the bride and groom's first dance.

As the opening bars of Luther Vandross's 'Here and Now' echoed across the room, Kris led Sally onto the dance floor where they rotated like figures inside a musical box. Anna had always thought such conventions excruciatingly awkward: a hundred pairs of eyes gawping at you whilst you attempted to gaze lovingly at your new spouse for a full five minutes and twenty seconds like some perverse kind of staring contest. She and Dan had barely made eye contact all day. It was going to be a whole barrel of laughs sharing a bed with him tonight, let alone a five-hour car journey tomorrow. She watched as he made his way to a table in the corner where he sat, pint in hand. Then the dance floor began filling to the B-52s' 'Love Shack', and she joined Julian, Phil and Jenny in 'ironic' retro dance moves that were alarmingly similar to those being made by other guests over the age of sixty.

It was 1am before they eventually staggered up the curved staircase to their rooms.

Dan had left the door slightly ajar. She crept in quietly, stumbled over the shoes he'd left in the middle of the floor and cursed aloud. The shape in the bed stirred. Anna removed her clothes, folded them in a neat pile, and slipped under the covers. The sheets felt cool against

THEN

her skin. After a while, her eyes began to adjust to the darkness.

A voice, muffled by sleep, said: 'I'm sorry.'

She turned to look at Dan, who was facing her on his side. His eyes were still closed. An arm snaked through the sheets and came to rest around her waist. She heard his breathing become deeper and more regular. Wordlessly, she placed her hand upon his and felt his little finger curl automatically around hers. Her body felt heavy, like the mattress was trying to pull her into itself. She gave herself up to the sensation and the oblivion of sleep.

In the morning, after a communal full English, there was an orgy of hugging and kissing and promises to stay in touch. Dan looked over at Anna, laughing and joking with Phil. At least she'd spoken to him this morning. He appeared to be forgiven. He made his way to the car and heard her crunching over the gravel behind him.

'Do you want to head straight back or stop off at the services on the way?'

She shrugged. 'Don't mind. I've got a bottle of water and a Mars bar in my handbag.' She got in, rested her forehead against the window and closed her eyes, shutting him out.

After an hour of silence, to keep himself awake, he reached over to the well between the seats, pulled out a cassette tape and slid it into the player.

Anna opened her eyes as the tape clicked, whirred, and Springsteen came blasting from the speakers. With perfect synchronicity, they joined the song at the chorus, bellowing that tramps like them were just 'Born to Run'.

They looked at each other and burst out laughing.

Anna stretched her legs in the footwell. 'Not quite the same in a Ford Escort, is it?'

'No,' said Dan. 'But you can strap your hands across my engines any time.'

Anna gave him a look. He was clearly irredeemable.

Like migrating birds in reverse, first Sally and Kris, then Dan, headed north. Even Claire had handed in her notice, answering the call for qualified teachers in Australia. Anna felt restless, like she couldn't settle in her own skin. She spent her days teaching or writing up chapters of her thesis. In the evenings, as the light faded and became melancholy, she would walk for miles as if trying to walk free from her own self, listening to the sound of her feet on the pavement, emptying her mind of any thought.

The weekend after the wedding, she and Rory had been standing in the kitchen making a Greek salad when he'd asked her about it. She'd shared a few amusing anecdotes: the best man's excruciatingly awful speech; the chief bridesmaid discovered with her face planted in the bottom tier of the wedding cake, drunk; her relief that the car Dan had borrowed no longer had a bungee cord holding the passenger door closed.

'How long have you known each other?' Rory asked, casually.

'Dan?' Sally thought for a moment. 'I don't know, years. Since I was a student.'

THEN

'And how did you meet?'

'In halls, where I met all of the gang – Sally, Phil, Jenny, Julian, Dan, of course, and the Hulk.'

Rory gave her a quizzical look.

'He's massive.' Anna stretched her arms vertically and horizontally by way of illustration. 'And Scottish. But we tried not to hold that against him.'

He smiled, absently.

Anna poured some white wine vinegar into a screw-top jar. 'Can you pass me the olive oil?'

She looked at him. His knife was resting against a piece of cucumber, mid-way through the act of chopping.

'Rory,' she said, gently. 'The olive oil?'

He looked at her, surfacing from deep thought. 'Sorry,' he said. 'I was miles away.'

If, at that time, Anna sometimes felt like a kite – floating, directionless and dangerously close to the outer edge of the Earth's atmosphere – then time spent with Rory was a reassuring anchor.

One day, they decided to take a trip to Stonehenge.

'It's Britain's most famous ancient site,' he said. 'I can't believe I've never seen it.'

'Well, let's go,' she said. 'But don't get too excited. The mysticism is slightly compromised by the roar of traffic from the A303.'

They packed up a picnic and sat on the grass overlooking the stone monoliths as they cast dark shadows across the ground.

Rory held the guidebook in his hands, occasionally reading aloud theories of how the huge sarsens or smaller bluestones had been transported to the site. Anna knew this already. Her mother had gone through a hippy phase in the '70s and she had been brought here often as a child. She was bored. She picked up a piece of chalky stone and began drawing shapes on Rory's jeans. His head was still deep in the guidebook, but eventually he peered over the top to see what she was doing.

A deep, vertical line formed between his eyebrows. 'Hey, what are you doing?'

Anna looked up. She'd not heard that tone of annoyance before – he'd always been gently affectionate, often indulgent and occasionally adoring. She ran her hand down one thigh of his jeans, over the shapes she had made.

'It's OK. It'll come off.'

He put down the book abruptly and leant forwards, brushing irritably at the chalk marks until they began to fade. Anna turned away, selected a strawberry from the punnet at her side, and held it in front of his mouth: a peace offering. He shook his head, not looking at her. In silence, she began returning the picnic food to the rucksack. She sensed then the beginning of an ending.

The final straw came much later, as they were leaving her flat to spend a weekend in Bath. Rory was heading down the front path with her overnight bag when the postman stopped him. Standing in the doorway, Anna noticed his shoulders fall slightly. She locked the door behind her and got into the car.

'Post,' Rory said, tossing it into her lap. There was an electricity bill and a postcard featuring a picture of a whippet. On the back, Dan had written:

THEN

WANT TO COME UP AND HELP ME CHOOSE A FLAT CAP?

Anna laughed.

'That's the first time I've ever heard somebody laugh at an electricity bill,' said Rory, starting up the engine.

'It's the postcard.'

'What's with the whippet?'

'It's sort of a private joke.'

'Oh, a *private* joke.'

Anna looked at him. 'You know, because he moved up north. The land of flat caps and whippets. He thinks I'm such a *southerner*.'

'Well, you *are* a southerner.'

There wasn't much she could say to that.

The weekend wasn't a complete disaster. They strolled along the Royal Crescent; they visited the steaming, sulphuric Roman Baths; they stopped at Sally Lunn's tea rooms and ate Bath buns. But although they held hands and made love, Rory was somehow distant; when Anna looked at him, his mind was elsewhere.

They arrived back in London late on Sunday night. Rory deposited her bag in the hall and hesitated.

'Aren't you coming in?' Anna said. 'A cup of tea before you head back?'

'No, I don't think so.'

'Oh, OK.'

He stood there, looking at her. 'To be honest, I think it's best if we call it a day.'

Anna was taken aback at hearing him say the words aloud but at the same time not at all surprised.

'To paraphrase Princess Diana,' he continued, 'I think there have always been three people in this relationship.'

She shook her head. 'No, that's not true.' But even as she said the words, she knew they were not entirely honest.

'I'm sorry,' he said.

She leant against the doorframe and watched him walk down the path to his car. A deep melancholy weighed heavily in her bones. As he drove away, she closed her eyes, breathed deeply and slowly drank in the cold, night air.

Christmas followed a predictable routine: the dog cocked its leg against the Christmas tree, her father grumbled about falling needles and it was suddenly acceptable to eat an entire box of After Eights for breakfast. An added excitement that year was the announcement of her little sister's engagement.

Anna stood next to her mother as they unloaded the dishwasher.

'Are you alright, love?' Her mother's face looked concerned.

'Yeah, why?'

'You just don't seem yourself.'

Tony Blair had been elected Prime Minister, BritArt and BritPop had made London cool and D:Ream had told her 'Things Can Only Get Better', but they hadn't.

'Oh, I'm alright.' She bent to put a saucepan in a cupboard.

Her mother stood, placing handfuls of cutlery in a drawer. She gave her daughter a quick look.

'Why don't you move back home?' She saw Anna's

THEN

back stiffen. 'Not with your dad and me,' she added. 'Just closer to home. Sell the flat in London and get your own place. You could get a house down here with the money.'

Anna sighed. 'OK, I'll think about it.' Yet moving home felt like an admission of defeat, somehow, even if she wasn't living with her parents. Whenever she had bumped into old schoolfriends and they'd asked what she was doing, she'd say, 'Oh, I work in London,' and they'd looked impressed. It lent her a certain cool glamour and sophistication by association. In the local pub, they'd say things like: 'I suppose it's all champagne and cocktail bars in London,' and she'd laugh and smile.

But the day after New Year's Day, she'd walked back into her empty, echoing flat and knew that she'd had enough. She was no longer in her twenties and London no longer seemed so glamorous and exciting. At work that Friday, she saw an advertisement in the TES for a teaching job just seven miles from her parents' village and applied for it on a whim. And that's how, months later, she found herself holding the keys to a new house fifteen minutes' drive from her new school.

'I'll help you move in if you like,' said Dan down the phone one night. 'When are you getting all your stuff out of storage?'

'This weekend,' she said.

'Alright,' he said. 'I'll drive down.'

Dan had none of Tom's smoothness and charm, but he did have a million-watt smile, and Anna's mother thought the sun shone out of his rear end.

'What a lovely man,' she said as Dan lugged heavy

boxes upstairs, 'coming all that way from Leeds to help you move in.'

'Yes, Mum, it's lovely of him.'

'And attractive, too. He's got a lovely smile.'

Anna gave her mother a look and made a 'tsk' sound.

'Well, I'm just saying.'

'Mum, give it a rest and help me hang these curtains.'

By early evening, curtains had been hung and most of the boxes had been unpacked.

'Well, I'll leave you two alone, then,' said Anna's mother, hovering on the doorstep as Anna's father waited in the car, tapping his fingers irritably on the steering wheel.

'Thanks, Mum. Thanks for everything.' Anna stood in the doorway with her arms crossed, a bouncer ushering her own mother into the street.

'It's been lovely meeting you, Dan,' her mother said, craning her head to look at him over Anna's shoulder.

'Lovely to meet you too, Mrs Thompson,' he said, in the voice he reserved especially for formal social occasions.

Anna turned to look at him, her tongue firmly planted in her cheek. He gave her a look as if to say, *What?* and she shook her head slowly.

'Oh, call me Denise, please,' said Anna's mother.

At last, her parents' car pulled away.

'I've assembled the double bed in the master bedroom,' Dan said.

'Of course you have.'

He smiled. 'You gotta have somewhere to sleep.'

'So where are you sleeping, then?' She looked over at the sofa.

THEN

Dan placed his hands in the small of his back and gave an exaggerated, pained stretch. 'It's put my back out a bit, lugging all those boxes,' he said. 'I need to sleep on something with a bit of support.'

'What about the floor? Nice and firm. Plenty of support there.'

He grabbed her around the waist. 'Anna Thompson, would you make me sleep on the floor?'

'No,' she said, laughing. 'I think you've earned the right to half a double mattress tonight.' She broke away from him, and he watched as she began sorting through another box, extracting a lamp and placing it on the coffee table. She removed sheets of newspaper wrapped around a painting and held it up.

'Not sure what to do about that,' she said.

'I'll put up a picture hook for you,' he said. 'Where d'you want it?'

Anna hesitated. Earlier that day, her father had nearly had a heart attack as he'd spotted Dan about to bang a nail in the wall without using an electrical wire detector first. 'I thought you said he had a brain,' he said. 'Bloody idiot could have electrocuted himself.' It was fair to say that Dan was not the most practical man in the world.

'You know what?' she said. 'I think I'll leave it.'

'Nice picture, though,' he said. 'Where did you get it?'

'Rory bought it for me.'

'Oh.' They sat awkwardly for a few seconds. 'Yeah, I was sorry to hear about you two breaking up.'

That was a lie. Dan had barely been able to conceal his delight that she was no longer with the posh twat and had in fact needed to resist punching the air as she'd told him down the phone.

'Oh.' She shrugged. 'I don't think it would have worked out. He was too nice and well-adjusted.'

Dan completely missed the implied insult.

'Isn't that what most women want?' he said.

'I don't know.' She shrugged. 'I'm not most women.'

He watched her rub the tip of her nose absent-mindedly, smearing it with a black smudge of newspaper ink. It made her look somehow feline, and he had the urge to draw whiskers on her cheeks. He wanted to kneel down next to her on the floor and kiss her little feline face.

Instead, he said: 'I've set up the TV for you.'

'Brilliant. We'll get something to eat and see what's on the box tonight.' Then she sighed, pulling down the corners of her mouth. 'I haven't got any food in, though.'

'Chip shop?' he said, hopefully.

They sat, surrounded by partially emptied boxes and sheets of newspaper, a bottle of warm, white, corner-shop wine and chip wrappers at their feet, laughing at *Men Behaving Badly*.

'I don't know why I'm laughing,' said Anna, laughing. 'Gary's an absolutely tragic character, really.'

'Tragic? He's a legend! In what way is he tragic?'

'*Well*,' she said, slowly, 'he's sexually insecure, he has an unfulfilling job, he feigns laddish behaviour to avoid confronting any deeper feelings...'

'Yeah, like I said, a complete legend.'

She shoved him, then he put out his arm and she curled into him.

THEN

Dan stared absent-mindedly at the TV screen, feeling Anna's body next to him as it shook with laughter, and thought about what she had just said. She hadn't looked directly at him, but she'd spoken the words in a very *deliberate* way, as if she was trying to make a point. But what point was she trying to make? *He* wasn't sexually insecure – quite the opposite – as far as he was concerned, he'd always delivered the goods on that score. And feigning laddish behaviour? Well, what was suddenly wrong with behaving like a bloke? Unlike women, blokes didn't waste hours of their lives talking about their feelings with each other. What was the point? And who had deep feelings all the time anyway? There were more interesting things to talk about, like football and cloning and artificial intelligence. He had very deep feelings about those things, in fact. And his job – well, it wasn't at all unfulfilling. The people with whom he worked were, admittedly, a bunch of introverted, antisocial nerds, but that was OK because what he was researching was cutting edge, absolutely cutting edge.

'Penny for them.' Anna was looking at him.

'Mmm?'

'What are you thinking about?'

'Nothing.'

'Probably about artificial intelligence or whether Manchester United will win the FA Cup.'

Sometimes, it was scary how well she knew him.

'So, are you ready to occupy your half of the mattress yet?' he asked.

'Yeah, alright,' she said. 'Let's have an early night.'

The bed creaked alarmingly as she sat upon it. She

looked at the bedside table, on top of which were two screws and a screwdriver.

'Dan, why are there two screws on the table?'

'Yeah,' he said, 'I dunno. Bit weird, that. Maybe there were two spare screws.'

She sighed. It was the same bed she'd brought from the flat in London, and there hadn't been two spare screws then. As she lay down next to him, the bed creaked again like a wooden ship in a storm. *Oh well*, she thought, *at least if it collapses, we won't have far to fall.*

***

The wedding day had been a long time in the planning.

Every detail had been agonised over, from the invitations (heavy cream paper; golden butterflies), to the wedding cake (a triumphant solution for the indecisive: a layer each of fruit, chocolate and vanilla sponge), to the flowers. And even those decisions paled in comparison to the greatest decisions of all: the bride and bridesmaid's dresses. Anna's sister was dangerously close to turning into a monstrous Bridezilla. It felt like Anna had trailed around every wedding boutique within a hundred-mile radius. She began to consider breaking in a pair of walking boots and fortifying herself with Kendal Mint Cake. Even their own mother had bailed out, exhausted, after the fifteenth boutique.

'You carry on without me,' she said. 'I'm slowing you down. I don't have the stamina I once had.'

Lightweight, Anna thought.

THEN

With steely determination, she pressed on through the satin shoes, lace and taffeta, despite the fact that there seemed to be no end in sight. And then, one day, when Anna was close to uttering the infamous words: 'I am just going outside and may be some time,' Jess finally stood in the bridal shop and said: 'That's it!'

Anna looked at the mannequins: a tasteful, ivory-coloured wedding dress that looked exactly like all the others Jess had previously rejected, next to which was a bridesmaid's dress in shiny gold satin. She was speechless with horror.

'I look like the toffee finger in a tin of Quality Street,' she told Dan that night.

She could hear him laughing down the phone. 'I'm sure you'll look fine,' he said, 'you've got a lovely figure.'

'Nobody could look good in that dress. Shiny gold! I mean, does that flatter anyone?'

'It worked for Martin Fry.'

'He was wearing that suit ironically. At least, I hope he was.' She huffed, grumpily. 'Anyway, do you want to be my plus-one? You can spend the day talking to your one-woman fan club.'

'Yeah, I'm happy to spend the day talking to you, as you've asked me so nicely.'

'Not me! That fan club folded in 1989. I meant my mum.'

'Yeah,' Dan said fondly, 'I like your mum.'

'Well, the feeling's mutual. So, will you come?'

'Yeah, all right then, I'll come.'

'And you'll need to get a new suit. You're not wearing the graduation suit again.'

'What's wrong with it?'

'What's right with it more like. For a start, no one wears double-breasted suit jackets anymore. Secondly, you can't do up the trousers.'

'I can,' he said, unconvincingly.

'I'll come up in a couple of weeks and we'll go shopping for a new one, OK?'

He knew there was no point in arguing. 'OK.'

In order to get to menswear, it was necessary to walk through the women's lingerie department. Anna knew that this would make Dan uncomfortable, which was all the more reason to take her time. She kept stopping, fingering a delicate lace bra or tiny panties as he walked behind her. It was a peculiarly public form of torture: every time she held up an item, he imagined her wearing it and felt an uncomfortable stiffening in his groin.

'You all right?' She was clearly enjoying his discomfort. 'Hey, you know what this reminds me of?'

'*It's Ireland's biggest lingerie department, I understand,*' they said in unison.

'God!' Anna laughed. 'Your Irish accent is terrible!'

'You have an unfair advantage,' said Dan. 'You worked with Irish nuns for years.'

'I'll bet you've never set foot in a women's lingerie department before,' she teased.

He stared back at her, defiantly. 'Actually, that's not true. I've bought lingerie for a woman – quite recently, in fact.'

Anna was dumbfounded. In all the years that she had known Dan, she'd never heard him so much as mention

THEN

another woman, let alone seen him dating one. She felt irrationally jealous. She'd taken it for granted that she would always be the object of his desire. She wanted to ask who the woman was but didn't want to give him the satisfaction of thinking it mattered to her.

Instead, she said: 'Yeah, well, buying vests for your granny doesn't count. Come on, let's get to menswear and find you a suit.'

On the day of the wedding, Dan looked at his reflection in the hotel window as he made his way towards the reception desk. He didn't look too bad after all, if he did say so himself: a navy suit with a fine pinstripe; a blue and gold tie. Anna had left the house hours earlier – her sister had booked someone to do their hair and make-up. Entering the foyer, he saw her standing at the bottom of the stairs with another, largely built bridesmaid, also in gold satin, and a little girl in a cream dress. She looked up, smiled, and walked towards him. *She was right*, he thought, *she looks just like the toffee finger in a tin of Quality Street.*

'Hiya,' she said. 'You're the first row on the left, next to my mum.' She saw a smile playing on his lips as he looked at her dress. 'Don't say a word. It's bad enough having to wear it.'

'It could be worse', he said, looking over her shoulder at the other bridesmaid. 'You could have come as the toffee penny.'

She smiled and shook her head. 'Go and take your seat. I'll see you later.'

He shuffled along the row next to Anna's mother, who

was delighted to see him, and made polite small talk. Then they heard the opening bars of the 'Wedding March', and he turned to look down the aisle. Anna was walking behind her sister and her father looking very serious. When they reached the registrar, she gently dropped her sister's train to the floor and slid along the row next to him. He noticed how tightly her dress fitted on the bodice. They sat, thigh to thigh, knees touching, Anna fiddling with the petals in the floral bouquet.

After the ceremony, they made their way to the garden. Anna was ahead of him, holding the hand of the little bridesmaid. On the lawn, he watched her crouch down to the child's eye level to talk to her. Her face was animated, and she was pointing to a small copse. He could see the child's eyes widening in excitement. Anna stood, removed her golden shoes, and, picking up her skirts, raced the child to the trees. After a few minutes, he saw them walking back towards him.

The little girl looked up at him, her expression serious but full of wonder. She extended her hand, in which was a mouldy old acorn cup.

He looked at it, underwhelmed. 'An acorn cup.'

'Pixie cups,' she corrected. 'Anna showed me where the pixies live.'

'Right,' said Dan, looking at Anna for clues as to how he should respond.

Anna widened her eyes, signalling for him to play along. 'But it's not just any old cup,' she said. 'It's a special cup for special ceremonies, like when they crown the Pixie King. They all dance beneath the trees in the hour before

THEN

dawn, before we humans are awake.' She crouched down next to the little girl and looked into her eyes. 'Now, Ella, you have to promise me that you'll keep the cup safe. It's very precious treasure.'

The little girl nodded, her mouth hanging open, her fist clenched tighter around the object in her hand.

Anna pointed towards another wedding guest who was looking over towards them. 'Go and show it to Mummy. Tell her what you've found.'

The little girl went running off, her skirts flying.

She stood up. 'Where did I leave my shoes?'

'Over there.' Dan watched as she located her shoes, put them on and walked back to him, then he said: 'How do you think up all that stuff?'

Anna shrugged. The guests were being called to the wedding breakfast, and they moved across the large expanse of lawn towards the orangery. The little girl ran up to Anna and flung her arms around her thighs.

'I've been hearing all about the *pixie cups*,' her mother said, winking, then added, 'she was so excited about the wedding, she kept us up half the night.' She looked from Anna to Dan. 'Do you want to keep her?' She laughed, wearily.

Dan smiled. He thought how good Anna was with children. She would make a wonderful mother. He was in his thirties now. He'd heard of women having biological clocks, although Anna had never mentioned one ticking, but for a while now, he had seen men of his own age playing football with their sons in the park or carrying their children on their shoulders and had experienced a powerful desire to become a father himself.

That night, as they lay in bed, he turned to her.

'You know, you'd be a wonderful mother.'

She looked at him, her brow furrowed. 'What on earth makes you think that?'

'You were great with that little girl today.'

'Yeah, well, it's easier when you can give them back.' She shifted to lie on her back.

'Have you never thought about it?'

'What, having a *baby*?'

He nodded.

'Maybe. In the early days with Tom.' She exhaled loudly. 'Imagine how much more of a nightmare that would have been if a child had been involved.'

He lay in silence for a few minutes, letting the statement hang in the air.

'Not all men are like Tom,' he said. 'You know, if we had a kid…'

She finished the sentence: '…*with my looks and your brains, it couldn't go wrong.…*'

He turned to her, astonished. 'How did you know I was going to say that?'

'You said it to me once before, when we were in bed together one morning in 1989.'

'*Did I?*'

How the hell could she remember something he'd said to her that long ago?

'Yep.'

He thought about that for a while, trying to recollect himself saying it, but when he turned his head to speak, her eyes were closed, her mouth had fallen open, and she

THEN

was fast asleep. And so he never told her that it wasn't some glib statement.

He meant every word.

***

'I didn't realise that it could get so hot this far north,' Anna said.

'We're still a fair way south of the Arctic Circle!'

They were lying on the moors outside Leeds. Clumps of heather marked the bleak beauty of the landscape like purple bruises. It was stiflingly hot and there was no shade. Anna pushed her sunglasses up her nose and reached over Dan's lap for the water bottle, unscrewing the cap. She took a mouthful and wrinkled her nose: it was warm and tasted of plastic. She wiped the top of the bottle with her hand and held it up to Dan's mouth. He lifted his head to look at her, his eyes narrowing in the glare of the sunlight.

'Champagne tonight, I think,' he said, taking the bottle from her hand.

'Ooh, last of the big spenders!' Normally, Dan's idea of splashing out was a bottle of Spanish cava.

'Well, it's a double celebration.'

It was Anna's birthday, she'd finally finished her doctorate, and Dan's university lecturing post had been made permanent.

'Talking of which…' He sat up and pulled out a gift-wrapped parcel from his rucksack. 'Happy birthday!'

'Aww, thanks.' She pulled herself upright and leant in to kiss his cheek. The parcel was flat, but it was too light and soft to be a book. She tore open the paper and into her lap fell a cream silk camisole, and matching knickers. She stared at him, open-mouthed. It was the most intimate, romantic gift he had ever given her. She thought back to the day in the lingerie department when he'd told her that he'd bought lingerie for a woman, and she'd felt so jealous. Of course, she reassured herself, the lingerie had been for her all along.

'Do you like it?'

'I love it.' She looked at the label. 'How did you know my size?'

'Well, I didn't, so the shop assistant lined up some of her colleagues and I had to say whether you were bigger or smaller.'

Anna laughed, but she knew how painfully embarrassed he would have been. The fact that he had endured this for her sake was touching. She kissed him again.

'If that's the reaction I get, I'll have to buy you lingerie more often.'

That night, they sat opposite each other in an upmarket Italian restaurant. Teardrops of wax slid down the candle in the middle of the table. Anna held a flute of champagne by its stem and took another sip. Her face took on a dreamy expression as she gazed out of the window.

Dan thought how lovely she looked. She was wearing a white linen dress, and she had caught the sun, making her skin appear almost golden in the early evening sunlight. She twisted strands of her hair absent-mindedly around

THEN

the finger of one hand. He wasn't sure what love felt like, or indeed if he'd ever felt it, but he knew that she was the woman he desired. In all those years, there had never been anyone else.

He wondered what she felt about him. He was sufficiently self-aware to remember that he had hurt her once, badly, back when they were students, but he wasn't the same person now. Neither of them was.

He watched as Anna set the champagne flute back on the table and rested her hand on the tablecloth. He placed his hand over hers and squeezed it very tightly. It was such an unusual thing for him to do, stone-cold sober and in public, that she looked up. His expression was serious, as if he was about to tell her something of great importance.

'You know, I've lusted after you for the best part of a decade,' he said, and then came to a halt. He couldn't find the right words to express what he wanted to say.

She waited. His words felt like the preamble to something else, but he simply continued looking at her, so eventually, she said: 'I know.'

Anna wondered how it was that she had known Dan for so long, she could often accurately predict what he would say or do, but that in many other ways she didn't know him at all. Of course, she knew how he felt about football and politics, science fiction novels and films with foreign subtitles, but they had never really spoken about their feelings for each other. Dan didn't like talking about his emotions and there was an unspoken acknowledgement that the subject was off-limits. She wondered why he had gripped her hand so tightly and why he was looking at her so intently if all he had to say was that he lusted after her. She already knew that.

Dan saw the waiter hovering behind Anna, waiting to clear the plates, and his hand sprung apart from hers like he'd just received an electric shock. His face coloured with embarrassment.

'Where to after dessert? Pub or my place?'

They went on to a pub. She had drunk too much champagne in the restaurant, and it had made her flirtatious. Back at his place, he watched her slide off her dress and reached over to touch the warm silk that clung to her skin. She looked up at him, her face flushed and smiling. In that moment, he wanted her very badly; he didn't stop to put on a condom. It felt like one of life's wonders to be enclosed in her flesh. He moved inside her until her breath became ragged and, as she came, he looked into her eyes and released himself deep inside her. When eventually he had to leave her body, it felt like a kind of bereavement.

Anna didn't immediately notice that her period was late. She'd been busy and preoccupied at work and had begun a redecoration project on the house. For a while she had felt a heavy, bloated feeling deep in her abdomen – the feeling that always came before her period was due – and so she assumed that it was on its way. Then, one weekend, she was in Boots with Dan buying some cleanser when they walked past a shelf full of pregnancy testing kits. She hesitated, and Dan nearly collided with her back.

'What's up?'

THEN

'It's probably nothing.' He followed her gaze; she was looking at the pregnancy tests.

'What's nothing?'

'I'm just a bit late this month, that's all.'

He froze as he remembered the night he'd forgotten to use a condom.

'How late?'

She thought for a bit. 'I don't know, about ten days or so.'

'Is that normal?'

'No, not that late. But it's probably nothing. I mean, we always use condoms.'

She saw the expression on his face and her stomach lurched. She thought back to the weekend of her birthday, when she'd drunk too much champagne and had become outrageously flirtatious.

They stood looking at each other as customers pushed past them.

Dan broke the silence. 'I think we should buy a test, just in case.'

She felt a wave of nausea move from her stomach to her throat. She couldn't bring herself to do it. If she did, it might make things real. Her mouth felt dry.

'You buy it. I'm going outside to get some air.'

He placed a hand on her shoulder. Her face looked ashen. 'Are you all right?'

'I'm fine. I just need some air.'

'OK, I'll buy the test and meet you outside.'

She nodded and handed him the bottle of cleanser.

Dan selected a test from the shelf and made his way to the tills as Anna made her way outside.

SOMETHING CHANGED

The sky was a cloudless, very pale blue and a fresh breeze was blowing. She perched on the edge of a bench, gripping its wooden slats tightly, and hung her head over her knees. After a few minutes, she felt someone standing over her. It was Dan.

'Come on. Let's go home. You look as white as a sheet.'

He put his arm around her, and they walked back to the car. In the passenger seat, she wound down the window, desperate for more air. She moved her face into the current and closed her eyes as it whipped her hair around her face. She could sense Dan glancing over at her, but he said nothing.

Back at the house, they stood immobile in the hall, the carrier bag bunched in Dan's fist. He passed it to her.

'I think you'd better do the test.' He looked up the stairs towards the bathroom.

She felt a wave of nausea again and didn't know if it was nerves or because she really was pregnant. Her knees felt weak as she climbed the stairs, like her legs might buckle under her at any moment. She shut the bathroom door and collapsed onto the toilet seat. For a while, she stared at the carrier bag at her feet, feeling numb. Then she reached out, opened the box and read the instructions. She removed the plastic cover from the absorbent stick, peed on it and snapped the plastic cover back in place. Then she placed the test on top of the cistern, washed her hands and went downstairs.

Dan was waiting in the living room, pensively. He looked up as she entered.

'Well?'

'It takes a few minutes. I've left it on the cistern.'

THEN

She looked so pale; she seemed to have retreated into herself.

He moved towards the kitchen. 'I'm going to make myself a coffee,' he said. 'Do you want one?'

She shook her head.

Anna tried to imagine the possibility of a new life, a new human being, growing inside her body but failed. Before an image could form, it slid away from her, as if such a possibility was too fantastical. She thought of all the times in her life that she had experienced the urge to walk free of her own body – and not just her own body, but her very self. She wondered how this same body could ever be a vessel holding a new life.

She heard the metallic clinking of a teaspoon in a mug as Dan made coffee in the kitchen. He seemed so sure that she would make a good mother. She wondered what he saw in her that she could not.

Dan stood in the doorway, coffee mug in hand. Two furrow lines appeared between his eyebrows.

'Are you going to see what it says?'

She didn't move. Finally, she said. 'I can't. You do it.'

He placed his mug on the table and climbed the stairs. The test was lying on the cistern. He took a deep breath and picked it up. Running through the window on the stick was an emphatically deep, blue line: the test was positive. He experienced a feeling of terror and exhilaration as he realised that this one small line had the potential to change his life forever – to change both of their lives forever.

Clutching the test in his hand, he descended the stairs. Anna was standing, looking out of the window. She turned as she heard him behind her. He saw her eyes grow wider as he held up the test with its deep blue line. All those years of longing and lust and hurt; the years of sarcastic banter and sharp put-downs and words unspoken. All those years had crystallised into this one moment, this single blue line, this new life.

She looked up at him, fragile and vulnerable. 'Do you want this baby?'

Their eyes locked together, and Dan nodded his head firmly. 'Oh, yes.'

There was so much that was still uncertain, but that was something of which he was absolutely sure.

All the tension left her then and her body seemed to sink into his. They stood there for some time as he held her, his hands encircling the body that, miraculously, contained their child.

NOW

Jack removed an earbud from his ear, letting the wire dangle over his shoulder.

'Sorry, what did you say?'

Dan raised his voice slightly. 'I said, is there anything else you want to see?'

Jack shook his head. 'No, I don't think so. I've done the lecture, talked to some students, seen the accommodation. I'm good.'

Dan looked over at Anna and she shrugged.

'Right,' he said. 'We'll head off, then.'

The car was parked in a residential backstreet; the run of Victorian terraced houses was interrupted by a low-rise block of flats that had grown up in the place where a wartime bomb had obviously fallen. A small child rode a yellow plastic scooter round and round on the paved area outside.

The car lights flashed as Dan pressed the key. They sat with the doors open for a few minutes to let air circulate, then the driver of a large van sounded his horn, trying to get past. They slammed the doors shut, enclosed in the stifling air.

SOMETHING CHANGED

Dan opened Google Maps on his phone, entered a destination and started the car.

'Take the next left,' instructed Sat-Nav Lady, 'then turn left onto the A32 zero-zero.'

The air conditioning began to kick in as they approached Westminster Bridge. The Houses of Parliament stretched out before them, duplicated by the shimmering surface of the Thames and bookended by Big Ben. It was a view that looked like one of those postcards you could find on wire racks outside tacky souvenir stalls selling fridge magnets and Union Jack T-shirts.

They skirted the edge of St James's Park, emerging at the side of Buckingham Palace. Anna swivelled around in her seat and nudged Jack's leg.

'Buckingham Palace, Jack!'

He looked up, glanced out of the window, smiled at her, then returned to his phone.

When they got to Wellington Arch, she didn't even bother to try to attract his attention. It was no match for YouTube.

Soon enough, Dan pulled up in the drop-off area outside Paddington Station.

'You'll have to be quick,' he said. 'I can't stay here for long.'

Anna turned around to attract Jack's attention. 'Come on, love, we need to get moving!'

She opened the passenger door a few centimetres, waiting for a break in the cars moving past, and then leapt out.

Dan wound down the window and leant his head towards Jack, who was standing on the pavement, a bulging university tote bag slung over his shoulder.

NOW

'I'll see you next weekend, OK?'

Jack nodded. His father said the same thing every weekend.

'And be good for your mother.'

Jack completed the routine. 'I will.'

Dan watched his son put his arm around his mother as he loped alongside her towards the platforms. They were a tight knit unit, those two. There was a time, when Jack was tiny, that he would refuse to be parted from her, clinging tightly to her leg. In those moments, Dan had sometimes felt like an interloper. But in adolescence he had sensed their son gradually growing away from them both, like a young sapling that has discovered another source of light, and that was as it should be.

Dan saw Anna give Jack a good-natured shove – probably, he imagined, in response to some sarcastic comment – and he could see them both laughing. He'd been right, all those years ago, when he and Anna had stood in each other's arms and the future had solidified before them: she was a wonderful mother, and Jack was a wonderful son.

A cacophony of car horns sounded behind him; it was time for him to move on. He picked up his phone and checked Google Maps: there was some congestion around Brent Cross before he could join the M1. With any luck, he should be home by early evening. He'd treat himself to a takeaway beef madras for dinner. All that saturated fat wasn't good for his waistline, but then, it was Saturday night, after all.

***

Anna swerved to avoid being hit by an enormous, wheeled suitcase as they made their way into the station.

'So, what did you think, then? Will you put it on your UCAS form?'

Jack nodded. 'Yeah, I think so.'

'I was right about the student union bar, though, wasn't I?'

'Yes, Mum. Great view. Though I'm surprised you recognised it in colour.'

She looked at him.

'Well, it was all black and white back in your day, wasn't it?'

She gave him a good-natured shove and laughed. 'I'm not that old, you cheeky devil!' Though sometimes, she felt it.

They headed towards the departures board, joining the passengers who, faces uplifted, were waiting for their platform to appear from above.

'Platform Two,' Jack said, touching his mother's elbow and steering her to the left.

They found two seats either side of a table, facing each other. Jack rummaged through the canvas tote bag and pulled out a deflated beach ball branded with the university's crest.

'What am I supposed to do with that?' He laughed. 'The university's nowhere near a beach. What were the marketing department thinking?'

She shook her head and smiled.

'I liked it, though. The course is good.' He paused. 'But perhaps I've been influenced by you and Dad. You had a good time in London, didn't you?'

NOW

'Well, it was certainly *eventful*,' she said, carefully. Like any parent, she'd only ever given him the edited highlights.

She remembered that period in her twenties as a time of great highs and dangerous lows. She was sure there had been dull moments in between, moments of boredom and tedium, but as is the way with dull things, her memory had erased them. In her memory, life then was an adrenalin rush, a rollercoaster that was simultaneously terrifying yet exciting. It was a time when the future was unpredictable, when anything could happen, when every time a new person came into your life, you thought: *is this the one? Is this the person who will change the course of my life in a way that I cannot yet know?*

Motherhood had changed her. How could it not? She was responsible for another person, another life, and she had been desperate not to fuck it up. The highs and lows had been replaced by a new equilibrium. There were regular mealtimes and bedtimes and playdates and swimming lessons and homework – a life of predictability that, she knew, made a child secure. And, most importantly, Jack was loved. They had both fallen in love with their son at first sight, scarcely believing that they were capable of creating something so miraculous, so perfect.

Lying in her bed decades ago, Dan had been right when he'd joked that, with his looks and her brains, their kid couldn't go wrong: Jack was handsome, intelligent, articulate and kind. Had he sensed then, on that chilly morning in the tiny flat in south London, that although they had barely known each other for a few months, they were destined always to be a part of each other's lives?

Or was it a throwaway comment that became prophetic only in retrospect? Anna wasn't sure that she believed in fate. Fate was romantic. Life was far more random and arbitrary.

She looked across at their son. He had taken out his copy of *The Great Gatsby*, an A level set text. She thought of the closing sentence: *So we beat on, boats against the current, borne back ceaselessly into the past.*

Perhaps, she thought, *as we get older, and our malleable forms harden like fired clay, there is an inevitability about the pull of the past; its accumulation of people and experiences that have made us who we are. We reach a point in our lives where there is simply more of it.*

As the train jolted, pulling away from the station, Jack put down his book and looked at her, suddenly thoughtful.

'Do you ever wish you could go back?'

She considered his question for a moment and then shook her head. Her younger self would recoil in horror from the regular, conventional rhythms that had become her middle-aged life. If they stood face to face in a room, they would not recognise each other.

Jack tried to tempt her: 'Cheap drinks? Clubbing? Late-night parties? Raging hangovers?'

'No,' she said, laughing, 'especially not the hangovers!'

He returned to his book then, and she turned to look out of the window. The backs of buildings flashed past as the train picked up speed, moving inexorably into the future.

AUTHOR BIO

Born and raised in Bristol, Julie has been writing stories since she was a child, when she would read them to her long-suffering little sister. After university, where she was lucky enough to be tutored in prose writing by Malcolm Bradbury and Rose Tremain, she went into teaching, and has enjoyed sharing her love of literature and writing with teenagers for over three decades. During lockdown, she decided to return to writing to keep herself sane, which resulted in *Something Changed*, her debut novel. She still lives in Bristol, where she loves going to gigs by indie bands, getting piggy back rides across the Clifton Suspension Bridge and generally pretending that she's still 21.